Pride Publishing books by Brian Lancaster

Single Books
Companion Required
Any Day
Salvaging Christmas

I0658907

SALVAGING CHRISTMAS

BRIAN LANCASTER

Salvaging Christmas
ISBN # 978-1-83943-760-1
©Copyright Brian Lancaster 2021
Cover Art by Fiona Jayde ©Copyright December 2021
Interior text design by Claire Siemaszkiewicz
Pride Publishing

SALVAGING CHRISTMAS

Dedication

Ask my partner and he will tell you that my love of Christmas is bordering on Hallmark card embarrassing. Our home gets turned into Santa's grotto with festive wreaths, ribbons, mistletoe, sparkles and anything I can get my hands on that I consider tastefully seasonal.

Since arriving in Hong Kong in 1998, we have always hosted a Christmas lunch for friends and colleagues who are often thousands of miles from home and who perhaps may not have the opportunity to celebrate the festive season with their families. We provide an extended family for them, a home from home, and lay on a full Christmas spread for everyone to enjoy.

Salvaging Christmas is my tribute to all the people out there who selflessly take on the role of making the festive special for others.

And in case you're considering putting together a playlist this Christmas, each chapter is dedicated to a favourite Christmas song of mine, the song list with the artists detailed at the end of this story.

Preface

Salvaging Christmas takes place at Christmas in 2017, before the coronavirus pandemic made an impact on our daily lives. In all honestly, I would have relished the challenge of setting the story during those difficult times, but there is another reason entirely for this decision. Those who have read *Companion Required* will recognise characters from this story appearing at the end, so I wanted to ensure I kept the timelines consistent.

Chapter One

Last Christmas

Trevor McTavish loved traditions.

Or, more to the point, new traditions built on old ones. After all, wasn't that what most of them were, a blend of old and new, built layer upon layer over time? They provided a foundation, something people could rely on, even when everything else around them broke down, or changed unexpectedly, or disappeared entirely from their lives — which seemed to happen to him all too often of late.

Traditions ensured continuity, and even with the few hiccups this year had brought, Trevor loved the Christmas tradition he and Cheryl had created for their friends.

As the sullen driver of the prepaid cab steered in silence through the early morning streets of London, Trevor rested his head against the ice-cold window. Gentle vibrations from the hybrid engine massaged his skull. Already the sky had begun transitioning from purest black as the night shift packed up and daylight took over. Fully alert despite the early hour, he looked for homes with their Christmas lights still burning and gardens or roofs decorated with seasonal figures. A part of him instinctively knew he would get along with the person who had gone to all the effort to put them up, most likely done to make other people smile.

Nothing could shake Trevor's upbeat mood as the cab turned into the familiar road where the Madison family lived. Since he'd packed last night, the sense of anticipation and excitement at the promise of a road trip with best friends had kept him pumped up and grinning like an inflatable snowman.

Six in the morning on that pre-dawn Friday in December, he climbed out of the overheated car and crunched down onto a pavement of overnight frost. After collecting his luggage from the boot, he pulled out a five-pound note from his wallet and tapped a fingernail on the driver's window. With a smile, he held up the banknote, ready to wish the man a heartfelt season's greetings. After all, if the poor guy had to drive a cab at this early hour, he obviously needed the money.

Without even bothering to acknowledge Trevor, the driver pulled away.

Left standing alone in the road, Trevor shrugged and put the fiver back. Perhaps the man had somewhere better to be. Not everyone shared his passion for all things festive.

Humming to himself, he manoeuvred his wheelie luggage up the broken-tiled garden path and prodded the front doorbell. Bing-bongs chimed from somewhere inside. Cheryl Madison's mother opened the door in her furry-hooded olive parka and mismatching navy Wellington boots. Further at odds with the ensemble, her pink floral nightie peeked out from beneath the jacket.

Trevor almost let out a giggle.

Until he saw the expression on her face.

After a furtive glance at the staircase behind her, Mrs M nodded sharply towards the Volvo out front while handing him a small but deceptively heavy cardboard box. Hauling a larger one from the floor, she strode past him and he trailed after her, the wheels of his luggage clunking arrhythmically on the broken pavement. Only as she unlocked the hatchback and placed her carton inside did she reveal the predicament.

"Hannah's not coming. She broke up with Cheryl last night. Met someone at their Christmas office party on Tuesday night. Supposedly."

The way she articulated that final word said everything. Trevor dropped onto the tailgate — causing the car to bounce — and placed his container next to hers. Mrs M stood there studying him, arms folded, appearing to wait for his response. Instinctively, he mirrored her body language and sighed. Of all their friends, he understood only too well the devastating effects of being dumped. Right before their long-anticipated Christmas trip, too. Hannah had always possessed a selfish streak, an immunity to the sensibilities of others. She had often manipulated Cheryl but he'd never thought she would stoop so low.

"Shit. Poor Cheryl. How's she coping?"

"You'll see in a minute. Putting on a brave front. I tried to sound surprised when she told me, but something's not been right for months. The important thing, Trevor, is that we're down by one more guest."

"Double shit," he said, staring down at the road between his legs.

"I'll let you think about that before I bring out any more boxes, and while I go and put the kettle on," she said, before heading back to the house.

So much for the *Yuletide Gay Club*.

They had started the group five years ago. Cheryl, his best friend since high school, could take credit for the idea and him for its successful implementation. Sick of hearing in January how many of their gay friends had spent the holiday season either alone or with families who barely tolerated them, they had created their own tradition.

Six couples shared the cost of renting a country cottage in rural Britain. Seven or eight days spent enjoying Christmas their own way, with their own people, in the countryside.

Far from the maddening crowds.

At first nobody had known whether bringing together couples who were occasional friends would work. That first time, the gathering in the six-bedroom farmhouse in Devon had turned out to be nothing short of a miracle. Everyone had gelled quickly and mucked in together, laughed and got drunk together, played games like Cards Against Humanity until sunrise and raved about the break well into the New Year. So good was the experience that Trevor had already had the next event booked up by February. The same thing had happened the following years, with the small group growing closer.

Except this year—the fifth—grim providence had made a personal appearance. Tragically, Mrs M's seventy-two-year-old Scottish girlfriend, Monica, the only other person allowed in the kitchen at Christmas and the life and soul of the party, had succumbed unexpectedly to a brain aneurism and passed away in late January.

Next up, at the beginning of March, they had received a cryptic email from regulars Johnny and Frank. Both having quit their jobs, they'd decided to take a hiatus from the rat race, managed to rent out their home, and set off on their travels. Finally free, they'd also committed to a technology-free tour of the world and their last handwritten postcard had been sent from somewhere in the Middle East.

As the year progressed, the casualties had continued to fall like autumn leaves until the usual company of twelve had dropped to five.

Then in April, Trevor's husband of two years, Karl, had not only announced his newly discovered heterosexuality, or bisexuality, or sexual fluidity — he had yet to settle on a label — but admitted that he had fallen in love with a woman. Four years together, and Trevor's spouse had woken one morning and realised he had been wrestling for the wrong tag team.

Which left four of them. Initially, they had considered cancelling the event. But without consulting any of them, Hannah had tactlessly filled one space with a new girl from her office, twenty-year-old Jessica, who, in turn, decided that bringing along a male colleague would be perfectly acceptable.

Could things get any worse?

Apparently, they could. After Trevor had signed the online divorce papers, there had followed a doorstep altercation with Karl about which artwork, pillows, bed linen, dishes and cutlery he was entitled to take in the divorce. Not thinking straight, Trevor had succumbed to all his demands. In addition, for their Christmas excursion, Karl had seen no reason why he should be ostracised, why he should not still be invited with his new partner. Maybe because of dwindling numbers, or more likely the result of a temporary lapse in sanity, Trevor had capitulated.

Cheryl had refused to speak to him for three weeks after he'd told her.

By the beginning of December, the promise of a seasonal sanctuary, which used to be the epitome of a cosy, warm and cuddly Christmas Hallmark movie, had morphed into the awkward, dysfunctional cast of characters befitting a Woody Allen feature.

"The question remains," came the voice of Mrs M. Lost in his thoughts, he jumped when she perched down beside him. "Is it too late to cancel?"

Trevor huffed out a steamy breath and searched for seasonal inspiration along the row of terraced houses. All year he had been looking forwards to their getaway. But this wasn't only about him.

"Technically, it isn't. But we won't get a refund, so we'll lose the full amount, deposit and all. I'll also need to ring around and let everyone know pretty swiftly before people set off tomorrow. And I'll try, but I'm not sure I can contact the owner. Apparently, she has her own family gathering abroad."

Two nights ago, he had received an email from Mrs Mortimer-King telling him that she would not be in Scotland to meet them, but would arrange for someone to hand the keys over and settle them in. Even though he'd never met her, he liked dealing with her, enjoyed her clear instructions, efficiency and her friendly communications.

"I had a long talk with Cheryl last night," said Mrs M. "She still wants to go. Doesn't want to spend Christmas at home sitting around moping."

"Understandable. How about you?"

Mrs M provided another smile before gazing wistfully to the heavens.

"No matter where I am, I'm going to miss having Mon by my side. She always made this time of the year special. Might as well be busy in Scotland as stuck here with too much time on my hands. Cheryl can help me in the kitchen. How about Karl?"

"Karl? What about him? He's going to be there."

"That's my point. How do you feel about that?"

"It's fine. I'll deal."

Total nonsense, of course. Privately, Trevor prayed his ex-husband would do the decent thing and not show up, or perhaps the new significant other would be better at talking him down from the ledge of his principles. Most of all, he dreaded the idea of seeing Karl fawning over a new partner. Over the years Trevor had grown to love the man, had looked to their life together. Karl suppressed his emotions well and had never been afraid to put on a front and fight for what he believed to be right. Trevor had never been a fighter. He had felt emotionally volatile during their doorstep argument. After Karl had gotten everything he came for, he'd promptly turned on his heel and headed back to the comfort of his newfound relationship. That evening, Trevor had curled up on his side of the double bed he had managed to keep, feeling so painfully alone and pathetic. All night he had lain awake, wondering why Karl had never fought for him the same way.

"In different ways, we've both lost someone this year, Trevor. But you know we'll be there for you, Cheryl and me, don't you?" said Mrs M, as though hearing his thoughts.

"And I really appreciate that, Mrs M. But if they do show up, promise me you won't let the break turn into an us-and-them fiasco. You know what Karl's like when he becomes militant."

"Wouldn't dream of doing so. But I'm also not standing quietly and letting him order anyone around. Like he usually does." She pushed a lock of grey hair from her face before turning to him. "He's still going to the SLAGO meetings. Turned up at the Christmas fundraiser. Did he tell you?"

Karl had said nothing, but Trevor was unsurprised. His ex might have woken up one day and realised he wasn't gay anymore, but he still loved a cause, a fight to champion. Hence his unfailing loyalty to the Surrey and London Association of Gay Organisations. After the break-up, Cheryl had mused somewhat unkindly whether Karl had ever really been gay, whether he had decided to call himself queer because he needed to wear a badge of honour, to fight on the side of something subversive and radical, become a member of the Great British LGBTQ Cause Club. Trevor knew different, because their relationship had not been a sham even if Karl had shunned affection outside the bedroom. Trevor accepted those things because they meant having someone to care for, to love and share a life with. And more than anything, even after everything that had transpired, Trevor still respected Karl as a person.

"What he does now is his own business. Lots of straight people go to those meetings," he offered. He didn't want an argument about Karl. "Helping young gay kids who are chucked out on the streets by their families, kids with nowhere to go. Karl's still supporting a worthy cause."

Mrs M didn't appear to want to listen. In some ways, she was just like her late partner.

"Lesbians that convert and cross over to the hetero side are labelled 'hasbians'. What do you call men who denounce their homosexual status?"

"He's not calling himself straight, if that's what you're asking. So I don't think he's entirely forfeited the title."

"Mon would have called him a *fecking wee Judas*."

Trevor let out an exasperated breath. Had she been alive, Monica would have probably gone round to see Karl and given him a piece of her mind, and would at the very least have withdrawn his invitation.

"Look, I know you're supporting me, Mrs M. But if we're going to get through this holiday, let's keep our thoughts to ourselves and try to struggle through with the minimum of casualties."

After a glance, she chuckled a steamy breath into the morning.

"You're really selling this holiday, aren't you? But I'm deadly serious, Trevor. If you want to back out now, we're with you all the way."

He stared into the distance and thought about something Cheryl had said recently to him. Quoting the five stages of grief, she believed Trevor should be going through the anger stage by now, showing signs of betrayal or issuing threats of revenge. But that was never going to be his style. Others had made their thoughts and feelings known about Karl, but Trevor wasn't built that way. Yes, of course he had wallowed in self-pity at first, but he had also had nine months to use up those emotions and now felt wrung out, emotionally exhausted, and resigned to living out the rest of his days as a bachelor gay. And a holiday far away from the city smoke could be just what the therapist ordered — if he'd had one.

"Stuff it, no. Let's do it, Mrs M. If not for us, for Monica. She loved this time of year. And we're gathering in the land of her ancestors, the Caledonian Celts."

"Oh, baby," she said, putting her arm around his shoulders and hugging him tightly. "You have such a good heart. I promise never to mention this again for the duration of the holiday, but Karl was neither right nor good enough for you."

"You're obligated to say that. It's written into the mother charter under the 'Cheryl's best friend' subsection. So how many are we now?"

"You, me and Cheryl."

"Three."

"Karl and his new — is she his girlfriend?" asked Mrs M.

"Partner, I think."

"What's her name?"

"No idea. But that makes us five."

"Jessica and this guy she's bringing. From Hannah's office."

"Seven then. Are they a couple?"

"Not according to Hannah."

"How are they travelling there?"

"Train, I think. Not our problem, is it? They have the address."

"Are they even gay?"

"Don't think so."

"Heaven help us," Trevor said, shaking his head. "This keeps getting better and better. Seven of us in a seven-bedroom converted lakeside lodge — sorry, *lochside* lodge — that sleeps up to eighteen. Obscene, really. Mind you, the place looks amazing, especially the kitchen. Did Cheryl show you the latest website photos? Modernised, but they've still maintained its vintage charm, especially with that huge Aga cooker."

"Never trust photographs. Remember the Lake District? All mod cons, my foot. Just because they provided a four-slice toaster and a heated towel rack. And I've tried cooking on many an Aga, and recall what a temperamental pain in the backside they can be."

"That's your superpower, Mrs M. Wrestling temperamental pains in the backside. I suppose you've packed enough food to feed the whole village?"

"You might thank me if we're snowed in."

"The way the weather's been playing up, we're more likely to experience heat stroke."

At that very moment, Cheryl emerged from the house, juggling three mugs of something hot and steaming. Decked out in her faux-Versace beige-and-burgundy silk dressing gown and pink slippers, she came to a stop before the garden gate. With a mimed roar, she issued a steamy yawn into the morning.

"Trevor Oswald McTavish," came her familiar voice. She was the only person he would allow to use his full name. Sometimes his friends called him Mac, because nobody—*nobody*—ever referred to him as Trev. Not unless they wanted to be ghosted. Considering everything that had gone down over the past twenty-four hours, she did not look too bad. "Thought I heard your dulcet tones. Well, don't sit there like pigeons on a pole. One of you open the gate for poor, lonesome old me. Can't you see my hands are full?"

"Someone's cheered up," whispered her mother. "Must be hearing your voice, Trevor." Standing up from the tailgate, she went over and unlatched the access. "I thought you were showering. You told me we needed to be on the road early, to beat the traffic."

"I didn't know if you and Trevor had decided to pull the plug. But judging by your smiling faces, I guess not. And anyway, there's no rush now. I just checked the satnav app and listened to the latest traffic report." Cheryl handed a mug of deep brown tea to her mother, and a milkier version to Trevor. "Looks as though people stayed home. So we may as well do the M25, M40 then hit the M6. If we leave by nine, with an hour's stop for lunch, we'll reach the lodge between eight and nine this evening."

"Perfect," said Mrs M, taking a sip from her mug and pulling a face. "Means we'll arrive in time for a quick shower and a bite to eat before bedtime. Then a whole day getting things ready before the others arrive."

Trevor studied Cheryl as Mrs M spoke. She seemed far too bright and perky considering everything. Either she was putting on a brave face or, more likely, the news had not been unexpected.

"So what's gonna be the theme this time, Martha Stewart?" Cheryl asked him.

Each year, Trevor had been tasked with decorating the venue in readiness for the rest of the troupe's arrival. If Cheryl's mum excelled in the kitchen, his forte was in decorating spaces. On the first trip he'd created a freedom rainbow theme, conceptually tricky but accomplished without making the place seem too tacky, or like a set from *My Little Pony*. In subsequent years, other people had pushed their choices — *Frozen's* pure white, and blue for Johnny and Frank, after their favourite Christmas song, *Blue Christmas*.

This season Trevor had consulted nobody. But he always remembered Monica's reaction whenever he unveiled one of his creations, a simple, *'Nice, Mac, but what's wrong with normal decorations?'* This year, he had decided to go with a conventional Christmas theme, fresh and natural, incorporating whatever he could find around the lodge. Hopefully this would entail a visual and fragrant display of branches of fir, evergreen and pine cones, items he could fix together and finish off with the red or tartan ribbons he had brought from home. No gaudy colours, no artificial paints or glitter this year, just earth colours and raw materials.

"Trade secret. But let's just say I'm not taking requests this year."

"Whatever you do," said Mrs M, patting him lightly on the shoulder, "I'm sure it will be lovely."

"Not sure anyone will notice," Trevor muttered to himself as she shuffled off, a move clearly meant to leave space for Cheryl and him to talk. As she managed the latch on the garden gate, Cheryl moved to take the place beside him. They sat for a few moments, each sipping their drinks, before either broke the silence — an honour given to Cheryl.

"Mum and I talked last night. As long as you were still on board, I'd be driving the first leg until Birmingham," she said, the ordinary topic surprising him. "Mum's insisting on doing her bit, but her eyesight's getting worse. So I suggested she take the second leg for a couple of hours until mid-afternoon before the light starts to fade. After that, you can take over."

"Fine by me."

"Told her you're the only one who's been to Scotland and knows back roads."

"I've been there once. To Edinburgh by train. When I was ten."

"She doesn't need to know that. Besides, we have my trusty satnav app."

They sat in comfortable silence again until he peered at her.

"Why didn't you call me last night? About Hannah?" he asked. Few of the people who knew Cheryl got to see the morning version—pale and makeup free and, quite honestly, looking like she needed a blood transfusion. She held her mug before her in both hands but refused to look at him as she took a big sigh and replied.

"She called at midnight. And I didn't want to bother you. You're still working through your own relationship aftermath." Cheryl smoothed an errant lock of her long mousy brown hair over her right ear, a trademark habit. "I'm angry, Mac, of course I am. But the truth is we've been drifting apart for months. Last night wasn't a knife to the heart so much as the final squeeze that stopped the heart from beating. Worst of all, everyone saw what was happening but me. Maybe because I'd hoped that if I didn't say anything, things might eventually turn themselves around. But everything makes sense now. I wanted us to marry, she didn't see the point. I wanted to move in together, she preferred her own space. Can't tell you how many times she voiced her dislike of kids, as though letting me know not to even dare ask. All the signs were there. I was just deaf and blind to them."

"Yeah, well, love can do that."

"I'm not even sure what we had was love. More like comfortable familiarity. This was my wake-up call, my epiphany, telling me it's time to grow up and move on."

Trevor reached across to squeeze Cheryl's hand.

"Must say, you're taking this like a trooper."

"Really? Right at this moment, I feel like standing up on the bonnet of this car, getting my Adele on and belting *Make You Feel My Love* into the morning at the top of my voice."

"Please, no. Think of the sleeping neighbours. Besides, no karaoke before midday."

Both chuckled, Cheryl bumping her shoulder with his, before she sighed deeply.

"I've no idea who she is," she said. "This girl she's supposed to have met at the work party. Not even sure there is anyone. If you want my guess, she needs time alone over Christmas, or at least the company of her own family."

"Could have picked better timing," said Trevor. "I'm not sure we'd have gotten a refund, though, if —"

"Doesn't matter. I paid her share," said Cheryl.

A heavy silence hung in the air between them.

"They say bad things come along in threes," said Trevor.

"Threes?"

"Monica, Karl and now Hannah. Although your mum's loss is hardly comparable to ours. How's she doing?"

"You know Mum. She tries not to let anything get to her, puts on a brave front for everyone. But I know she's hurting. I know she misses Monica terribly. A couple of times I've heard her talking to herself, in the bedroom or the bathroom. Until I realised she was actually talking to Monica."

Trevor breathed out a sigh and let the sadness sink in.

"Poor Mrs M. Our worries pale by comparison, don't they? I suppose things gets better, over time."

"So they say. Do you still miss Karl?" asked Cheryl.

Trevor stared at his feet. *Every day*, he almost blurted. For five of their six years together, they had lived under the same rented roof, shared the same bed, watched the same television shows, cooked and cared for each other — in sickness and in health. On the other hand, each had stuck with their own set of friends outside of their home and the two camps had rarely mixed. He and Karl had only ever showed up as a couple on the rare occasion, such as family gatherings or meetings with their support group friends.

When Karl left, Trevor had holed himself up, and the flat had become a tomb. Apart from visiting Cheryl's place on occasion, he hadn't felt brave enough to step out on his own.

"Sometimes," he lied. "But I'm finally comfortable with my own company. At least you didn't get married then get dragged through the gutters of divorce."

"True enough."

"All those years the gay community spent chasing marriage equality. And once we finally won the right, we totally forgot that marriage comes with that evil and twisted twin lurking in the shadows, waiting for an opportunity to pounce. We forgot that once you get the main prize, there in the wings like a vicious predator, hungry to get its fangs into anything you have and stamp on anything you ever felt, lies good old-fashioned divorce."

"And *finally* Trevor's anger raises its ugly head —"

"You think you know somebody until you're threatening to strangle each other over throw cushions, nylon quilt covers or placemats decorated with the heads of Lenin, Mao and Che Guevara. Even a novelty penis bottle opener. I'd love to know what my replacement has made of that little gem."

"What's her name, by the way? This new girlfriend."

Cheryl's mother had asked him the same thing.

"No idea. We'll find out tomorrow. Unless the pair of them come to their senses and decide not to show." Trevor stared at his mug and gently shook his head. "I'm twenty-eight, Cheryl. There's this guy the same age as me who works for one of my clients. He's married to another man and they have a kid he walks to school each morning."

"And your point is?"

"When am I going to grow up?"

"*We*, you mean. And to be honest, I hope we never do. At least you get to cross marriage off your list." Cheryl placed the mug against her cheek and sighed deeply. "Is this trip going to be a disaster?"

"Are you giving me permission to burst into *My Heart Will Go On*?"

Cheryl checked her wristwatch.

"Sorry, Mac, still morning. No karaoke. Your rule, not mine."

Once again, they grinned at each other, and Trevor felt his bravado swell through their shared humour and adversity.

"You know what, Cheryl? Your mum asked the same thing, and I'll tell you what I told her. We're doing this. We may not have the usual crowd, but your mum's still serving up her amazing Christmas fare, there are plenty of rooms for privacy, and we'll be in walking country. So if anyone starts to get on our nerves, we can find each other and go for a long walk in the glen. Or a hike to a local pub. Or go for a swim in the bloody loch for all I care."

"I am so not packing my swimwear," she said, horrified.

"Wimp," he said, nudging her shoulder.

"Bloody right. But I'll happily cheer you on as you cut a hole in the ice and dive in. I may even help you out, if you can find the hole again," she replied with a mischievous smile. "And I am going to eat and drink whatever I want, no calorie counting and no judgement."

"And no disagreement from me. I am with you one hundred percent."

"God," she said, breathing out a long sigh. "Maybe we should just get married to each other. If celebrities are alleged to be able to make marriages work, I'm sure we can. Sex isn't everything, is it?"

Trevor took the question to be rhetorical.

"Love you as I do, Cheryl, we would only ruin a perfect friendship. We'd end up killing each other over which TV programmes to watch, acceptable toilet seat etiquette, whose turn for the karaoke machine, duvet hogging — any number of things. Besides, not only am I never getting married again, I am never falling in love. And you can quote me on that."

"Oh, trust me, I will."

"Now, let's get our arses into gear. We've got a long road ahead. But just so you know, I'm not booking anything next year. Takes too much effort. This is definitely going to be the last."

"Last what?"

"Last Christmas. And no, that was *not* your cue for a song!"

Chapter Two

2000 Miles

Five hundred miles and three pit stops later, they left the A82 to circumvent Britain's highest mountain, Ben Nevis, and hit the small B-road heading for Loch Arkaig. Winter's night had comfortably settled in. Rainclouds had cleared along the route, and the otherwise rain-washed lanes glistened with a magical sheen of ice, headlights and moonlight.

After handing over the driving to Trevor at the final stop, Mrs M had taken the back seat and promptly fallen asleep, leaving Cheryl to navigate. Trevor enjoyed driving, loved to be focused when the pure act emptied everything else from his usually busy mind — especially the thought of running into Karl again. When he turned the Volvo onto a small gravel track at almost precisely eight-thirty and bumped towards the silhouetted structure of Stratham Lodge, Cheryl was the first to spot another car parked on the far side, the lights on and engine still running.

"Must be the owner's contact. Right on time."

"Let me sort the keys out," said Trevor as he parked up and switched off the engine. "Looks freezing out. Stay here in the warmth with your mum. Once I've got the door unlocked, I'll come and fetch you."

"Go on. I need to check my phone for messages now we've stopped moving."

They had in common that neither of them could read text in a moving vehicle without feeling carsick. Trevor half suspected that Cheryl wanted to check if Hannah had been in touch. When he pushed the door open, chill air invaded instantly, so despite stiffened joints, he hurried out and slammed the door behind him. Across the parking area, seeing his approach, the driver's door opened and the silhouette of a man unfolded into the night.

"Trevor, my man. How're they hanging?" came a familiar Irish voice.

"Johnny? Johnny Reilly?" Either because of the chill air or the sudden surge of emotion, Trevor's eyes began to well up. "What the hell are you doing here? We thought you weren't coming. Aren't you and Frank supposed to be on a beach in Iran or Lebanon — or somewhere like that?"

"See, Frank, you dickwad," said Johnny, leaning down to address his companion, who had sensibly chosen to remain in the warmth of the car. "I told you the card we sent from Istanbul never arrived. Bet the bloody thing's still behind the hotel reception. We never said we weren't coming, Mac. Truth is, we wouldn't have missed this for the world. *Umph.* What's that for?"

While he had been talking, Trevor had strode over and pulled him off balance into a fierce hug. Finally, something good had come out of their potential catastrophe. He held tight and pushed his face into Johnny's collar.

"You have no idea how pleased I am to see you guys."

"Mary and Joseph, sounds like someone's got a story to tell," said Johnny softly, before pushing an arm around Trevor's shoulders and squeezing, staring with concern. Not wanting to worry Johnny, Trevor pulled away and shook his head before taking the set of keys offered by his friend. "We gave your name to the young fellow-me-lad from the big house and he left those with us. Headed off a few minutes ago but said he'd be back to check on us late morning tomorrow. We were going inside and see if we could light a fire, but apparently the place is centrally heated. He said the heating's on a timer and already running. He also said you were due at any minute, which is why we decided to wait."

They made a good team. Johnny used his phone torch to shine a light on the lock, while Trevor tested each of the keys in an attempt to open the front door. Behind them, the East London voice of Frank sounded.

"This hotel travel geezer in Turkey managed to get us a standby from Dalaman to Edinburgh. Hope you're impressed. We've just flown two thousand bloody miles to be here, 'cause Christmas wouldn't be the same without a dose of Mrs M's Christmas nosh. When was the last time we saw you, Trevor? February, March? Much happened since then?"

As the right key finally fit in the lock, Trevor turned and offered Johnny a world-weary shrug, probably wasted in the virtual darkness.

"If you'd hadn't sold your phones before you left, you'd already know," he called out.

"Digital detox, Trevor," said Johnny. "That's what we told everyone. Total absence of technology. Why do you think you got postcards, not emails?"

"Although, to be fair," said Frank, "we bought a couple of cheapo phones and SIM cards at Edinburgh airport before picking up the rental. So we're back online, kind of. I've got almost a year's worth of email and text messages to trawl through."

"Well, you can delete all of mine and we can do that over dinner," said Trevor. "Let's get unpacked first. Go in and switch the lights on while I fetch Cheryl and Mrs M."

Back at the Volvo, he opened the door wide and broke the news to Cheryl, her reaction much the same as his. Together with the cold air, her squeals of joy woke Mrs M. Once he had brought them both quickly up to speed, they grabbed their luggage and headed to the sanctuary of the lodge.

The front door opened into the lodge's left side, into a small anteroom with hooks for coats and racks for shoes. As Mrs M opened the next entry into the kitchen, a wave of pleasant warmth hit them, evidence that the owner had indeed activated the central heating. For some reason, neither Johnny nor Frank had turned on any lights. Cheryl found the switches first, but when she tried them, nothing happened.

"What the hell?"

"Not working," came Frank's voice as a flickering light from his phone announced his arrival. "We've been scouting around for the fuse box, but this place is a bleeding maze. Do you have the number of the owner, Trevor? I'll take another look around, but all they need to do is tell us where the fuse box is."

Trevor dug out his phone and noticed two things. Not only was the battery almost dead, but the device barely registered a signal. Without a word, he marched back out into the cold night, where the reception appeared strong and stable. Eventually he found an email from the owner with the telephone number, but the call went to voicemail each time he dialled.

"Bloody marvellous. Nobody's answering," he called to the darkness inside the house.

"Looks like there's no electricity. Except for the built-in fridge, which is a little baffling," said Cheryl, as Trevor entered and shut the door behind him. Using his phone light, he joined Johnny and Cheryl at the kitchen table. Both had their phone lights shining on their faces like something out of a low-budget horror film.

"Maybe some devices are on a different circuit," continued Cheryl. "I just tried to plug in the kettle for a cup of tea, but no luck. The heating must be gas-fired. How about the Aga cooker, Mum?"

"Apart from not knowing whether this is gas or oil-fired," said Mrs M, "from my limited experience, they take hours to get to a reasonable heat. I'll tackle the monster first thing in the morning when there's more light."

"What are you saying, Mum? No tea?" came Cheryl's whiny voice.

Despite groans from Trevor and Johnny – Frank was still lost in the lodge somewhere – Mrs M started chuckling. After her silhouette placed a cardboard box down by the sink, she turned to them, hands on hips.

"Honestly, you kids. Surprised none of you have checked to see if there's a pizza delivery service nearby."

"You don't think – ?" began Cheryl hopefully.

"Of course not. But just as well I was a Girl Scout in my youth. Along with food supplies I brought a big box of candles — large red ones for the Christmas table, but I think our need is greater right now. And my camping gas stove is still in the car from an old field trip. Come on, let's get busy. Fill a saucepan with water, Cheryl. Trevor, use your light to hunt around for cups, saucers and a teapot. Johnny, find out where the plates and cutlery are stored and get some for each of us. I'll go and fetch the cooker from the car."

Once they had followed Mrs M's orders, Cheryl and Trevor set about lighting candles, placing them in saucers and arranging them in the centre of the kitchen table while Mrs M set up the make-do stove. After setting a large pan of water to boil, she sent them off into the lodge with their phone lights to claim their bedrooms.

Trevor picked the one nearest the kitchen. According to the website, this more compact bedroom had a small double bed and would be perfect for one person. Larger bedrooms with adjoining bathrooms were situated on the first floor with views over the loch. No doubt Johnny and Frank would be first to bag one of those.

When he returned to the kitchen, the candlelit dining table looked like something out of a Dickens novel, brightened by a floral China teapot and matching cups and saucers. Mrs M had her back to him, the large pan on her portable stove hissing and spitting, the scent of frying bacon filling the air. Everyone wandered back in dribs and drabs, enthusing about their rooms but even more about the smells coming from the kitchen. Mrs M knocked up a very palatable meal of fried eggs, bacon, sausages, tomatoes and mushrooms – more like breakfast really, but nobody complained. At the end of the meal Trevor led the round of compliments to an amused Mrs M.

"This may sound weird," said Frank, leaning back, his arms folded over his stomach. "But this already seems right. I feel completely at home here."

"I know what you mean, Frank," agreed Johnny. "Candlelight, cups of tea and a fry up. And darned good company. Good to be back, to be sure."

"And it's good that you two are here to help," said Mrs M, nodding at them. "Cheryl needs a hand getting some last-minute things in town tomorrow morning. Give you a chance to have a look around the town and get yourselves lunch. More importantly, I don't want you under my feet while I'm trying to find my way around this kitchen."

"She means you," said Frank, nudging Johnny.

"She means all of us," said Cheryl. "Except Trevor. He needs time and space to work his decorating magic."

"Exactly," said Mrs M, clearing plates away. "Now how about telling us what mischief you two reprobates have been up to since you disappeared off the map."

"In which case," said Johnny, standing up from the table and getting a bag he had left on the kitchen floor, "can I tempt you all to some after-dinner Turkish delights? And I'm not talking about the sugary, squidgy, sweet version. Frank, while I do the honours, tell them about us almost getting arrested in Sudan."

While Frank mesmerised them with their world adventures, Johnny produced two bottles of Lebanese red wine and a selection of Turkish cheeses that he said he had been saving for Christmas Day. Impressing them all, while unwrapping the cheeses, he recited the names of each in turn—Kaşar, Tulum, Kelle, Dil, Örgü, Van Otlu and Kuymak—until Frank held one of them up to a candle and pointed out that the shopkeeper had written the names on the paper wrappers. While everyone else groaned, Trevor couldn't help but smile. More than anything, he hoped the sense of fun and optimism would remain tomorrow evening when everyone else arrived.

With his spiked black hair, permanently creased forehead and quick dark eyes, Frank Ward had developed a roguish charm. Born in a rough housing estate in East London, his mother had left home by the time he was six. Shorter and quieter than his three older brothers, he was bullied relentlessly. When Trevor first met him, Johnny Reilly told the story of the days fifteen-year-old Frank slept rough after being chucked out by his dad for coming out, but not before being kicked and punched by his brothers until they had broken two of his ribs. Frank rarely talked about those dark days, only ever quipped about the *Irish ginger knob*—Johnny—who volunteered as a counsellor at the gay shelter and had offered to take him in temporarily until he got himself back on his feet. Turned out Frank had an innate knack for electrical work and, after fixing up Johnny's small flat then breezing through a couple of examinations, got himself a comfortably paid job as a sparky with a building company. By then, Johnny, three years his senior, had fallen for him so hard that rather than letting him leave, he'd pleaded for him to stay.

"Why didn't Karl and Hannah come down with you?" Frank asked during a lull in the conversation, while topping up Frank's tea cup with Merlot. "Is Karl working?"

Trevor stared into his tea cup as nobody answered. For the first time since they had sat down together, the mood dropped and Trevor realised they had some explaining to do.

"Hannah and I split up," said Cheryl. Typical of her to come straight to the point while Trevor sat there quietly, unsure how to tell them about him and Karl. "She's not coming."

"Oh feck. So sorry, Cher."

"Let me guess. Hannah met someone else, didn't she?" said Frank. At best, he and Hannah had tolerated each other for the sake of keeping the peace. When Cheryl nodded, he muttered something under his breath that nobody could hear.

"Karl's coming tomorrow," said Trevor, ignoring Cheryl's candlelit glare. Johnny and Frank knew nothing about what had happened earlier in the year, and he didn't want to dampen the upbeat mood. At least, that's what he told himself.

"Come on, Trevor," said Cheryl from across the table. "You're going to have to tell them. May as well rip off the bandage and come clean."

"Tell us what?" said Frank, mirroring Johnny's posture and leaning back in his chair, his hands folded behind his head.

Trevor studied them both, wondering how much he should tell them about his dreadful year. But then, maybe they would understand, because the two of them had lived through far worse.

"Come on, buddy boy," said Johnny. "Spill the beans. What's Karl Marx been up to this time? Not been in the slammer, has he? Arrested for throwing his soiled Y-fronts at UKIP supporters."

"I wish it were that simple. But the truth is, we're not together anymore. He's just, he…"

Trevor faltered and breathed out a sigh, wondering when explaining Karl's act of marital treason to people was going to get any easier.

"He switched sides," finished Mrs M loudly, turning around from the sink. "Decided he's not gay anymore. So he walked out on Trevor and now he's shacked up with a woman."

"He's what?" asked Johnny, aghast, thumping forwards in his seat, his thick red eyebrows scrunched together. "Tell me you're pulling me fecking weasel?"

"No, Johnny. Mrs M's right. We broke up. And he's already moved in with his new girlfriend."

Silence fell across the table. Cheryl stared down at her hands. Mrs M stayed at the sink, looking fierce but saying nothing more. Frank, who had been quiet all this time, was the first to speak, far too calmly for Trevor's liking.

"Well ain't that a kick in the nuts? Yours was the first gay wedding we ever attended. Was the little bastard stringing you along all this time? Because next time I see him, mark my words, I'm going to break his nose. After I've given him a piece of my mind. See if I don't, the traitorous little —"

"That's why I didn't want to say anything," Trevor interrupted, squeezing the bridge of his nose in sympathy for Karl. "He wasn't stringing me along. He simply identifies as bisexual now, among the lower scores of the Kinsey scale I'm guessing, and that's not something any of us can change. He's clearly taken with this new girl and, more importantly, they are probably going to show up here tomorrow. So can I ask you—can I *beg* you all—to please not start any trouble?"

Once again, an awkward silence descended on the table. Despite Johnny's angry glare, Trevor noticed him stifle a yawn behind his hand. Trevor had begun to feel the same creeping tiredness.

"For the love of Jesus," said Johnny, folding his arms. "I thought the whole point of this Christmas tradition was that we shared the place exclusively with our own fabulous people. Had a chill time together."

"Times change," said Cheryl.

"You can bleeding well say that again." said Frank, getting up from the table and placing a hand on Johnny's shoulder. "Come on. Let's get you to bed."

After nodding and taking one of the candles, Johnny's words came back from the corridor, his voice carrying clearly.

"Ah well, Frankie boy, if there's one thing us gay boys love more than a good time with old friends, it's the promise of a bit of drama."

Trevor lowered his face into his hands.

Chapter Three

Deck The Hall

The central heating kicked in early the next morning — without the luxury of hot water. When the group reconvened in the kitchen for breakfast, Frank informed them that neither the electric showers nor the central boiler was working, both most likely on the same circuit. Everyone but Mrs M and Frank cursed the owner then grumbled about having to wash in cold water. Trevor assumed Mrs M's camping days had hardened her to the idea of a cold shower. Frank would happily bathe naked in the loch if only Johnny would let him.

Having the room closest to the kitchen, Trevor had woken early to the sound of Mrs M moving around next door, opening and closing kitchen cupboards. She appeared to be the most resourceful. Cheryl had been the one to remark on her mother's success in getting the gas-fired Aga going. All morning he'd noticed a calm contentedness about Mrs M, especially when she'd turned the morning moans into murmurs of delight by producing a breakfast of mugs of hot tea accompanied by scrambled eggs and smoked salmon on wedges of buttered golden toast.

At ten o'clock, leaving their dishes on the table at Mrs M's insistence, Cheryl, Frank and Johnny went off to change for their trip into Fort William. Even though his pride had taken a beating, Frank had eventually been dragged away from trying to locate the man fuse box in cupboards and wardrobes. Before heading off to change, he told Trevor he suspected the box had been artfully hidden behind a secret panel somewhere during the lodge's renovations.

When the front door closed and the engine started up, Trevor waited for Mrs M to meet his gaze. They sat at the kitchen table, hands wrapped around mugs, listening as the engine faded off down the lane.

"Okay, Mrs M. Spill the beans. You know something, don't you? Did you manage to find the fuse box?"

"No, dear, I have no idea about those kinds of things. I'm just a clueless old lady," she replied before levelling her gaze at him. "But I do know a thing or two about Aga cookers."

"And?"

"And how some are set up to provide hot water for a house, although I think this one only serves the kitchen. The owners kindly left me a laminated instruction sheet — very nicely done, too — showing me how to start the old girl up. So if you want some hot water for the bathroom, you can fill up a saucepan or a bucket from the hot water tap in the kitchen sink. Water's piping hot."

Trevor tipped back his head and laughed.

"If I'd told my Cheryl, I know I'd never have gotten rid of her. She would have spent the morning going back and forth from the kitchen, filling a bath, then the rest of the day getting under my feet."

"I wondered why you told them to leave their dishes. On all our other holidays, you've ordered us to clean up after ourselves."

"On all the other holidays there's been a working dishwasher."

"In which case, let me do the honour of washing up. I don't have an adjoining bathroom, so I might just wash my face at the sink once I'm done."

"Let me fill up a saucepan, and I'll leave you alone."

They had always worked well together, Trevor mused as she headed off into the lodge. Left alone to wash dishes in hot water felt like a special treat and he had everything completed, including all surfaces cleaned and cleared and himself flannel-washed, by the time she reappeared.

"Now the Aga's heated up, I'm going to start baking. Having no electricity doesn't affect that, but the electric appliances like the toaster and coffee machine are more convenient than using the Aga each time. Might be good if you could call your contact again and get the power switched on."

Trevor closed his eyes in frustration.

"My phone died last night. And I couldn't plug in my charger. I know you don't have a mobile phone, so I meant to ask Cheryl for hers before she left, but completely forgot—"

"Look, dear, I know I'm not a technical wizard like all you youngsters, but could I make a suggestion?"

"Of course."

"Do you think maybe that old telephone contraption on the wall over there might still be of use?" asked Mrs M, pointing to a grey wall phone fixed next to a backboard. "I know they worked fine back in my day for old ladies like me."

"Okay, Mrs M. Enough with the smartass for one morning. I didn't know that was there. Yes, I'm sure it works fine, but I still have the email with all the key phone numbers and contact details on my dead mobile phone. I didn't think to print off a paper copy, and they didn't leave anything in the lodge. Doesn't matter anyway. Last night, I remember Johnny saying the contact would come over this morning. So while we wait for them, I'm going keep myself busy decorating the place."

"Good plan. Are you putting anything up in here?"

"Just a few things."

"Maybe get that finished before the rabble returns. I've a feeling we'll be spending a lot of time in this room. But first, give me an hour to get some things started then come back and I'll help you."

Within the hour, Trevor had strung up the garlands and tartan ribbons he had spent hours assembling at home, and although they looked fine, they seemed lost in the huge living space. At some point he would need a ladder to reach higher places. As he worked, wonderful smells of pastry and cinnamon and other spices began to creep through the lodge. When he eventually entered the kitchen, Mrs M had countertops full of pots, pans and food. Between checking the Aga and furiously kneading dough, she helped him with the minimal kitchen decorations, leaving him to head back to the main living space.

Standing in the entryway, he studied the space with a critical eye. They had chosen well this year. The photographs on the website did not do the lodge justice. At the far end stood the building's focal point, a magnificent semi-circular communal area with floor-to-ceiling windows providing stunning panoramic views over the loch. In the centre, a modern faux-log gas fire encased in a circle of red brick and covered above by an enormous steel flue made the whole ensemble appear almost ceremonial. A semi-circle of comfy settees in beige cotton surrounded the fireplace. Where the windows ended either side of the vista, the owners had built dark oak bookcases. Only the long bar of mahogany built into the left wall interrupted the walls of books. Using dark wood in the living area had been masterful and drew the eye to the natural light filtering into the room and out to the rugged but spectacular scenery beyond.

Even when he had first entered the room that morning with Cheryl by his side and both had gasped at the sheer magnificence of the space, he'd known instinctively that a traditional Christmas theme would work perfectly. But to do the lodge justice, he would need supplies from nature. They had been promised a Christmas tree as a part of the holiday package, and Trevor was disappointed to find the owners had left them nothing. Cheryl's joke that the tree might be hidden away with the fuse box had done nothing to lighten his mood. For someone recently dumped, she seemed to be coping better than him. Although he said nothing to her, he wondered if the lack of power and the absence of a Christmas tree were further signs that they should never have agreed to come.

At eleven o'clock, with his wellies tugged on, plastic garden sacks in hand and a forced resolve, he set out to scavenge the grounds around the lodge.

As the overnight frost burned off, a cloudless morning began to bathe the ground in steamy warmth. Trevor climbed the small path to higher ground, partly to forage for holly, evergreens and fir branches, but also to get an open view of the lodge. He stopped to catch his breath under a blazing sun, removed and tied his coat around his waist and even thought about taking off his woollen jumper. Finding the perfect vantage point, he perched down cross-legged in the rough grass and took in the view.

Whoever had planned the lodge's renovation had attempted to keep the original building's essence and merge old with new. Maybe that had been a condition of the planning permission if, as Trevor suspected, the lodge was a listed heritage building. Whether purposely or by coincidence, the building had been forged into the shape of a Celtic cross.

At the newly built end facing the lake, the architect had created the circular communal living area on the ground level with the huge glass windows and outside porch. Three bedrooms jutting out from the floor above had balconies overlooking the scenery. Despite attempts to blend old and new stonework, the lower floor of the building followed a traditional design, restored and updated in places, but the same structure as the original building, which culminated in the extended kitchen and the car park. All anxiety about the holiday began to melt away with the frost, and Trevor started to treasure being in this little corner of paradise.

On his stroll down another lane towards the lodge, he noticed a cluster of wild purple thistles over a barbed wire fence. In his mind he had planned the theme as Christmas scarlet and green, but seeing them growing wild he decided the Scottish national flower should have a place in their temporary home.

Even leaning carefully over the barbed railing, using his coat for protection, he couldn't reach the plants. Undeterred, he carefully pushed his arm through the wire and stretched forwards with a gloved hand. Just as he had grasped a couple of prickly stems, his foot slipped on the slope of an unseen ditch, the arm of his woollen jumper snagging on a barb, and, with a gasp, he fell up to his groin in ice-cold bog water. With one arm trapped and the other clutching uselessly at flora — but otherwise unharmed — he stopped panicking and took a few steadying breaths.

And that's when Trevor saw him.

In the distance, a man — gloriously shirtless — on a shiny black horse moved leisurely along a dirt track through the glen, hauling a small cart laden with what appeared to be a pine tree. For some reason, the sight struck Trevor as vaguely comical, but as the man neared, Trevor's breath caught at the smooth masculinity. Broad-shouldered and upright in the saddle, he wore his hair short beneath a black cap, college-boy style, and had a dark dusting of stubble. Even from a distance Trevor could make out the thick, muscular thighs in jodhpurs and the carved lines in the pale skin of his hairless chest, muscled arms and rippled stomach. Waking himself from his fixation, he realised he needed to get the rider's attention. Until he saw the man already heading his way even though he appeared in no hurry. As he neared, Trevor could have sworn the rider was trying to control an amused and frankly rather handsome grin on his face.

"You enjoying yourself down there?" he called, his voice a pleasant baritone with a trace of a Scots accent.

"Having a bit of trouble, actually."

"Aye, you surely are."

"Sorry, can I ask why you're not wearing any clothes?" said Trevor. He hated sounding like his grandmother but seemed unable to stop himself. "You'll catch your death."

Almost upon Trevor now, the man pulled on the reins and unhurriedly brought the horse to a stop. After a glance down at his own body — as though noticing his semi-nakedness for the first time — the man levelled a humoured gaze at Trevor.

"First of all, I was not expecting to see anyone else out here today. And you may not know this if your accent is anything to go by, but it's a rare hot day for this part of the world. So I thought I'd get some sunshine. D'you not consider this hot?"

An inappropriate response to the question formed in Trevor's head.

"As you can see, I've been otherwise preoccupied."

Even though the young man didn't laugh, he looked away to smile into the sky. He had a strong profile — formal, solid and defined, something Trevor's grandmother might have referred to as 'good breeding'.

"Aye, you surely have."

"Don't suppose there's any chance of a hand?" asked Trevor.

"Give me a minute."

In one limber movement, he dismounted the saddle and landed lightly on the ground. After watching a moment, Trevor unpicked the sleeve of his jumper from the metal thorn, and when he turned, the man stood towering over him.

"If you could just give me your hand and help me to —" he began, but before he could finish, the man had reached down, placed a hand under each of his armpits and hauled him effortlessly out of the ditch. When Trevor finally regained his composure, red-faced, wellies full of water, standing in a puddle on the path, he could barely find the courage to look his handsome rescuer in the eyes.

"I'm Rudy Mortimer," said the man, holding out a hand. "And you are?"

The words 'I'm ruddy mortified' sat on Trevor's tongue, but once again he managed to restrain himself from speaking them aloud.

"Hang on. Mortimer?" he said instead, shaking the strong, warm hand. "Any relation to Mrs Mortimer-King, the owner of Stratham Lodge?"

"Her son. Or one of them."

"In which case I'm McTavish. Trevor McTavish. I'm the one renting the place."

"Oh, yes. McTavish. That's a good Scottish clan name you have there. Do your folk hail from this way?"

"You know, I'm not really sure where they come from. Apart from Balham in South London. That's where my mum's parents grew up. Maybe my father's parents came from Scotland. They died before I was born."

"I'm sorry to hear that. Anyway, welcome to Arkaig, Trevor McTavish."

"Are you the one who handed over the keys last night? To my friends?"

"Yes, I am."

"The same person who never answers his phone?"

"Sorry?"

"I tried calling you last night. On the number your mother left me. I think it's a mobile phone number."

"That'll be mine. Forgot to charge my phone last night. Those unknown calls I missed were from you, then?"

"Unless you have any other holidaymakers who arrived last night and who have no power in their holiday home."

Rudy Mortimer had the decency to turn a shade of beetroot, the colour rising from his neck to his cheeks and making him look positively adorable.

"Och, I'm sorry. Please, don't tell my mother. She'll surely kill me. I told her I had everything under control. I'm on my way to the lodge now, to make sure you settled in all right."

"In all fairness, we did. And as you were kind enough to stop and help me out of the ditch, let's call it quits. But if you could show me where the fuse box is so that I can switch on the electricity, we would all be really grateful. I think I'm going to need a hot shower when we get back. Is that our Christmas tree?"

"Aye. Freshly cut down this morning."

"Perfect. With everyone else arriving later this afternoon, I'll have plenty of time to decorate."

"I really do apologise, Trevor," he said guiltily. "This is entirely my fault. I remembered to sort out the heating during the day, but completely forgot to switch on the power. How did you manage last night?"

"Candles and a camp stove. My friend's mother, Mrs Madison—you'll meet her soon—is incredibly resourceful. She managed to produce a breakfast feast last night and again this morning."

"Well, I'll need to apologise to her, too. Can I ask, how did you end up standing in the ditch?"

"I was being impulsive, leaning over the fence attempting to pick heather and thistle. To use for decoration in the lodge."

"If it's heather and thistle you're wanting, there's a whole field full of yon prickly weed around the back of the lodge. Come, I'll show you."

"Before you do, I have one request."

"Of course."

"Can I empty my Wellingtons?"

After doing so and removing his socks, and after a surreptitious glance at the tight backside remounting the horse, Trevor strolled alongside, chatting companionably.

He learned about Rudy being the youngest son of Mr and Mrs Mortimer-King. His parents had gone to look after his mother's older sister in Vancouver over the Christmas season but would be back on New Year's Eve, Hogmanay. Rudy's horse was called Troy and lived in the stables up at the old house. Whenever he said the words 'old house' he pointed a thumb back the way he had come. Over the holiday season, Rudy had been left to fend for himself, but didn't seem to mind. Trevor filled him in on their little group of friends, about the regular get-together, omitting to mention what they had in common, about them batting for the gay team. Fair enough, too, because for the first time in five years not all of them did.

Instead of leading them to the lodge's front door, Rudy steered the horse to the other side and, just as he had stated, a field opened before them. After a brief chuckle, Trevor stepped in and used the scissors he had brought with him to collect healthier specimens, placing them into his plastic sack. Without a word, Rudy guided Troy off, this time heading towards the back of the lodge. Once Trevor had finished, he hurried to catch up, finding Rudy now wearing a white polo shirt tucked into his jodhpurs and tying up the horse in the car park. Mrs M stood at the door, staring as Rudy unloaded the tree. When Trevor reached her, he stood at her shoulder, having turned to study Rudy.

"You need a hand?" Trevor called out.

"No, I'm good."

"You most certainly are," muttered Trevor, as Mrs M snorted and bumped her shoulder against his. They watched Rudy unload the Christmas tree and drag the evergreen towards the front door.

"Are you Mrs Madison?" asked Rudy as he approached.

"I am," said Mrs M, folding her arms. "What of it?"

"I'm Rudy Mortimer, the owner's son," he said, lowering the tree to the ground before removing his cap and holding out a hand. Trevor noticed his hair and brows then, a deep, dark shade of red. "And I need to apologise to you. I should have switched on the power yesterday, and because of my mistake, I put you out. If there's anything I can do, please let me know."

She studied him for a moment then looked to Trevor for reassurance.

"Is he for real?"

"What Mrs M means," said Trevor, grabbing Mrs M's hand and making her accept Rudy's outstretched hand, "is that she's not used to dealing with such well-mannered people. And to thank you for bringing the tree."

Rudy dropped the tree off in the main room, then walked Trevor and Mrs M through the house, pointing out little features they could easily have overlooked during their stay. By the end, they knew their way around the lodge, where to find the fuse box and lights for the bar counter — hidden behind a wall panel just as Frank had guessed — the switch to illuminate the outside porch, how to fire up the central fireplace and where the remote controls were located for the television sets in each of the rooms.

Back in the kitchen, Mrs M set about making tea. Rudy offered to stick around to help Trevor put up the tree and the decorations, in recompense for his forgetfulness.

"I took the bedroom next to the kitchen," said Trevor, to make conversation before wondering why he had shared that particular snippet.

"Good choice. Best room in the lodge."

"Not sure about that. But it's the nearest to the kitchen."

"I take that room whenever I stay here. Bet you didn't discover its little secrets, did you? Mind if I show you?"

Even before Trevor shrugged his approval, Rudy had already started moving towards the door. Inside the compact room, on either side of the bed, floor-to-ceiling wood panels covered the walls much like the rest of the lodge. The owners had placed a small bedside cabinet with a lamp on the right side of the bed, but nothing on the left, near the small window. Trevor had thought nothing of this, putting the lack of furniture down to fact that the room only slept one person. Rudy stepped around the bed and stopped at the bare wall on the left.

"Unless by accident, you probably wouldn't have discovered this," he said before placing his palm on the panel and pushing. The wall moved inwards softly and soundlessly, a hidden door leading into darkness. Reaching a hand inside, Rudy pressed something on the wall and bright light flooded the space.

Turning to Trevor, he beamed and said, "Come take a look."

A modern bathroom had been fitted inside with a tub, a shower cubicle, sink and toilet. Rudy stepped over and turned the sink's hot tap. Even though they had only just switched on the lodge's electric immersion heaters, steamy hot water gushed into the sink.

"Best of all, the old lodge used to be heated from a fireplace in the kitchen — pipes still run at the back and through the Aga — so if you ever have a problem with the boiler, or if you have a power cut, this room will always get hot water. I love staying here when we have too many guests up at the old house. You may think you got a bum deal on the oldest and smallest bedroom in the house, but I guarantee, you'll not get cold, because the pipes run beneath the bedroom floor."

While Rudy talked, he had placed a hand on Trevor's back, making his body stiffen slightly at the intimacy. When he left the warm hand there, Trevor turned to grin conspiratorially at him. Eventually Rudy let go, but the place where his hand had touched remained warm.

"Does that mean I can finally get out of these wet clothes and take a quick shower?"

"You need a hand?"

Trevor grinned at Rudy and the comment slipped out before he could stop himself.

"Might not be so quick if we're showering together."

"I meant with the shower controls," said Rudy, baffled, his smile draining away.

Instant mortification. Usually Trevor had better filters and would never be so openly playful with someone he had just met. Not for the first time in his life, he had misjudged the situation, and now he had embarrassed Rudy. This time, he felt the deep burn of a blush on his cheeks.

"Um, sorry. Bad joke. Ha-ha."

"Let me carry on with the tree in the main room," said Rudy, backing out of the bathroom. "I'll hang around until you've finished. Give you a hand with the decorations, as I promised."

As soon as Rudy had gone, Trevor squeezed his eyes closed and shook his head. *Well done, Trevor.* Not even a day in the place and he had already embarrassed the host and made a fool of himself.

Once he had figured out the shower controls, he undressed and stood beneath the water, wondering if he should apologise again, or write the stupid comment off as a bad joke. He decided on the latter.

After towelling off and changing into dry clothes in record time, he joined Rudy back in the main room.

Fortunately, Rudy seemed unfazed and appeared to enjoy the challenge of decorating. Over the next ninety minutes, with a quick break of tea and freshly baked mince pies from Mrs M, they hung up decorations and integrated the flora Trevor had collected. Even though their conversation had faltered, they worked seamlessly together. Most of the time Trevor directed Rudy, sending him to the top of a ladder and guiding him where to pin things, which worked well because Rudy knew his way around the room. Even using conscious effort, Trevor couldn't help ogling Rudy stretched out at the top of the ladder, or when his muscular arms hauled boxes out of their way. Both were so caught up in the work that neither realised how much they had accomplished. Not until they heard Mrs M's soft gasp from the edge of the living room. When Trevor turned, she stood there frozen in her flour-dusty apron, with a hand placed over her mouth.

"What's wrong, Mrs M?"

"Beautiful," she said through her fingers. "If only Mon were here. This is what she had always wanted. Come over and take a look, the both of you."

Once they moved to stand next to her, Rudy drew in a sharp breath and, probably without conscious thought, placed a hand on Trevor's shoulder. Trevor said nothing, and tried to dismiss the gesture as nothing more than kinship at a job well done, even though the warmth and pressure felt as nice as before. To distract himself, he cast a critical eye around the room.

Tartan bows of scarlet and green, or mauve and green, those they had fixed at regular intervals to garlands of fir, provided the central theme above the windows and around the circular fireplace. Bunches of purple thistle or sprigs of holly and mistletoe, arranged with simple gold ribbons, added another focal point. To one side of the window, the Christmas tree continued the simple theme, but with the bonus of white lights that twinkled and faded softly in and out. Rudy had accomplished that without his help. If anything, the overall effect came across as naturally rustic, exactly what Trevor had envisaged, totally fitting the lodge and the location. Not only that, but he knew the moment Cheryl returned and saw the decorations, and after her squeals of joy had died down, her entire repertoire of over five hundred Christmas carols and songs would begin to issue through her Bluetooth speaker.

"Pure dead brilliant, Trev. You've a rare talent for this," said Rudy, and for the first time in his life, Trevor warmed to a nickname he usually despised. Perhaps because on Rudy's tongue, with his soft accent, the word sounded nice, sexy almost. Heavens, he thought, what with that and the warm hand on his shoulder, Rudy could ask for anything right now and he would give it to him.

"Yes, well," he replied, to keep his voice steady. "This is not all me. You did your bit, too."

"Just what you told me to do," Rudy said before absently checking his wristwatch. "Och, will you look at the time. I should be going. Mother's calling the old house around four and I haven't fed Troy yet."

"Come on then," replied Trevor. "We'll see you out."

On the way to the door, Rudy commented on the delicious smells coming from the kitchen, and Mrs M, a sucker for compliments, asked him to hang on while she picked out some freshly baked scones and cakes for him to take home. Trevor stood in the doorway, watching as Rudy went over to pet Troy, readying to mount again.

"So, Trev. What is it you're wanting for Christmas?"

Be still my beating heart, thought Trevor unable to stop his smile, *and for heaven's sake stay my errant tongue.* He could tell Rudy was teasing him, but he didn't mind. Trevor almost asked him if he might have a gay twin brother hidden away that he could borrow for a Christmas fling.

"The usual. Peace and goodwill to all men. And women, of course. More to the point," said Trevor, "what plans do you have for Christmas? Do you have someone cooking for you up at the — um — big house?"

"No," said Rudy, and something fleeting passed across his gaze. Just at that moment, Mrs M appeared with a large brown paper bag. "It'll just be me. Family's away, but even when they're here we're not big on Christmas. As I said earlier, we tend to save our celebrations for New Year's Eve."

While Trevor's mind wrestled for some way to respond, to offer up an olive branch and invite him over to join them, Mrs M must have been reading his mind as she walked over to hand him the bag of goods.

"Well, you're not staying on your own," she said. "You'll come and join us for Christmas lunch, even if I have to squeeze into my boots and drag you here myself."

"Seriously, Rudy," said Trevor. "Decline an invitation from Mrs M at your peril. More to the point, if you think I'm good at decorating, you should taste her amazing cooking."

As he bounced into his saddle, an incredible smile lit up Rudy's face again.

"That's very kind of you, Mrs M. Can I call and let you know?"

"As long as it's to say yes," said Mrs M, her arms crossed, making Rudy shake his head with amusement.

"I'd best be going. Let you get ready for your guests. Thanks, Trev. I really enjoyed helping. And thanks for the cakes, Mrs M. See you soon, eh?"

"I hope so," murmured Trevor, lost in his smile again and almost convinced Rudy had winked. "I really do hope so."

Chapter Four

Mary's Boy Child

Just before six o'clock that evening, Cheryl and Trevor finished decorating and laying the kitchen table for dinner. While each enjoyed a glass of sparkling wine, they sang along to Christmas carols and played a game of *'what would you rather?'* His mood had improved considerably since Rudy's visit, although he had kept the details to the bare minimum when telling Cheryl and the boys. Mrs M worked quietly in the background, occasionally snorting at their responses but mainly concentrating on checking the progress of the lamb joint and roast potatoes in the Aga, and getting the Yorkshire pudding and selection of vegetables ready to be dealt with last.

"Would you rather have car sex or shower sex?" asked Trevor, as Justin Bieber came to the closing bars of *Mistletoe*.

"Easy one," said Cheryl without pausing to think. "Shower sex. Especially in this weather. Would you rather have a small penis that can ejaculate, or a big one that can't even get an erection?"

"Exactly how old are you two?" asked Mrs M.

"We're on holiday, Mum. We're allowed to be juvenile. Come on, Mac. What would you rather have?"

"Small penis," said Trevor, then he started giggling as the opening bars of Bruce Springsteen's *Santa Claus Is Comin' to Town* started up. "What's the point of having one if it can't get hard? Would you rather French kiss with melted Cadbury's Creme Eggs or a melted marshmallow Wagon Wheel?"

"Either. No, both!" blurted Cheryl, making even Mrs M laugh aloud. "Would you rather get voted off in the first round of *Great British Bake Off*, or go all the way to the final of *Hell's Kitchen*?"

"I know my answer," said Mrs M, who had a strong aversion to bad language.

"Easy. *Bake Off*," said Trevor. "I'm out. You got any more?"

"Last one. Would you rather live your life over again as a twelve-year-old girl but with all your current memories intact, or continue your life as a twenty-eight-year-old man with untold wealth and respect, but with no memory beyond yesterday morning?"

Trevor had to stop and think. Life hadn't exactly gone to plan, but would he want to lose all memory of the past? Some people might want to forget, might want to try life as the opposite gender, but if he was going to be completely honest, he had enjoyed his male years so far.

"Can I choose car sex?" he replied, then noticed Mrs M had suddenly gone still and had turned her head to listen at the window.

"What time are these friends of yours arriving?" she asked Cheryl.

"Any time now," said Cheryl. "Why?"

"Listen."

And right then Trevor heard the crackle of tyres on gravel and a car engine being killed in the parking bay outside the kitchen window.

"Who do you reckon?" asked Cheryl, staring with concern at Trevor.

Trevor's heart sank, the lightness he had been feeling evaporating. Trevor knew Cheryl had played the game partly to divert his anxiousness about Karl showing up with his new partner. Taking a deep breath, he resolved to put on a brave front, for all their sakes.

"Whoever it is, we're not going to let them spoil our fun. Agreed?"

"Quite right, Trevor," said Mrs M, already back to work.

"Cheryl?"

"Of course."

So far, things had gone well. Cheryl and the boys had arrived back from Fort William laden with goodies and in high spirits. Mrs M and Trevor had listened patiently for more than an hour over mugs of tea as they'd recounted their day trip. Frank and Johnny had bought extra Christmas pressies to cover all the guests, as well as cases of beer, wine and spirits, and had also contributed generously to the fresh food shopping.

While the boys had enjoyed drinks over lunch in a local pub, Cheryl had remained sober, agreeing to be the designated driver, but planned to make up for lost time that evening. Only as they'd finished talking and laughing, and as the sun began to sink, had Trevor led them all into the living room and shown them the illuminated decorations. Reactions had been varied but not unexpected. Frank and Johnny had shared a couple of amazed expletives while Cheryl had gasped and hugged the breath out of Trevor before running to her room and rushing back to hook up her Christmas music.

With darkness descending, stars sparkling off the dark surface of the loch, lights twinkling on the tree and The King's Singers filling the air, their holiday lodge finally became the perfect Christmas setting. At around five-thirty, the boys had gone off for some private time while the rest of them had begun preparing food for the evening.

When the doorbell sounded, Trevor felt his face drain of blood. Cheryl must have noticed his reaction because she leapt up from the table.

"I'll go."

Above the sound of Christmas music playing, he could hear the exchange of voices at the door. One male, the other female. But the male voice did not belong to Karl. Cheryl appeared first, trailing two young people behind her, and treated Trevor and Mrs M to a dramatic roll of her eyes.

"Mum. Trevor. These are Hannah's co-workers, Jessica and Antoni."

With a relieved sense of reprieve, Trevor jumped up from the table and greeted the pair. Of the two, Jessica seemed the more forthcoming and friendly, while Antoni stood in her shadow. They made an unlikely couple — if they were a couple. Even in heels, she barely reached over five foot. She seemed to laugh easily and Trevor thought perhaps nerves played a part. From her complexion, he wondered if she might be second generation Indian, and although he had never met an Indian girl with the name Jessica, contemporary naming conventions tended to be more eclectic across the country. Towering behind her, the black-haired boy stood taller than Trevor's five-ten, probably touching six-two. He wore thick-framed spectacles, the old-fashioned type, and every few seconds he screwed up his nose and pushed them back up the bridge.

"Welcome to Christmas at Stratham Lodge," said Trevor, marvelling at Jessica's firm handshake. "I'm Trevor. Cheryl and I organised the break."

"Call me Jess," said the girl after releasing his hand. "And he's Antoni with an i."

Behind her, the boy craned awkwardly over her shoulder to shake hands.

"Antoni Kaminski. Dad's Polish. Food smells amazing. In case you needed to ask, neither of us have any food allergies and we'll eat anything. Lots of anything. Am I rooming with you?" he asked Trevor.

"No, there's plenty of space," said Cheryl. She had taken her seat back at the table, having played her part. "We all have our own rooms. I've put Jessica on the top floor, up the central staircase to the right, and you're on the ground floor, directly below. Oh, and my mum's the cook. But you can call her Mrs M."

"I can show you to your rooms," said Trevor. "Anything else you need to know?"

"What's the Wi-Fi password?" asked Antoni.

Of all the questions he could have asked, that one caught Trevor unaware. He'd forgotten to ask Rudy if the place had Wi-Fi. When he stared over at Cheryl for help, she merely shrugged and shook her head.

"Uh," said Trevor, passing on the shrug, "I'm not sure we have Wi-Fi."

"What?" said Antoni, horrified, his mouth dropping open as though Trevor had just told him they had no indoor toilets.

"Yes, we do," said Mrs M, coming to the rescue, a small piece of paper in her hand. "Rudy made sure the router was working and left this with me. The network is Stratham4G, and he wrote the password up on the kitchen blackboard. It's all gobbledegook to me. Just a series of number and letters."

Rudy hadn't said anything to him, but there, as Mrs M had said, in a neat script were chalked the words 'WIFI Password (case sensitive): B1gluvG@ynoH8'.

Included beneath was his WhatsApp handle—RudyMKing—and a mobile number in case of emergencies. When Trevor turned back to Antoni, the young guy had visibly deflated with relief.

"Does that mean we're not going to see you for the rest of the holiday? Except at mealtimes?" asked Jessica, glaring up at him, her hands on her hips.

Even though he could tell she was half-joking, Trevor understood. Something about Antoni screamed awkward introvert, someone who would happily hole himself up in his room. Maybe he had some sword-wielding, fantasy role-playing buddies he needed to keep in touch with to ensure the survival of the human race.

"What? No!" Antoni said, taken aback. "I have a marketing proposal to get out by Wednesday. And I need to get into the system at work for research materials."

"Honestly, he works all the time," Jessica said with a huff.

Okay, thought Trevor, *so I need to reel in the stereotyping critic in my head.*

"While Ms Wilkinson swans off on holiday to Tenerife for Christmas. Do you think she's working? Yuh, I don't think so. Getting a tan, more like."

"Wilkinson?" asked Trevor in all innocence.

"Your friend. Hannah Wilkinson? The one who pushed us to come on this holiday."

"Hannah's gone to Tenerife?" asked Cheryl, plucking the glass away from her mouth, the flare in her eyes nothing short of molten. Trevor had been on the receiving end of that look once or twice.

"Jess," hissed Antoni to the back of her head. "You weren't supposed to say anything."

"Oops," said Jessica, a hand held over her mouth. "Sorry. My bad. Forgot you two used to be an item. Think it was a last-minute thing, if that helps."

"They were an item until two days ago," added Mrs M, slamming the Aga door closed. At least Jessica had the decency to look embarrassed at her admission.

"I really am sorry," she said for Trevor's benefit, while Mrs M went over to comfort Cheryl.

"Think I'd better show you to your rooms," said Trevor, wanting to give Mrs M space to console Cheryl and time to vent.

Twenty minutes later, after getting Jess and Antoni settled and demonstrating the features of their rooms that Rudy had shown him, he returned to the kitchen. As he approached from the hallway, he spied Johnny and Frank standing shoulder to shoulder, arms folded, glaring at the front entrance as though a wild animal had happened across the threshold. Cheryl and Mrs M were nowhere to be seen. Only as he entered did he spot the cause of the men's hostility.

Karl.

Beneath the permanent seriousness etched on his face, he still looked good, if a little tense and tired around the eyes. When he turned and saw Trevor, his features softened. His wild, shaggy brown hair and dark eyes had always captivated Trevor, even when they had disagreed with each other. Now sporting a trim beard, Karl had also tamed and styled his hair, and lost some weight. Togged out in his old tan leather bomber jacket and denim jeans, Karl had cultivated a hot but casual look befitting a GQ model. Not that Trevor could tell him, but he no longer had the rough edges of the male Beat Generation authors he loved so much, and right now wouldn't have looked out of place in a boy band line-up.

"Everyone, this is Rosemary," said Karl, stepping to one side. Trevor could tell by the way his ex-husband's eyes flitted from one face to another that he was anxious, but in true Karl style, he stuck out his chin in defiance. "But she prefers plain Mary."

The moment small, unsmiling Mary stepped forward, Trevor could tell she was anything but plain, and either morbidly obese or heavily pregnant. From her thin face and the way she pushed a hand into her lower back, he assumed the latter. Right then a hundred and one thoughts hit him. Was the baby Karl's? And if so, why hadn't he said anything? Had he planned the child or had it been an accident? Had they been sleeping together while he and Karl had still been married? Why the hell had he brought her to Scotland in that condition? But then her strident schoolmarm voice brought him back from his meltdown.

"Which one of you is Trevor?" she asked, looking from Frank to Johnny and finally to Trevor.

"I-I am," he said, raising his hand. With something bordering distaste, she looked him up and down like a sergeant major inspecting one of her troops — and disapproving on every level.

"Are we the last to arrive?"

"Actually, you are."

"I see. Well, first of all, thank you for arranging everything. I know these things don't happen all by themselves," she said and appeared genuine. For a moment he began to think everything would be fine, even though her words seemed to come out a little contrived. "Secondly, I hope you haven't assigned rooms yet, because we'll need our own private bathroom. Not that any of you would understand, but in my condition, there is no way I can share. And when you heat the place, can you make sure the temperature is comfortable, not more than twenty-five degrees. Pregnancy sends my body temperature soaring, especially at night. Obviously, I'll regulate our bedroom heating myself, but in the communal areas I'd appreciate your cooperation. Thirdly, do any of you smoke?"

Nobody answered. Everyone stood in stunned silence.

Until Johnny piped up, "Cigarettes?"

"Yes, of course. What else? Oh, cigars, you mean. Do you smoke either?"

"No."

"Does anyone?"

As one, Trevor, Johnny and Frank obediently shook their heads. Trevor felt sure pot-smoking Johnny had not been referring to cigars.

"Good, because I refuse to share a living space inside or out with baby-killers. Fourth, from a food perspective, I am a vegetarian, so have brought my own provisions, which I trust none of you will touch. You'll need to assign me dedicated shelves in the refrigerator. At meal times, please wash and move your pots, pans, glasses and chopping boards out of the way when you've finished, so that I can prepare my own meals. My husband tells me you are all carnivores. Whether I approve or not, that is your choice, but I would appreciate your understanding and cooperation in this matter."

"Did she call him her husband?" whispered Cheryl to the back of Trevor's head. She must have returned while Mary distracted everyone with her monologue. "Did you know?"

Trevor shook his head gently, and Cheryl hissed out a sigh behind him. In the meantime, Mary had been surveying the faces in the room to see if her words had provoked any reaction, and only then did Trevor realise Mrs M was missing. No doubt she would have something to say about these demands.

"Finally," continued Mary, turning back to Trevor, "I know this — situation — isn't perfect and might be a little awkward for you, for us both, but we're just going to have to muddle through. For my part, this is my one last chance of a break from routine before our baby boy comes. Something I would really like to make the most of. So let's clear the air right from the start."

"There's really nothing — " began Trevor.

"Karl is with me now. And as you can see, we are about to bring another life into the world. So I would appreciate you keeping your judgement to yourself and not arguing with him over — "

"Okay, that's enough," said Johnny, piping up and not even attempting to mask his contempt. "Karl, are you sure you and Rosemary's Baby here wouldn't be more comfortable in a hotel? We drove past a nice one on the outskirts of Edinburgh."

"Johnny, Edinburgh's four hours' drive away — oh," said Frank, catching on.

"You see?" said Mary, rounding on Karl with an exaggerated sob. "*You see*? I told you we shouldn't have come. Told you we wouldn't be welcome."

"If we'd been given the chance, any one of us could have told you that," said Johnny. "If only your — husband, is it now? — communicated instead of keeping secrets from his friends."

When Trevor looked over, he noticed Karl's anguished gaze frowning at the kitchen flagstones. Maybe he was deciding if this was such a good idea, whether to cut and run, to turn and flee, follow Johnny's advice, but Trevor felt a sudden and overwhelming surge of compassion for him.

"No, Johnny," said Trevor, quietly but firmly. "I invited Karl and his — Mary. Me. If you want to have a pop at someone, then have a pop at me. But while they're here, I'm going to make them as welcome as every other one of our guests. And I'd like you and Frank to do the same. Understood?"

At that Karl peered up, and the ghost of a grateful smile touched his lips.

"For you, Mac, happily. I'll share the place, surely I will," said Johnny, his Irish accent ramped up to the max. "But don't ask me to be civil. There'll be no sympathy for this devil. Not from me."

Mrs M appeared just as the Frank and Johnny headed out, giving them a quizzical gaze as she entered the kitchen. As Cheryl followed not far behind, she patted a hand on her mother's shoulder but said nothing.

"What did I miss?" came Mrs M's cheerful voice — which then dropped a tone or two when she spotted Karl. "Oh, it's you. Hello, Karl. Just in time for the evening meal. Dinner's at seven. Go and fetch your bags from the car while I check on the food. Then I'll show you and your girlfriend up to the bedroom."

"Up? Are there stairs?" asked Mary.

Mrs M sized up the new arrival, her arms folding. Trevor decided to pick that particular moment to slip away.

"That's usually how we get to the first floor," came Mrs M's humoured voice as he passed her by. "What were you expecting, dear? A chairlift?"

Once secured in the sanctity of his room, Trevor shut the door. Karl and Mary must have gone out to get their luggage, because Trevor heard no more voices until after he had showered. He had almost forgotten about the paper-thin walls between his bathroom and the kitchen. When he stood at the mirror, brushing his teeth, he could quite clearly hear two female voices talking, both of them raised.

" — and as I have already stated. In my condition, I cannot be expected to — "

"Stop right there," came Mrs M's distinctive voice. "That's just about enough from you, young missy."

"I haven't finished — " began Mary.

"*Oh, yes, you have.* Now be quiet and let me run through a few house rules. First of all, the kitchen is my domain. If you want to prepare your own food, that's fine. But you go through me. However, I am more than capable of handling vegetarian meals, something I have done for many years. What type of vegetarian are you?"

"What do you mean, what kind of vegetarian am I?" came the derogatory voice. "I don't eat meat, of course."

"Do you eat cheese and eggs?"

"Of course."

"But no red meats, poultry, fish or shellfish."

"I have eaten fish occasionally. And some shellfish. Prawns and shrimps as long as they're cleaned thoroughly. For the protein."

"So you're a pescatarian? Not strictly vegetarian."

"Mostly vegetarian."

"One of our previous guests was the same, so I can create dishes specially for you. I'm happy to do that. Alternatively, you can prepare your own. But if you do so, you work to my schedule, and eat with the rest of us. Are we clear?"

"I don't see why—"

"*Are we clear?*"

Even though they had probably only been together since April, Trevor could hear how Mary had already adopted Karl's rebellious tone. But nobody—*nobody*—messed with Mrs M.

"Fine," said Mary, the word expelled like an expletive.

"Secondly," said Mrs M in quick succession, "Cheryl and Trevor went to a lot of trouble organising this holiday, something they've done for years, one they've invested time and energy planning, and something to which—"

"Look, Mrs M. We understand—" began Karl.

"—*something to which* we have been kindly invited. So you will both show them respect and think yourself lucky they've agreed to include you. You will not walk in here and start throwing your weight around just because one of you is pregnant and hormonal. That was your choice. I've been there and out the other side. My Cheryl is living proof of that. And when I was a mum-to-be, I shared one bathroom with a family of eight. I know what it's like better than anyone in this lodge.

Which is why you have been allocated a bedroom with an en suite bathroom on the first floor. We have a long-standing informal arrangement on our holidays about room allocation, meal times and kitchen duties, use of communal areas, smoking policy, eating and drinking and other things that form a part of our annual get-together. Everyone follows these simple rules and so will you. Karl can fill you in as well as anyone. And if you decide to stay, you'll be kind enough to keep your mouth shut and your opinions to yourself. Am I making myself clear?"

"I don't see why —"

Trevor thought he heard Karl mutter something to Mary.

"Am I making myself clear?"

This time, Trevor would have been surprised if everyone in the lodge hadn't heard Mrs M.

"Yes," came both Karl's and Mary's sullen voices.

"If you find our basic rules too much for you, Johnny tells me there are numerous small hotels around Fort William. You can drive there tomorrow. And I'm sure Trevor can arrange a refund for you. Now let me show you to your room, so you can freshen up for dinner."

As he tugged on his jeans and thin sweater, Trevor felt increasingly nauseous, wondering if Mrs M's harsh words would make things better or worse. He almost felt sorry for Karl. Was he destined to be henpecked for the rest of his life? But then Karl had made his bed. Surely he had solid feelings for her, and wasn't about to ditch her if he found himself unable to handle the pressures of marriage or, worse still, fatherhood. And more immediately, how the hell were they going to get through dinner tonight without there being casualities?

Heading to the empty kitchen early, he decided he needed a fortifying drink or two before round two.

Chapter Five

Winter Wonderland

Round two began ominously.

Trevor sensed Mrs M's coolness the moment she marched back into the kitchen and began carving up the chicken and leek pie. He wanted to say something, to apologise for caving in and allowing Karl to come, and for the inconvenience Mary would cause her, but he could see she was in no mood to talk. Instead he helped out by laying the table in silence, placing down baskets of freshly baked rolls and taking an occasional tug from his bottle of designer beer. Cheryl came in and helped him partway through, still a little red-eyed, but smiling as she snatched the bottle from him and took a swig.

Eventually, people began to trail into the kitchen, each of them selecting drinks from the fridge and their places around the table. Within a matter of minutes, sides had been drawn. Mrs M held court at the end, with Johnny and Frank next to her, across from each other. Trevor and Cheryl also sat opposite each other, inadvertently providing a no-man's-land in the middle.

Jessica and Antoni, oblivious to the earlier heated words, took seats next to each of them. Karl and Mary sat at the far end.

Blatantly ignoring the tension in the room — something all of them must have felt by the unusually subdued chatter — Mrs M remained seated but called for silence while she kicked off proceedings.

"Welcome everyone, old friends and new. I trust we've all settled in. Before we start eating, it's customary for me to say a few words and lay down some ground rules for the holiday. I'll start with meals because that's my domain. Breakfast buffet and dinner will be prepared by me and I will write the day's choices of both vegetarian and non-vegetarian meals on the kitchen blackboard. Unless otherwise instructed — such as Christmas lunch — each of you will be left to fend for yourselves for lunch. But if you want to use any kitchen equipment, please make sure everything is washed up after use or placed in the dishwasher, and all surfaces cleared and cleaned before three in the afternoon, when I begin dinner preparations. If there are no questions, I'm sure you're all hungry so I'll start dinner. Frank, give me a hand."

"Vegetarian?" whispered Jessica, sitting next to Cheryl but loud enough for Trevor to hear. "Does your mother think I don't eat meat?"

"Not you, Jessica. Mary at the end. Don't worry. Mum had already pre-prepared a batch of meat-free dishes for Hannah," Cheryl whispered back. "Pies, quiches, bean casserole. Brought them anyway, rather than waste the food. They just need heating up. But don't tell her ladyship."

"Her ladyship?" asked Jessica, before following Trevor's gaze to the end of the table where Mrs M handed Mary a plate with a large Brie and sun-dried tomato tart and a selection of vegetables. "Oh. I see."

"And one final thing," continued Mrs M, back her seat. "Especially for the newer and younger guests joining us. Mobile phones are a necessary evil in this day and age. While we're happy for you to take photos of the food or decorations or the rooms, no photos of people should be posted on social media without their express permission. And that includes videos. Isn't that right, Frank?"

Drinking from a beer bottle, Johnny began to choke.

"Fair do's. Point taken, Mrs M," said Frank, about to stuff a piece of bread roll into his mouth.

Two years ago, during a Christmas break in Wiltshire, Frank had recorded and posted an after-lunch video of Mrs M and Monica sat next to each other on the sofa, their heads tilted back, fast asleep, snoring at the ceiling. He had called the post 'the Christmas Snorus Chorus'. Monica had been furious and despite it having over four hundred likes, they had pressured him into taking the post down.

After Mrs M's final pronouncement, the meal proper began. Compared to the relatively lively affair of the cobbled-together meal the night before, conversations took place in lowered voices. Apart from the occasional whispered word to each other, Karl and Mary scarcely spoke throughout and Trevor assumed they had either decided to play along or were planning to escape in the morning. If he managed to get Karl alone at any point, which seemed unlikely, he vowed to get the truth out of him. For the time being, he was grateful Mary had drawn in her claws.

Between dinner and dessert, Antoni had asked Trevor about the origins of their seasonal escape and had been given an account of the first year. At the end, after a lull, Mary finally took the opportunity to wade in.

"If I'm going to be honest, I find this whole members-only tradition not only antiquated but slightly offensive. Strikes me as its own form of discrimination. Yes, I understand from my husband the argument about privacy with like-minded people, but isn't there the counterargument of equality and inclusion, and that by creating this private members club, you are guilty of the very thing you've been fighting against for years. As a vegetarian I don't see the need to lock myself away with other vegetarians. Nor would I want to. And we are ostracised and marginalised in much the same way as members of the LGBTQ plus community—"

"Oh, come on. You can't compare the two," said Johnny with disgust. "They're hardly the same—"

"They're exactly the same. You don't hear me refusing to share the table with meat eaters—"

"I wish you would—" muttered Cheryl, next to Trevor.

"Although I do expect them to respect my life choices—"

"How the hell can you compare them?" said Frank, thumping his chair back down from the two legs he had balanced on, his face drained of colour. "How many vegetarians do you know who have been scared shitless of telling their family, their father and mother and siblings, about their food choices because of the repercussions? Did they have to keep copies of specialist food magazines carefully hidden away for fear of being found out and screamed at, or worst still, punched and kicked until they had to be taken to hospital? Were they thrown out of their homes and forced to sleep rough on the streets? Or packed off to conversion therapy retreats to force them into becoming what their family or faith considered normal? I have no doubt some of your community have had to deal with hostile situations, but for every one I can show you a thousand gay or lesbian kids who have suffered a hundred times worse."

"Calm down, Frank," said Trevor.

"No, Johnny. Mary needs to hear this," said Frank. "We mix with other people the whole year round, in our jobs, in our social interactions and out in the world — some of us more than others. We have to put up with the veiled homophobic asides or jokes in the workplace or threats on the street, and listen to ignorant politicians who are still intent on nailing us back in the closet. So if we decide to enjoy the company of like-minded people over Christmas, in a safe place where we don't have to filter what we say, where we can be ourselves, then that's our freedom of choice. The people we choose to holiday with share our values. None of us have to be on best behaviour in case we get judged for saying something to offend bigoted people's homophobic sensibilities."

"That sounds rather holier than thou, don't you think?" said Mary. "Are you trying to tell me people in the gay community don't judge?"

"Of course we judge," replied Frank. "We're still human. But our judgement is not expressed with hatred and violence. Within our own community, we criticise each other plenty. Although with our friends, it's usually more of a gentle ribbing, done in a lighthearted way."

"Karl," said Johnny, "feel free to wade in any time you want."

"I don't understand," said Antoni calmly. "Surely who we love or what we eat should be our choice alone. Nobody should dictate either. As long as we're not hurting anyone else. Isn't that the whole point of a free society? Honestly, my friends and I are sick of labels. One day, I hope we won't bother with them anymore. When you can love who you want, irrespective of race or orientation or religion, and eat what you want, without being ridiculed, because nobody will care."

Everybody sat quietly after Antoni's words.

"Amen to that," said Mrs M. "If only everyone thought like you, Antoni, then perhaps one day we might enjoy a brave new world. But for now, I wouldn't hold your breath."

Even Jessica tuned in to the tension, because after a few moments of awkward silence, she distracted Mary with chit-chat about her older sister's recent pregnancy, offering advice on water births, best-buy nappies, breast milk pumps and postnatal depression. Trevor tried his best not to listen in. At one point he glanced up and caught Karl's eye, receiving a warm smile that he refused to return and which soon dissolved.

Barely a moment after a dessert of peach and strawberry crumble with vanilla ice cream had been polished off, the four newest arrivals rose from the table and disappeared to their respective rooms, claiming travel fatigue. Left behind, the five remaining friends finally breathed a collective sigh of relief.

"Would you rather have an incurable disease that caused you pain every day for the rest of your life, or live with that woman?" asked Cheryl.

"Looks like Karl Marx has already chosen the answer to that one," said Frank.

After helping to clear up, they followed Frank's suggestion and headed to the main living room to enjoy a glass of one of the bottles of Taiwanese single malt whisky he and Johnny had bought at the airport duty free. And for the first time that evening, everything felt like old times. Sitting around the open fire, red-faced from the heat and the alcohol, they polished off two bottles, the rest of the night becoming a blur of catch-ups and memories and laughter.

* * * *

The next morning, Trevor woke with a gasp in a strange bed, in a darkened bedroom, to the sound of someone trying too hard to open and close cupboards quietly in the kitchen next door. His heart raced instantly, bringing on a pounding headache from a hangover he absolutely deserved, relieved only slightly by the chill air of the bedroom. Not as arctic as the frostiness that had hung over the dinner table the evening before, but just as sobering.

At barely seven in the morning, instead of trying to fall back to sleep, he decided to get up and shower. While towel-drying his hair and brushing his teeth, he checked his fully charged phone to find a strong Wi-Fi signal.

Right then he heard soft tapping.

At first he wondered if the sound had something to do with the old plumbing, before realising the knocking was coming from his bedroom. Back inside the dim room, standing barefoot on the warm floor, he stared at the door and waited. Once again the rapping noise came, but from the window, not the door. When he pulled the curtains aside, he gasped and stepped back when he discovered the smiling face of Rudy Mortimer filling the frame. Unlatching the pane, Trevor allowed a frozen breeze of air to invade the room.

"What on earth are you doing?" he asked.

"Needed to drop off a basket of goodies. Instructions from Mother. Then I was going for an early morning stroll. Wondered if you fancied joining me? Show you some of the sights around the moor?"

"Early riser, eh? Is that a habit?"

"Och, no, not really," said Rudy, his smile slipping. "Just don't sleep much these days."

Trevor might have been mistaken, but that tiny admission appeared to carry a whole depth of personal pain.

"Tell you what. Why don't you go round to the kitchen. I can hear Mrs M starting to fix breakfast, and I know she'll be delighted to see you. Grab a mug of tea, and pour me one — milk with one sugar — and I'll be out in five. Deal?"

"Deal," said Rudy, blowing into his hands. "Going to snow today."

"No, I don't think so."

"It's not a question, Trev. I'm telling you, it's going to snow."

"When every weather person in the country says there's going to be no snow across the British Isles, Rudy Mortimer begs to differ. Is this some Scottish myth, like when the cows lie down in the field with their legs in the air, farmers know it's going to rain?"

"If a cow's lying on its back with its legs in the air, Trev, in my experience it's probably dead. No, I'm talking about snow. Lots of snow. You wait and see."

"Okay, I believe you. Now bugger off so that I can put some trousers on."

Rudy's laughter lit up the morning and was almost worth having let the sub-zero air into the bedroom.

When Trevor entered the kitchen togged out in a thick woollen jumper and jeans, Rudy was sitting at the kitchen table with Mrs M, the two of them chatting happily. Rudy appeared so at home there, maybe because this had been his home from time to time. Midway through talking to Mrs M about the basket of goodies he had left—a local brand of Dundee cake and a bottle of whisky, the sight of which made Trevor nauseous—Rudy looked up and held out a mug to Trevor before offering another of his knee-trembling smiles.

"What time will you be back?" asked Mrs M.

Trevor turned to Rudy and shrugged.

"Around nine-thirty, if that's okay, Mrs Madison," said Rudy.

"Fine. As long as you agree to call me Brenda."

"Of course. I wanted to show Trevor the moors before the weather turns."

"Weather turns? What do you mean?" she asked, turning to the unblemished sunshine outside the kitchen window. "It's going to be a beautiful day today."

"That's what I told him," said Trevor. "There's not a cloud in sight."

"For now," said Rudy, grinning as though he had some secret knowledge.

* * * *

On their walk along a trail behind the lodge, Rudy explained how he had stumbled upon the perfect viewpoint of the area in his youth, and Trevor felt a tinge of honour that he felt comfortable enough to share the spot with him.

Rudy insisted on leading from behind on the way up from the trail—safer that way, he said—although he was probably being a gentleman and wanted to let Trevor sample the climb without having anyone in his way blocking his view. Not that Trevor would have minded having Rudy's backside in his sights. He could think of a lot worse.

A fallen tree provided their perfect perch on the crest of a steep hill, although Rudy chose to remain standing. Beneath them, the landscape stretched out like a patchwork quilt of earthen browns and moss green. Scotland's wild flora and fauna fought for existence against a backdrop of dark granite. Even without prompting, Trevor could make out the lodge's Celtic-cross shape nestling against the loch. But Ben Nevis stole the view, rising from the earth like a leviathan and dwarfing everything around. To the north of them, what looked like a French castle or fortress painted beige and built into a hill proudly dwarfed the smaller dwellings, the humble cottages that huddled near the loch or around the small road circumnavigating the mountain.

"Is that a castle?" asked Trevor.

"No," said Rudy quietly. "That's Mortimer Hall."

"Mortimer? As in Rudy Mortimer? Are you shitting me? That's the house you live in?"

"Please don't, Trev. It's our ancestral home. Nothing more."

"Ancestral home? Oh my God," said Trevor, slapping his hands on his thighs and staring in wonder. "Tell the truth, Rudy. Are you descended from royalty? Or titled, at the very least? And should we be referring to you as 'my lord' or 'your highness'? Oh no, should a commoner like me be kneeling in your presence right now?"

Trevor rocked forward from the log, onto one knee, while an unamused Rudy folded his arms.

"You're going to get thumped in my presence, if you keep that up."

Sitting back on the stump, Trevor tipped his head back and laughed, and Rudy soon joined him. He had a nice laugh, and Trevor liked that he had a sense of humour.

"Have to say, it's beautiful," said Trevor, appraising the building. Nature had been reshaped to accommodate the structure, but the end result seemed to blend beautifully into the landscape.

"Aye, it surely is. But something so grand can also be lonely," said Rudy, a tinge of sadness in his voice, before inhaling a deep breath. "Ah well, at least there's going to be snow today."

Trevor heaved out a steamy sigh and turned to study him. Quite a pleasant task, if he was going to be totally honest. With his dark red hair and brows, flawless pale skin and moss green eyes, he almost melted into the scenery.

"This again? Am I going to need to find a psychiatrist? What is this obsession of yours with phantom snow?"

"Just humour me, and I'll explain how I know."

"I'm all ears," said Trevor, mirroring Rudy's folded his arms and crossing his legs at the ankles.

"Where does snow come from?"

"Is this a trick question?"

"No, come on," he said, dropping down next to Trevor and bumping shoulders — the way Cheryl often did. "Where does snow come from?"

"The North Pole."

"Come on. You're not a wee bairn, and this is not Nickelodeon. Think more scientific," said Rudy, nodding exaggeratedly upwards.

"From the sky. Snow is formed from water retained in clouds that freezes into ice crystals. Once particles become too heavy, they fall like rain — only slower."

"Correct." Not only did Trevor find Rudy's smile and earnestness infectious, but he also enjoyed the warm pressure from their shoulders pressed together. "So if you're going to predict whether it'll snow, the first thing you need to do is keep an eye on the sky. Am I right?"

"Which today is cloudless, and as flawlessly blue as the Mediterranean. What's your point?"

"That's the first thing. The second thing is to take a deep lungful of air in through your nose and hold for a few seconds. Then, when you slowly release, try to taste and smell what you inhaled. That's a bit more difficult for you, because you need to be able to tell the difference. I've lived here all my life, on and off, so I know the change. But when snow's coming, the air smells and tastes different."

Trevor did as asked, and he did notice an almost metallic scent in the air. Not that he was going to tell Rudy and let him off the hook so lightly.

"Next?" asked Trevor, causing Rudy to chuckle.

"Next, you need to listen," said Rudy. Trevor did as asked but could hear nothing.

"What am I listening for?"

"Just listen. What can you hear?"

Once again, Trevor strained to hear something, anything. All he could make out was the gentle rush of wind and the distant sound of a car engine navigating one of the small lanes around the loch.

"Honestly, I can't hear a thing."

"Exactly. Even in winter the birds would be chirping on a morning like this. So why aren't they?"

"No idea. Gone for breakfast?" Trevor's stomach rumbled in sympathy.

"Look up there. Hiding in the juniper tree," said Rudy, pointing to a branch in a nearby tree. At first Trevor could make out nothing, but then he noticed a row of birds bunched together. "They huddle when snow's coming. I've seen the same behaviour many times before. And the last thing is that if you'd stepped out of the lodge last night and looked at the sky — instead of getting bladdered on foreign whisky — you would have seen a halo around the moon. Sure sign of snow on the horizon."

"How did you know we had whisky last night?"

"I can smell it on your skin. That hike up the hill must have opened your pores."

"Wonderful. So I smell like a distillery?"

"You smell good, actually."

Trevor had no smart-ass comeback for that comment, but instead felt a trace of pleasure that went straight to his groin at the thought of Rudy noticing how he smelled. He tore his gaze back to the stately house.

"So you've lived here all your life?"

"As I said, on and off. Spent time here during school and university holidays. Moved back permanently almost six months ago to the day. For the past seven years I've been living and working in York. Studying and managing a sports centre."

"What happened?"

"Long story. I decided to come back home because —" Trevor could sense Rudy looking sidelong at him. Was he making up his mind whether to let on to the real reason? "Because of a bad break-up."

"Oh. I see."

"Actually, I don't think you do. How could you? But that's my problem. Let's just say we were together for six years — I'm twenty-nine now — and in all that time we never moved forward. Not really. I wanted to, but things were difficult, the timings and situation were never right. It didn't help that Debbie spent a lot of time working or travelling and I found myself alone too much. Even when we were together, we were never a proper couple, due to one thing or another. And after a while I realised that not only was I making all the compromises, but I felt as though I was slowly being suffocated. That's when I decided to cut and run, come back home, much to the consternation of my father. But now I'm helping him manage our portfolio of holiday properties, which is not particularly taxing but which nicely supplements our other family business — "

"Whisky distillery and cake baking, by any chance?"

Rudy turned to face Trevor, his eyebrows raised.

"How did you know?" he asked.

"Only just figured it out a moment ago. That castle down there — the old house — is showcased on the labels of the bottle and cake you brought this morning. Very generous of you, by the way."

"I should have dropped those off the day you arrived," said Rudy. "If she asks, don't tell my mother

I messed the gift basket as well as the electricity. What do you do for work, Trev? Sorry, I didn't ask earlier."

"That's okay. I'm a freelance chartered accountant. After I finished my exams, which took forever, I worked for a big firm for a couple of years. Hated every moment. They tend to own your life — well, the one I worked for did. More by luck than anything, my uncle working in the London restaurant trade put me in touch with a few owners who needed bookkeeping and accounting services. That was around five years ago. I've now got around thirty clients on my books, mostly based in Central London, and although sometimes I'm completely swamped at the end of the tax year, my time is largely my own. So I love my job, earn an average enough wage, but I'm also lucky enough to have great clients, who I think of more as friends."

"Friends as clients. Sound great. Talking of which, how are your friends settling in?"

Maybe because of the beautiful morning vibe, Rudy's opening up, or perhaps because of the whisky amnesia from the night before, Trevor had forgotten entirely about the dysfunctional group back at the lodge. He almost shuddered to think of them purposely ignoring one another around the breakfast table.

"Come to dinner tonight," he exclaimed, barely resisting the temptation to go down on one knee again. "Please, Rudy. I'm sure Mrs M will be fine. Don't make me beg. I'll do anything you want, just…please."

"Whoa there, pal," said Rudy, chuckling. The steadying arm he placed around Trevor's shoulders almost undid him. "What the hell happened?"

Trevor knew he was jabbering, but once the emotions began to tumble out and mix with words, he couldn't stop them.

"Let's just say I'm considering extending Hadrian's Wall across the middle of the kitchen table before dinner. Tempers. Moods. Tantrums. Where to begin? Last night was nothing short of a nightmare. Made worse by my ex showing up with his heavily pregnant wife. If only you'd left me to drown in that ditch yesterday. But at least with you there at dinner tonight, people are more likely to be on better behaviour. Maybe even be civil to one another."

"Trev, slow down, will you?" said Rudy, smiling at him. After a moment, though, the smile faded and he pulled his arm away. "Wait. What was that about your ex-wife showing up?"

"Husband," said Trevor, before catching himself and eyeing Rudy warily. "Oh, hell. I'm not going to lie to you, Rudy. Karl is my ex-husband. Who's now straight or bisexual or whatever. And remarried. To a woman this time. Who's also pregnant. And if you hadn't already worked it out through that verbal garbage, I'm gay. But clearly not very good at it. I'm sorry."

Rudy tilted his head back and roared with laughter into the sky. Trevor hung his head until he felt Rudy's arm land across his back. He took the gesture to mean that Rudy didn't have a problem with him.

"And you think I'm crazy," said Rudy, shaking Trevor by the shoulders, "because I believe it's going to snow?"

"Seriously, Rudy. I know it's an imposition, but if you could join us, you'd be doing me a huge favour. I'd need to check with Mrs M but I'm sure you'll be welcome, and more importantly you'll get to sample her incredible cooking. She's a wonder in the kitchen, and because it's Christmas Eve, she'll be doing her traditional beef Wellington dinner."

"So, what?" asked Rudy, folding his arms, his tone becoming serious. "Just like that, at the drop of a hat, you expect me to cancel my own long-standing dinner arrangements? Not sure that was part of the rental agreement. And just to keep you and your group of misfits from killing each other?"

"Oh," said Trevor, his cheeks burning. "Sorry. When you put it like that, I see what you mean. I assumed you would be alone in the house tonight. Don't worry. Forget I said anything."

"No, hang on," said Rudy, not letting the point drop. "You're seriously expecting me to leave my delicious can of tuna in olive oil unopened, just so I can be your dinner mediator?"

Once again Rudy's wonderful laughter sounded in the crisp morning air.

"Bastard," said Trevor, putting his head into his hands.

And once again Rudy thrust his arm across Trevor's shoulders, hugging their sides together and warming Trevor to the core. Never had he ever felt this connected to someone in such a short space of time, certainly not in all the years he had been together with Karl.

"Trev, my friend, it would be an honour. Of course I'll come. Now get me up to speed with this band of miscreants you want me to meet, or kill. Or both."

Chapter Six

Imagine

Before heading their separate ways, they agreed that Rudy would come over at six for pre-dinner drinks. Trevor also promised to confirm his invite by text after speaking to Mrs M, although he knew already she would be delighted to have him at their table. Rudy left Trevor at the top of the knoll and threaded a downhill path to the old house. Trevor watched him go for a while, enjoying the effortless grace of the man as he picked his way confidently along the route, down hidden trails and through the wild vegetation. Once he was out of sight, Trevor turned and made his way back to the lodge.

On the way back, grinning to himself, he kept replaying their conversation. The dose of highland air had all but cleared away any traces of a hangover. Moreover, he connected with this guy, found him pleasant company and easy on the eye. His mind wandering, he imagined having a boyfriend like Rudy, holding hands with him and watching everyone turn to stare in envy. He had to concede that Rudy being straight might be problematic. But he also believed that reality should never get in the way of a good fantasy. And at no point did Rudy seem to have a problem with Trevor being gay. They had gotten along so well that his new friend had even opened up to him about his past. And having magnanimous Rudy Mortimer there for Christmas Eve dinner was nothing short of a masterstroke, giving his warring friends a peaceful offering, a kind of impartial intermediary.

A definite win-win all round.

Just after nine-thirty, as he removed his boots in the anteroom and entered the kitchen, the lodge smelled of breakfast but seemed far too clean and quiet, with only the sound of Christmas music playing softly from a kitchen speaker. On the blackboard propped up on the kitchen counter, Mrs M had chalked up the day's fare.

Breakfast: Full English or Mushroom Omelette with vine tomatoes.
Dinner: Beef Wellington or Vegetarian Moussaka with assorted vegetables.

Trevor smiled at the sight.

Cheryl sat alone at the far end of the huge table, her hands cradling a mug. On seeing him enter, she peered up and managed a smile. Once again she had decided not to bother with makeup that morning, and although the absence made her appear more vulnerable, he had begun to enjoy seeing more of the real Cheryl.

"Morning, Mac."

"Morning, Cheryl. Breakfast finished already?"

"Frank and Johnny are nursing hangovers. Frank came to get coffee for them both, but said they'll be skipping breakfast to sleep in. Karl came down saying

Mary's feeling under the weather and is probably going to need breakfast brought to their room each morning. Can you believe? Mum just about hit the roof, and asked him to remind his wife that this is not a hotel and there is no room service, and what part of 'eat with the rest of us' did she not understand. I swear she's going to kill that woman before the week's up. I actually felt a bit sorry for Karl. He didn't explain himself very well. He meant he would bring breakfast to her each day. Anyway, after having a quick bite himself, he took a tray up to her. He asked after you, by the way. Jessica and Antoni looked better than anyone. They've been and gone, him to finish some work and I think she's showering and changing right now."

"What about your mum?"

"Same."

"Is she pissed off? That we didn't have breakfast together? Especially after her instructions last night?"

"Not really. Antoni and Jessica joined us. She figured the boys might not make an appearance this morning. I don't think she's holding out much hope of Karl and Mary being sociable. And she told us you were out having a guided tour. She saved you a plate of food. Being kept in the warm part of the Aga."

"So it's just you and me?"

"For now. Why? What's on your mind?"

"I just—I hope last night's antisocial dinner company is not a taste of what's to come," said Trevor, heading for the oven. There inside, piled high, he found a massive plateful of scrambled eggs, fried bacon, sausages, tomatoes and grilled mushrooms. "Heck, I can't eat all that."

"Don't look at me, I'm stuffed. I think she left that much in case your new friend came back with you.

Take what you want and leave the rest in the oven. The boys might be hungry later. I was about to go and shower."

"Oh, okay," said Trevor, coming to the table with his plate and trying to mask his disappointment.

"But now you're here, I'm going to stay and keep my bestie company."

"Thanks," said Trevor, smiling and taking a seat across from her.

"And grill him about what he's been doing with this apparently smouldering hot lodge owner's son all morning. Who has yet to be introduced to me."

Trevor poured himself a mug of coffee and smiled at the table. When he offered to fill up her cup, she placed a hand over the top and tilted her head to one side.

"Nothing to tell. He asked me to join him for an early morning stroll while the rest of you were sleeping off your hangovers. Wanted to show me the lay of the land, help me get my bearings while we're here."

"I bet he did," said Cheryl, and he knew her well enough to decipher the tone. "Mum says that on the day we went into Fort William he rode over the crest of the glen, bare-chested, and helped you out of a ditch. The way Mum tells the story the only thing missing is his shield, a sword and a maiden to save."

"You should have seen him, Cheryl. Talk about heroic wet dream. But he's not aloof at all. He's down to earth and easy to talk to. And very funny. He's our kind of people, you know? He's also straight, with an ex-girlfriend back in York."

"Is that what he told you?"

"It is."

"And you believed him?"

"Why wouldn't I?"

"Well, if she's out of the running, turn him. If anyone deserves to drag one over from the other side, it's you. Mum really likes him. She called him *dashing*, whatever that means. Makes him sound like he's in a hurry."

"Makes two of us, then."

Trevor laughed at his own joke, and Cheryl joined in.

"As much as I'd love to convert him, the real world doesn't work that way," he said, sighing and forking a sausage with undue vehemence. "You'll get to meet him tonight. I invited him to our Christmas Eve dinner."

"You didn't?" said Cheryl, looking aghast. "After what you just said? If tonight's anything like last night's séance, you'll probably never see him again."

"I'm hoping that having a third party at the table might thaw everyone out a little. I already gave him a download on the lot of us."

"Everyone? Karl and Mary?"

"Everyone."

"And he's still coming?"

"I think so. I hope so."

"Poor Rudy. Doesn't know what he's letting himself in for. That's a whole lot of pressure."

Trevor hoped Rudy would come, most of all because he enjoyed his company.

"Enough about me. Did you call Hannah?" he asked.

Cheryl thrust herself back from the table and testily scooped hair over her right ear.

"Tried last night. She didn't answer. I eventually spoke to her mum. She really is in Tenerife, can you believe?" she said, swinging her gaze away. "Do I have 'stupid' written on my forehead? Don't answer that. I gave her an early Christmas present this year. Cash, she asked for, rather than a present, to pay off credit card debts. Eight hundred pounds, to be precise. Paid in November."

"How can she have debts? She's got that high-paying marketing job."

"Yes, and spends every penny she earns. Trust me, Mac, we've had that conversation so many times over the years. She never saves a penny."

"So she didn't pay off her debts?"

"She did," said Cheryl, the annoyance plain on her face. "Then promptly booked a holiday to Tenerife with this new girlfriend. I got a text this morning saying she'd booked the holiday last minute. A lie, of course. I caught up with Antoni this morning and he ended up confessing that she'd been bragging about flying to the sun since early December. Looking forward to getting a tan over Christmas. Clearly she had no intention of coming to Scotland with us."

Trevor said nothing. Even though he would never let on to Cheryl, he agreed with Frank about Hannah. People like her needed partners to keep them in check, to be the parent or guardian to their child in the relationship. If Hannah fell, Cheryl would always be there to pick her up. If anything ever happened to Hannah, Cheryl would be there to bail her out. But if anything happened to Cheryl, would Hannah have been there for her? Trevor found the notion hard to imagine. How long would it be before Hannah had racked up all those debts again and came crawling back? And how long before Cheryl caved in and welcomed her? At least Karl had always shared the burden of their marriage, had always been on the level with him, even about his change of orientation. A small concession, maybe, but something in Karl's favour.

"What are you thinking?" she asked. They knew each other far too well.

"You don't want to know."

"You think I'm an idiot."

"No, I don't," he said, putting his fork down and pushing his plate away. "You're caring and thoughtful, Cheryl, and that's a good thing. What I was thinking is that it's probably time we both moved on."

"I'll drink to that. In fact, let's have a glass of bubbly on it tonight."

"After last night, I'm thinking the nearest I'm getting to bubbles is sparkling water."

"On Christmas Eve?" she said, taking his plate and going to the sink. "Over my dead body. And anyway, you'll need alcohol to survive dinner. I've brought those two bottles of special reserve Paullac I won in the office party raffle. A vintage you said you'd love to try. It'll go wonderfully with beef, you said. You are so not going on the wagon tonight. I'm back to eating carbs and drinking whatever I want, remember? For the holidays, anyway. And you are my partner-in-crime."

"Fine. As long as you promise to be nice to Rudy."

"When am I ever not nice? Don't answer that. Anyway, it'll be good to finally meet him. I'd normally tell you to clear the invitation with Mum first, but I don't think that'll be necessary."

"Clear what with me?" came Mrs M's voice as she bounced into the kitchen.

"Is it okay? I invited Rudy over to dinner tonight."

"You know my answer already. That lovely boy is welcome here anytime, day or night. Nice to have somebody with lovely manners around the place."

While Mrs M busied herself at the sink, Cheryl smiled sweetly at Trevor with her smug 'I told you so' smile.

"Hope you're not alluding to us," said Trevor.

"You know exactly who I mean."

"I've already told Rudy to come, but I'll text him later to confirm," said Trevor. "He's still saying it's going to snow, Mrs M."

"Is he now. Has he seen the weather? Not a cloud in sight."

"That's what I said. But he told me all the signs are there."

"See?" said Cheryl, smiling. "There is a God. Maybe hot Rudy has the manners of a gentleman and is as cute as a cupcake, but clearly his lift doesn't go all the way to the top floor."

They all laughed together, even Mrs M, and Trevor marvelled at how nice the shared laughter felt.

"Okay, come on, you two, we're not staying in the kitchen all day," said Mrs M, her back to the sink. "If Mon had been here, we'd have been outside on some crazy jaunt by now—a treasure hunt or sailing boats on the loch. I've already recruited Jessica and Antoni. But the door to Frank and Johnny's bedroom is nailed shut, and I think it's best to leave Karl and her ladyship to their own devices. Go and scrub up, Cheryl, while Trevor helps me put plates and cups into the dishwasher. Then we're going to scout out the area."

"I'll help with the dishes, but I'll pass on the exploring, Mrs M," said Trevor. "I've already done that with my local guide. It's my turn to chill. And I also need to text Rudy."

Trevor didn't miss the exchange of looks between mother and daughter as he headed to his room.

* * * *

Coming back to the empty kitchen half an hour later and making some fresh coffee, Trevor decided to sit out on one of the loungers along the porch outside the main living space. After walking up and down, he found the door to the balcony at the end of the floor-to-ceiling windows.

Despite frail sunlight from overhead, the cloudless sky provided a beautiful panorama that reflected off the loch's surface. Chill breezes occasionally drifted over the extended deck, and Trevor had to drag a throw from an inside sofa to drape over his legs. Sitting alone, he typed up a text message to Rudy then hit the send button. A habit of his, he waited to see if Rudy had picked up the message and whether Rudy would respond straight away, but nothing happened. When he looked up, he spotted a lone bird, white-breasted with beautifully patterned brown-and-white wings, almost chequered, swoop down gracefully and skim the surface of the loch. The lodge's website had mentioned ospreys inhabiting the area. Rising in a perfect arc, the bird came to rest on the branch of a tree to resume its silent vigil. Alone and fending for itself, the creature sat there with no other birds snuggling up. Trevor felt an ache of sadness, of solidarity at the bird's loneliness.

"Trevor," came a deep voice from the balcony door.

Until his dying day, he would recognise that voice.

"Hi, Karl," he said without turning, still taken by what he had seen. After a few moments without getting a response, he craned around to see his guarded ex standing there, his hands thrust deep into his baggy jeans.

"Everything okay?" asked Trevor. "I hear Mary's not feeling too well."

"Morning sickness. Which should be renamed any-time-of-the-day sickness. Burning essential oils helps. And foot rubs. She's sleeping right now. Gets tired very easily."

"Must be tough," said Trevor, trying to sound sympathetic.

"She's a fighter. Thirty weeks along," said Karl brightly, not picking up on Trevor's lacklustre response. "Seven months. In her third trimester. Going to be a March baby, by all accounts, if the baby comes on time. Pisces. Same as you."

Karl stood there looking goofy, entirely out of character to the often cold and serious man Trevor had married. As Karl had been speaking, Trevor's accountant brain had been working back the dates, and he hated himself for doing so. What good would come of knowing Karl had cheated on him? But the simple truth was that even though the divorce hadn't been finalised until July, they had already separated when the baby had been conceived.

"Do you want to sit?" asked Trevor, nodding to the adjacent recliner.

"Is that okay?"

"For heaven's sake, Karl. You never used to ask permission."

Karl came forward and sat gingerly on the lounger's edge, his hands still in his pockets.

"That's because I can see how things have changed. Last night showed me that. You of all people know how much I look forward to these seasonal excursions. I always felt part of our exclusive group. I enjoyed time away from work and family as much as the rest of you, enjoyed eating and drinking with people I admire, people I could talk to about anything. You heard Mary last night, she tried to get me to change my mind. But I persuaded her to come, told her you were nice people and that we'd be fine once the group warmed to us. After last night, I'm not sure that's ever going to happen."

"Are you surprised? You know how fiercely loyal our friends are."

"Your friends now. They've clearly taken sides."

"What did you expect? You bailed, Karl. Not just on me, on them, too. You have everyone's contact details, the same as me. You had Frank and Johnny's email address. You could have sent them a message. Instead you dropped out of everyone's lives, leaving me to pick up the pieces and explain what had happened. So tell me honestly, what did you expect?"

Trevor realised he had been raising his voice and made himself calm down. Karl's brows had scrunched up, the way they did when he was trying to hold things together. Trevor took a steadying breath. He didn't want a fight with Karl, didn't want to make things tougher than they already were. Instead, he changed the subject.

"Pisces? Since when did you give a toss about horoscopes?"

Karl grinned and shrugged and at least had the decency to appear embarrassed. Trevor noticed a couple of grey hairs he hadn't seen before, and Karl definitely looked as though he needed a good meal.

"Mary follows them," he murmured.

"That's not long off, is it?" said Trevor after a pause, taking a mental step down and offering an olive branch. "Are you ready? I mean, have you thought of any baby names yet? For him or her? Actually, do you even know the gender?"

The question seemed to visibly relax and animate Karl, a sappy expression transforming his mouth and eyes.

"All along, Mary thought we were going to have a girl. But the ultrasound said otherwise. We're having a boy. If it was a girl, she wanted to call her Sugar. Sugar Ann. But now it's a boy, we're not sure of a name."

"Sugar Ray Robinson was a guy. Hang on, Sugar Ann? Did Mary take your family name, Spice?"

"She did," said Karl, grinning. "And I know what you're going to say. Sugar Ann Spice. Can you imagine the stick she'd have gotten at school?"

"Seriously, Karl. You need to pick a strong name, especially if it's a boy. You don't want the poor sod to end up having the kind of shit childhood I had to suffer through."

Trevor had put up with a lot of unimaginative name-calling all the way through school.

"If my son turned out anything like you, I'd be proud."

"But not out."

Trevor knew the remark was a low blow and instantly hated himself, except making it had felt cathartic.

"Okay, I deserved that," said Karl, hanging his head. "I know everyone hates me at the moment—"

"Not everyone, but we're getting there."

"And I understand why. But let me just say this. I never meant to hurt you, Trevor, never meant to hurt anyone. I needed to be honest, that's all. Not just with myself, but with you, too. And no matter what you think of me, I do genuinely love Mary."

"Lucky Mary. Does she know that's a first for you?"

That was an even lower blow, and Trevor fell silent, squeezing his eyes shut. Karl also quietened.

"Shit, I'm sorry, Karl. Feels like all these hateful thoughts have been bottled up and you being here brings them to the surface. Of course I can see how much you love Mary. I think everyone can."

"I loved you too, Trevor. I still do, if the truth be told. Just not in the way you would like. We had some good years together. And we did have our moments, didn't we?"

Trevor knew Karl had meant the sentiment to lighten the tension between them, and perhaps he should just have let the comment go.

"Did we?" he asked instead with a soft chuckle. "Maybe you should have woken me up so I could have enjoyed them, too."

What he had meant as a lighthearted comment came out as bitter. Time to bite his tongue. But if there was a goddess of love, thought Trevor, then she must be looking down on this little scene and laughing her arse off. How many wives had been through the same kind of scenes with husbands who finally decided to come out of the closet, telling them they needed to lead the life they were always meant to? Trevor felt sure the delicious irony of a gay man gone straight would not be lost on them.

"Do you really hate me that much?" asked Karl.

Trevor sighed a steamy breath into the air. Out across the loch, the sole osprey had decided to try his luck again. Still no bite.

Join the club, mate.

"No, I don't. Truth is I envy you. At least you can do normal things in public without anyone giving a damn.

People will even smile and coo at what a beautiful couple you make, especially when you're the one behind the pushchair. I know we're getting there, but I still don't feel I qualify for that privilege, no matter how far I believe society has come."

"You know I'll always fight against any kind of discrimination, don't you? And I'll try to instil those values in our child. No matter what you think of me, you must believe that."

"Of course I do," said Trevor with a sigh, and he did.

Into the afternoon peace came a plaintive cry. For a moment Trevor looked out across the loch, wondering if the sound had come for the bird he'd been watching. But the voice sounded again, female and very human. Weak and pleading, Mary's voice came from the bedroom above the balcony and carried Karl's name. Immediately Karl came to life, springing up from the lounger and excusing himself without another word.

Left alone, Trevor wondered if he'd ever had the same effect on Karl.

Chapter Seven

Let It Snow

A hollow chill seeped through Trevor's bones and into his blood. His osprey friend appeared to have given up the ghost and gone back to his lonely nest across the loch. Trevor's mind kept replaying the look on Karl's face when he had talked about Mary. Something magical had happened to him. In Mary, and in becoming a father-to-be, he had found his life's purpose. Had Karl been a friend instead of an ex, Trevor might have empathised more, shared more in his celebration. But the sight merely made him feel more inadequate and incomplete. Why couldn't he have someone look like that when they talked about him? Karl never had. To make things worse, he was sure Karl had no idea how besotted he looked and sounded when he spoke of his wife.

After doing his best to brave the weather, he finally surrendered and headed for the warmth and tranquillity of the lodge. Inside the Aga-heated kitchen, he washed his mug and emptied the dishwasher, making sure to clean surfaces for Mrs M. Standing in the middle of the room, hands on hips, he checked the time on the wall clock next to the blackboard. Almost two-thirty. His eyes trailed naturally to Rudy's number.

He'd still had no reply on his phone, although he could see his message had been read. With nothing else to do, he decided to head to his room and try to have an afternoon nap, or at the very least, listen to music on his phone. Fully clothed, he lay on top of the covers and hugged a pillow to his chest. On the ceiling, the silhouette of a dead moth lay trapped inside the flat surface of the drum-shaped light shade. Rudy had been right about the room, as warm and comfortable as the kitchen. But even though his body felt tired, his mind would not quieten, filling with questions and anxiousness centring around his inadequacies. Eventually, he managed to sleep fitfully, tossing and turning, before finally sitting up at the sound of someone moving around in the kitchen and at the ping of a text message.

RudyKing: Trev. I'll drop by a bit earlier if that's okay? Around five? So we can spend time together before everyone else appears. This is Rudy by the way.

Trevor read the message three times, sudden excitement filling his chest. *Some time together*. What did that mean? Had Rudy missed him? Or was that code for something else? Would Rudy rather it were just the two of them tonight? And what if Trevor were to push things later in the evening?

Sudden reality hit hard. Pulling the pillow into his face, he growled aloud at his overreaction, at his stupidity. In his desperation, he had misread the situation. Ignoring the plain logic and platonic nature of their meeting, he had allowed himself to become infatuated with Rudy. In the short space of time they'd known each other, Rudy had become an obsession. Those three words 'spend time together' meant nothing more than furthering their platonic friendship. Typical of Trevor, hungry for intimacy, he had reinterpreted Rudy's innocent offer of companionship to signify mutual attraction. If he didn't reel himself in, he would spend the evening staring doe-eyed at a man who only desired the company of other people on Christmas Eve.

Tonight, Trevor told himself, he would need to manage his emotions and distance himself, allow Rudy to chat to others and not selfishly and immaturely claim him as his own. He could almost hear himself introducing Rudy as 'my friend' with the words 'not yours' unspoken, which was precisely the notion that had begun to form in his fragile heart. No, he would need to play things cool. Unfortunately, Trevor had never been very good at putting on an act. Whenever he tried, he usually ended up wildly overacting — being cold instead of formal, rude instead of impersonal.

To make things worse, within the space of ten minutes, the one thing he'd been looking forward to all day — Rudy's company — was now the very thing he dreaded.

In an effort to distract himself, he decided to take a hot shower, but as he stood under the water, staring up at the showerhead, thoughts of a handsome, muscular, bare-chested horseman kept riding into his mind. Instead of fighting the vision, he gave in and allowed his overused right hand to bring about much-needed relief, hoping the expurgation might clear his mind of further unsavoury thoughts.

After the shower, with a towel wrapped around his waist and hands gripping either side of the washbasin, he stared at himself in the mirror, realising he needed a shave. Once he had finished the ritual, he heard the approach of a car. At the sound, his heart did a tap dance until he stared hard into the mirror and lectured himself to get a grip and get dressed.

Moving through the empty kitchen, Trevor could already see the signs of Mrs M's preparation and smell the aromas of the evening's dinner. If nothing else, tonight's meal would be memorable for Rudy.

Taking a deep breath, he pulled open the front door to the handsomely grinning Rudy, who had just arrived on the doorstep with carrier bags of unknown goodies. Despite the unflattering blue Barbour, which had seen better days, the tight denim jeans and body-hugging turtleneck sweater of grey wool that he wore accentuated his muscular form. Trevor tore his gaze away but then had to look instead into those fathomless green eyes. Swallowing hard, he hoped the warmth climbing his neck didn't show.

"Hey there, mate," said Trevor, far too upbeat, fixing a smile in place. *Mate?* the little voice inside enquired. Had he suddenly become Australian during the past few hours of mental turmoil? Fortunately, Rudy didn't seem to notice.

"Hi, Trev," he said. "Something smells nice. I'd give you a hug but my hands are full. You okay? You've got a wee bit of colour in your cheeks there."

Trevor continued to smile tightly, even though Little Trevor inside his head had just curled into a ball and rolled away into a corner.

"Do I? Just had a shower," he said, thinking on his feet. "Probably a bit too hot. And stayed under a bit too long. Hence the colour — you know? Come on in. Let me get you something to drink."

Over a bottle of beer each, they sat at the kitchen table while Rudy told a nodding and smiling Trevor about his day. He explained how their old housekeeper, Millie, and her husband, Tam, kept everything ticking over while his parents were away. And how his mother and father had called to say they'd booked their flights and would be back the day before New Year's Eve. In turn, Trevor managed to get Rudy quickly up to speed with more information about their guests, to which Rudy listened carefully without comment. Rudy wanted to know why the blinds in the kitchen had been closed. Trevor hadn't really noticed but guessed that Mrs M preferred to keep them that way in the evening, preferred to keep the atmosphere cosy. After all, he said, there wasn't much of a view over the rear car park. Right on cue, Mrs M entered the kitchen before anyone else, probably to check on dinner, and Trevor finally managed to breathe normally. Her smile gave her away the moment she spotted Rudy seated across the table from him.

"Rudy," she said, going over and patting his shoulder before heading to the oven. "Trevor told me you were coming. You're more than welcome at our table tonight, to celebrate Christmas Eve with us. And if anybody gives you any trouble, you just call me over. Okay?"

"Okay," said Rudy before looking bemusedly at Trevor.

"Get you a drink, Mrs M?" asked Trevor, trying to divert the conversation.

"Let me get this veggie dish into the wall oven first. Away from us meat-lovers' main event."

"Is that some kind of pie, Brenda?" asked Rudy, who had turned to watch.

"Vegetarian moussaka."

"How many of you are vegetarian?"

"Just her ladyship. Mary," said Mrs M, closing the oven door.

"All that for one person?"

"I'm sure if you ask her, she'll let you have some," said Trevor, grinning at Mrs M. "What do you think, Mrs M?"

"You can ask, but I wouldn't hold your breath," muttered Mrs M, with a phrase she clearly enjoyed using.

Rudy tipped his head back and laughed, the sound infectious and setting Mrs M off chuckling. For the first time that evening, Trevor laughed and some of the pressure he had been feeling melted away.

"Sounds like tonight's going to be a whole heap of fun," said Rudy, clinking his bottle with Trevor's.

"What's going to be a heap of fun?" came a familiar male voice from behind. "And who the hell are you?"

Karl strolled in and stopped at the head of the table, staring suspiciously at Rudy.

"This is Rudy Mortimer," said Trevor. "Son of the owner. He's joining us tonight."

"As Trevor's dinner date," said Mrs M, still at the wall oven, her back to them.

When Rudy exchanged a curious glance with Trevor across the table, Trevor felt a fresh wave of heat rise up his neck. He managed a strained smile and a nervous, barely noticeable shake of the head. Out of the corner of his eye, he saw Karl go over to the tall fridge, rip the door open with a loud clang and stare at the collection of bottles of soft drinks, beers and wines inside.

"Is he now," he said, as though to the contents inside. "And are the rest of us subsidising his meal?"

"Karl," said Trevor, appalled at his ex's words.

"I'm happy to contribute—" began Rudy.

"No, Rudy. You don't need—" said Trevor, then angrily to his ex. "Karl!"

"Yes, Karl. Why don't you keep your fat mouth shut!" Cheryl's voice sounded from across the room as she entered. For the first time since their trip down, she looked like her old self. Fully made up, but with her hair tied back tonight, she wore jeans and a maroon sweater. "We have a guest, and you're being rude."

"I'm just saying. Unless we're operating a soup kitchen that nobody informed me about, I thought everyone paid their way."

"He's my guest—" said Trevor.

"Yours, maybe. He's not mine, or Mary's."

"No, he's Trevor's, and therefore mine," came Cheryl's voice as she sat down at the table. "And I've paid in full for Hannah. For the whole holiday. Because, as you see, she couldn't come, which is also fortunate because your wife gets to eat her vegetarian meals. So tonight, Rudy's here at my request and, as far as I'm concerned, he can stay as long as he wants, and eat with us whenever he chooses."

"That's not the point. It's the principle," said Karl, now at his strident worst. Trevor remembered the tone well, understanding for the first time how insulting and demeaning he could sound. "Why are you suddenly inviting strangers into our group and to our table? Two from Hannah's work nobody seems to know much about, and now this random. I thought the whole point of this precious annual event was to enjoy the company of like-minded friends?"

"Me and Johnny keep asking ourselves the same thing. And we still can't figure out why the fuck you and Mary are still here," said Frank, also entering the kitchen and heading for a seat.

"Do sit down, Karl, dear," said Mrs M, craning around from the Aga. "In case you hadn't noticed, you're making a fool of yourself."

"The point is, Mrs M," said Karl, not giving ground, like a terrier with its teeth buried into a trouser leg, "this kind of thing would have been discussed and agreed between all of us in the past. And nobody has said anything to me about having another guest for dinner."

"That's because it's nobody's business but mine," said Mrs M, slamming the Aga door shut before turning to address everyone. "And in case you hadn't realised, Rudy, this delightful gentleman with no manners whatsoever is Karl. He used to be married to Trevor. But apparently Trevor wasn't good enough for him."

"Well said, Mrs M," said Frank.

"Mrs M, can we please—" said Trevor.

Everyone fell silent at the sound of Rudy's chair scraping away from the table. Even though he felt dismayed, Trevor understood. Why would anyone want to stick around after having witnessed their dysfunctional group and been insulted very publicly? If Rudy left now, Trevor would not blame him and would at least make sure to see him to his car.

Instead, Rudy stood and went over to Karl. Even Karl appeared momentarily taken aback by the imposing figure that approached him. Everyone waited for a few seconds. Maybe they, too, wondered if Rudy intended to thump Karl. But instead, he held out a hand.

"It's really nice to meet you, Karl," said Rudy, in his usual mannered way. "I don't want you to think I've gate-crashed your dinner and, as I say, I'm more than happy to contribute financially. Out of pure kindness on his part, Trev insisted I come tonight, knowing I'd have been alone this evening. My parents are away in Vancouver, you see. I'll try not to get in the way too much, and I promise to do my fair share of the kitchen duties. I've also brought presents for everyone, which is my way of saying thank you for letting me join you."

After shaking and releasing Rudy's hand, Karl stood dumbfounded for a moment before smiling and responding. Peripherally, Trevor noticed Mary enter the room and move to a seat near the table's end.

"He lets you get away with calling him Trev, does he?" asked Karl smirking. "That's a first."

"You don't like being called Trev?" asked Rudy quizzically, turning to Trevor. "Why didn't you say?"

"Most of the time I don't like people calling me Trev, that's true. But on your tongue, and with your accent, I don't know. Trev sounds quite nice. More of the cultured North. Less South London."

Everyone burst into laughter—including Karl and Mary—and even though Trevor had been deadly serious, he joined in, relieved at the change of atmosphere. Just then Jessica, Antoni and Johnny arrived, all of them smiling and more than likely attracted by the sounds of merriment.

"Trevor's always been a snob," said Karl, above the laughter. Karl had often called him out with the label in public, and Trevor usually ignored the slight. As he smiled around the room, he noticed Rudy had stopped laughing. Fortunately, nobody else had seen, and when they all sat back at the table, Karl had warmed to Rudy because he took the seat next to him. Not for long, though, because Rudy got up and went to introduce himself to the newly arrived guests.

At least with everyone chatting at the kitchen table, Trevor felt comfortable stepping away and helping Mrs M with the preparations. Only as he turned to survey the gathering did he notice how they'd all assumed the same seating positions as the night before, but this time with Rudy at the opposite end of the dinner table. Johnny stood up to get drinks for everyone from the large fridge, and Cheryl kept everyone amused with stories of their afternoon trek around the loch. At the other end of the table, Rudy chatted happily with the group, with even a pale-looking Mary joining the fun. Trevor set the table around them, keeping an ever-watchful eye on everyone. Jessica appeared to be taken with Rudy and flirted shamelessly. Trevor did his best not to stare. Every so often Rudy sent Trevor a private smile, one he either returned with a nod or tried to ignore. Before long, chatter around the table had reached a comfortable level.

"Are you okay, dear?" Mrs M had placed the beef Wellington onto a chopping board to rest and now checked on a pot of vegetables. "You seem a bit distracted. Rudy can look after himself."

"I know that," said Trevor.

"He's a such lovely boy. And listen to that lot getting along, so different to last night," she said, lifting the steaming pot off the heat and taking the contents to the sink. "He clearly likes you, you know?"

"Yeah," said Trevor, helping her strain the contents with a colander. "If only 'like' did it for me."

"Oh," she said, her voice softening. "I see. Have you spoken to him?"

"Enough to know he's doesn't bat for our team."

"He said that?"

"Not in so many words, but he mentioned the name of an ex-girlfriend back in York."

"And having one more friend's not enough for you?"

"It's going to have to be."

Once again, Mrs M had outdone herself with the food. Trevor had tried making beef Wellington a couple of times but had always ended up with tough, overcooked meat and burnt puff pastry. Mrs M's meat had roasted perfectly to medium, and the pastry still maintained a healthy golden colour. Having carved the Wellington and taken all the other dishes to the table except for Mary's — Mrs M had already plated up and delivered hers — Trevor took his place opposite a laughing Cheryl. Mrs M was right. The group had gelled far better than the night before.

"Okay, everyone," said Trevor, standing and raising his beer bottle. "Top up your glasses or go the fridge and get yourself a drink. We're going to have our customary Christmas Eve toast. Mrs M, would you do the honours this year?"

As a rule, Mrs M preferred to stay out of the spotlight, to concentrate on cooking. She avoided their games and toasts and other silliness, but Trevor thought this year she might want to say a few words and nodded his encouragement. After a sip from her wineglass, she stood up at the head of the table, and everyone fell silent.

"Thank you, Trevor. As most of you know, I'm not usually one for speeches, but I will make a toast tonight.

So here's to our little Christmas tradition, which if I'm going to be honest, I didn't think would happen this year. But against all the odds, here we are, so I'd like to thank all those seated around the table, new faces and old. And finally, a mention to the people who, for one reason or another, couldn't be here with us this year. Let's put all those wishes together, and join me in a single toast to Christmas Eve, to present company old and new, and to absent friends."

Everyone echoed the toast, glasses clinking with others around the table. Chatter started up immediately, and Mrs M had to raise her voice above the hubbub.

"Now pile your plates up before the food gets cold."

"Did you help cook the food, Trevor?" asked Rudy from down the table, in all innocence, as he passed a piled china dish of golden roasted potatoes and sweet potatoes down the table.

"Mac?" said Cheryl, setting Johnny laughing across from him. All his friends knew about his ineptitude in the kitchen. "Are you kidding? A meal at Trevor's always entails takeout or delivery menus."

"Is that why you call him Mac?" asked Antoni, joining the fun.

"Come on, team. That's a bit unfair," said Frank. "He's good with microwave meals and scooping food out of tin cans. Isn't that right, Trevor?"

"What can I say? I am gifted in the use of can openers," said Trevor, familiar with the teasing. "Although the bastards keep making those ring pull cans these days, so mine is a slowly dying art."

"Trevor's the only person I know who can burn a Caesar salad," added Cheryl.

"And she's not talking about the croutons," added Johnny.

"Do you remember that shepherd's pie lunch he made in Kingsbridge?" continued Frank. "When Brenda and Monica had gone for a hike. Golden brown on top. Still frozen at the base. I don't even know how you managed that."

"I told you. It's a gift."

"Come on, lads," said Karl. "You're all being a bit unfair. He's always been adept at microwaving spaghetti hoops. If we ask him nicely, he might even agree to making us a late supper tonight. What do you think of him now, Rudy?"

"Yes, what do you think of him now?" asked Antoni, laughing along.

"You want to know what I think?" said Rudy then took a deep breath while putting his fork down.

In the silence that followed, Trevor stared down at his plate and willed the floor to open up and swallow him.

"I don't know him as well as you all. But I think you're missing what's important here. From my understanding, Trev's the one who made all this happen. My mother kept me updated, so I know the young man she often referred to is Trev, someone who carefully organised this holiday, sorted out the deposit and the final payment, arranged rooms and keys — even someone to come and switch on the electricity, which didn't go quite to plan through no fault of his. And it takes a lot to impress my mother, let me tell you. Not only that, but without prompting, he set about transforming the lodge and the communal areas with the kind of wonderfully festive Christmas decorations that businesses pay big money to achieve, and all for your stay, for everyone to enjoy—"

"He did that?" asked Jessica, her eyes wide. "I assumed the owners had put up them up. They're totally sick, aren't they, Ant? Why didn't you say anything, Trevor?"

"Again, I've only just met him," Rudy answered for him, "but I'd say maybe it's because he's selfless. Someone who doesn't do things for recognition and praise. Maybe Trev's the kind of person who just gets on with things, to make other people's lives that little bit easier, brighter and more bearable. You asked me what I think? I think you're all very lucky to have him as a friend."

A silence descended on those assembled. Left breathless, Trevor felt the need to defend his friends.

"They were only pulling my leg, Rudy. But I appreciate the sentiment—"

"Rudy's absolutely right," said Mrs M, standing. "And I propose another toast, this time to Trevor, without whom none of this would have happened. To Trevor."

Everyone else followed suit, scraping their chairs away from the table and standing.

"To Trevor," they all said in unison, grinning at him. Even Mary had a small glass of fruit juice raised in salute. Trevor, never one for public displays of affection, nodded to each of them before mouthing his thanks to Rudy.

"Before you get stuck into Brenda's wonderful meal," said Rudy, left standing as everyone sat, "and just so that you don't think I'm a complete arse for that last comment, I've brought you all a small token of thanks from my family, as a way of saying Merry

Christmas. Mrs M told me you have your own tradition about opening gifts on Christmas morning, but I'm sure you'll forgive this small break with convention. These aren't even wrapped and are largely from the family business."

And to the delight of everyone, Rudy started to hand out presents from the bags he had brought—a large snow globe each for Cheryl and Jessica, a miniature bottle of Mortimer twenty-year-old single malt whisky each for Johnny, Frank and Antoni, a full-length apron with a Mortimer Distillery slogan for Mrs M and thick hoodies with the same for Trevor and Mary.

Cheryl had already removed her snow globe from the box and now shook the scene to life, holding the ornament out for everyone to see.

"Let it snow, let it snow, let it snow," she sang.

"So that's what you meant by 'it's going to snow today'. You brought the snow with you," said Mrs M, laughing at Rudy, who stood enjoying the laughter.

"And finally," said Rudy, chuckling along, "when Trevor was giving me the lowdown on you yesterday—could you feel your ears burning?—he mentioned Karl being a rugby fan. And back in York, I knew someone who plays for the Bulls. So I've got you their annual calendar signed by the team, if you—"

"My husband?" said Mary, suddenly animated. "No, no. I'm the Bulls fan, not him. He can have the hoodie. I'm the one who goes to all their home games and most of their away matches—"

"It's true," said Karl, grinning affectionately at Mary. "She does."

"Wait," said Frank from the other end of the table. "You're a Bulls supporter, Mary? No way!"

"For the past ten years," said Mary proudly, before patting her stomach. "Never miss a game. And if it wasn't for junior, I'd have been to every match this season."

"Favourite player?" said Frank, shouting a challenge down the table.

"In the present squad? Has to be either Todd Mercer, François Debois or Damian Ingram."

"I meant from a 'performance this season' perspective. Not from the 'hottest player on the pitch' viewpoint."

"In which case, both."

"Jessica," said Frank, standing in his seat. "Sorry to ask this, but would you mind swapping seats? It's a matter of urgency. I can see my Christmas Eve duty is to help educate Mary."

"Bring it on," said a laughing Mary.

And just like that, not only did the whole seating arrangement change, but the temperature in the room thawed utterly and, in the true spirit of Christmas, foes partied with foes. Mrs M finished off the table by bringing gravy and assorted mustards for the meat and setting an individual dish of mixed vegetables in front of an intermittently beaming and happily arguing Mary.

Midway through the meal, amid the quiet buzz of chatter around the table, Trevor, who had quietly enjoyed his food, excused himself to get another bottle of white wine from the fridge. After taking the time to select a nice screw-top Chablis, he thumped the door closed to find Rudy standing there, a look of concern on his face.

"Did I do something wrong?" asked Rudy.

"What?" said Trevor, flinching. "No, of course not."

"Because ever since we sat down for the meal, you've been ghosting me. You could have asked me not to come if you don't want me here."

Trevor almost dropped the wine bottle, his shock deep and genuine.

"Of course I want you here," he said before nodding back at the table. "Are you kidding? Look what you've done tonight. Nobody spoke last night. Tonight they're all getting along like old friends. And that's thanks to you."

"Then why are you not happy? You can't even look at me."

Rather than meet Rudy's fierce gaze, Trevor's studied the floor tiles trying to find the right words.

"It's not that I'm unhappy, Rudy. Honestly. Quite the opposite, actually. It's just…" said Trevor, deflating and wondering how to explain himself without embarrassing them both. As the words formed, he stared hard at the wine label. "Okay, look. I'm giving you space to get to know everyone, and also making sure my smart-mouth comments don't scare you off again, like I almost did in the bathroom yesterday. I like you a lot, Rudy. And I mean, *a lot,* if you know what I mean? What I'm trying to say, in my not-so-subtle way, is that Jessica's not the only person in the room who's developed a bit of a crush on you."

In the short silence that followed, a crestfallen Trevor felt his new friend glaring hard at him. Eventually, unable to bear the tension any longer, he looked up into the beautiful eyes of a grinning Rudy.

"I'm sorry," said Trevor. "Please don't go. Are we okay?"

"You're a silly arse. And there's nothing to be sorry about," said Rudy, snatching the bottle from him. "Here, give me that before everyone dies of thirst."

Once the meal had ended, they passed used dinner plates to the end of the table and Rudy excused himself to use the restroom, but not before he caught Trevor's eye, smiled and winked at him. Once again, Trevor's heart fluttered, but this time he made sure to return a quick smile before watching Rudy go. In the absence, he sipped his wine and listened to conversations around the table. A few minutes later, Rudy's voice whispered in his ear.

"I need you. Can you come with me a moment?"

Trevor turned, concern on his face. "Is everything okay?"

"Everything's fine. I just—need you for a second."

Trevor got up and followed Rudy through to the darkened living room. Someone had switched off the main lights, leaving the room lit by the orange glow of the flickering log fire and Christmas tree lights. Just for a second, he stopped in the doorway, soaking up the festive and homey space, and barely heard Rudy call his name from the front windows. Soft strains of Nat King Cole's velvety voice singing *The Christmas Song* issued from Cheryl's speaker. When Trevor got there, Rudy's playful grin had his pulse racing all over again. Maybe he ought to warn his new friend about the effect he was having so that he might tone down any furtive glances and warm smiles—and ultimately the mixed signals he was sending. But something twinkled in Rudy's eyes right now, as though he had a secret he desperately needed to share with his new best friend.

"Come here," said Rudy, pulling Trevor to him and—with what had quickly become his trademark gesture — putting his left arm across Trevor's shoulders. "Look outside."

When Trevor turned, he could not help the gasp that escaped him. Without thinking, he snaked his right arm around Rudy's waist as his mind grasped at what it was seeing.

Snow.

Everywhere.

Drifts and swirls and fields of powdery flakes. Brilliant white, thick and fluffy. Falling in slow motion, settling on everything, onto the hard, icy ground. Masking everything in its purity. Just as Rudy had predicted.

"Now tell me I'm crazy."

"You're not crazy. It's beautiful," Trevor said to the view. "You were right all along. You're amazing, Rudy."

Next to him, Rudy's body stiffened slightly, and his arm tightened around Trevor's neck. Before Trevor realised what was happening, his body was being turned around. With an effort of will, he tore his gaze away from the scene as Rudy brought their mouths together. Trevor barely had time to catch his breath as the kiss turned from soft lips touching to open-mouthed passion. Almost as though a switch had been activated, Rudy's body came to life, hungry for Trevor, pulling their torsos together. Engrossed in the kiss, Trevor struggled to catch up and make sense of what was happening, especially Rudy's hard arousal pressing into him. When questions nagged him about Rudy's sexuality, he batted them away, not wanting to spoil the moment. Only when Rudy smoothed his hand down Trevor's back, venturing beneath the material of his jeans to cup one of his cheeks, did Trevor finally come up for air with a gulp.

"Are you okay?" whispered Rudy.

"Seriously? Are you *seriously* asking me that? I am being kissed by the hottest man in Scotland, against a backdrop that most photographers would kill to capture, and you're asking me if I'm okay? Rudy, this is fast becoming the best Christmas ever."

Rudy had started chuckling even before Trevor had finished speaking. Soft chortles rose and fell against Trevor's chest until Trevor stilled them with another kiss. Eventually Trevor slowed and pulled his head away, and marvelled at Rudy's closed eyelids, illuminated by the soft light. Still with their arms wrapped around each other, they swayed gently to the music.

"Do you think we should let the others know?" whispered Rudy, his eyes still closed and a satisfied smile on his lips. "About the snow, I mean."

"In a minute. The snow's not going anywhere. Let me be selfish and enjoy this moment a little longer," said Trevor, tightening his arms around Rudy and pulling him closer. "They come so rarely in a lifetime."

"Whatever you need, Trev," said Rudy, pushing his cheek into Trevor's neck and returning the embrace. "Whatever you need."

Chapter Eight

Dear Santa (Bring Me a Man This Christmas)

Not one person acknowledged them on their return to the kitchen. Everyone appeared caught up in the excited buzz of conversation and laughter around the table. Trevor insisted Rudy be the one to let them know about the change in weather because, after all, Rudy had been the one people had ridiculed. He should have the honour of saying 'I told you so'.

As they approached the table, he let go of Trevor's hand and moved back to his seat at the head. Trevor missed the warm pressure, surprised at the sudden loss of intimacy. As he took his seat, a wave of uncertainty hit. Rudy seemed to sense his disquiet because he smiled and winked from down the table, both still in their invisible bubble, something Rudy burst by clanging a fork on his wineglass.

After a full minute, waiting patiently for one conversation or another to wane, and accompanied by a couple of people shushing others, he announced the news. Chairs scraped instantly and noisily away from the table, excited murmurs rising as Jessica, Antoni,

Frank and Johnny rushed to raise the kitchen blinds. All those left seated craned forward or around, smiling at the heavy snowfall outside the window, illuminated by the internal lights. Following louder squeals of laughter, those on their feet headed outside, each vowing to throw the first snowball. Even Karl and Mary joined them, caught up in the fun.

Although Rudy trailed the others outside, he stopped on his way and placed a hand on Trevor's shoulder and didn't seem to mind when Trevor shook his head, indicating his choice to stay inside. Left to his thoughts, Trevor's head began to fill with questions. What had the kiss meant? Surely not just a reaction to the beautiful landscape of falling snow? And, more importantly, was this a one-off or was there going to be more intimacy? Rudy had admitted to having a girlfriend in his past. Maybe this was a first for him, a tentative bi-curious toe in the water to test his sexuality? Except nothing about the embrace had been hesitant, quite the opposite. Rudy's kiss had rocked Trevor's world.

"Are we going to join them, Mac?" asked Cheryl, her hand landing on his forearm.

Trevor flinched at the contact.

"Whoa," she said, lifting her hand away and leaning back. "Are you in the middle of a self-diagnostic? In which case, do you want to tell me what happened?"

Cheryl knew about Trevor's incessant self-talk. Even though apart from Mrs M, nobody remained in the kitchen to hear him, he leaned his head in close and paused, waiting for her to do the same.

"Rudy kissed me," he whispered.

"You converted him," said Cheryl, waggling her eyebrows and not understanding the depth of his freak out. "Congratulations, Mac."

"No, I didn't. I told him I liked him, but that's all. He instigated the kiss."

"And you kissed him back?"

"Yes, I kissed him back. I'm not stupid. You're missing the point. He's not gay."

"Do you like him?"

"Of *course* I like him. I told you already, he's my fantasy book hero come to life."

"Then if he likes you, I don't see the problem."

"We had a moment, that's all. I'm not throwing myself at him and making a fool of us both."

"You're impossible."

"Cheryl, you of all people know how much I've humiliated myself in this world. I'm not about to add another notch to that particular screw-up belt."

"Where's your sense of adventure?"

"In a mushy pile of blood and guts at the bottom of the Lover's Leap."

"Stop bickering, you two," came Mrs M's voice from behind them, "and help me clear the table, while the rest are occupied. Then I'm going to turn in and leave you to it."

Trevor found that moving about and keeping busy helped take his mind off Rudy. By the time they had cleaned all surfaces and brewed coffee, those who had ventured outside began drifting back to their seats, complaining about the bitter cold, the short-lived euphoria about snowfall over. Trevor noticed Rudy making an effort to keep everyone entertained, the man of the hour, and he barely acknowledged Trevor. A couple of times Trevor observed a slightly drunk and smiling Jessica leaning into Rudy, but then later she seemed to transfer her affections to Antoni.

As the evening wore on, everyone except Mrs M made their way to the living area to watch the animated winter scenery from the warmth and comfort of the lodge. Cheryl, sitting next to Trevor, must have decided to liven things up, because she leapt up from her seat and stood in front of them.

"Frank, Johnny," she said, swaying along to the Christmas song. "Come on. Karaoke time. I brought a playlist. Are you up for the challenge?"

Rudy sat next to Mary, gaping up at Cheryl. Trevor noticed Karl roll his eyes, familiar with Cheryl's antics.

"Karaoke," said Antoni, his eyes growing wide. "Sick. I'm in."

"Hang on, Antoni. You may want to hear Cheryl out," said Frank, making Johnny laugh, then addressing Cheryl. "Can we choose our own songs, Cher?"

"Of course you can. As long as they're on the playlist."

"And who put this playlist together?"

Trevor laughed, knowing where Frank was going with his questioning. Same thing every year. And just as well, too. He did not want to end up making an arse of himself singing out of key in front of Rudy.

"I did, of course. All my favourite songs of all time without the lead vocal."

"And all in your personal key?" asked Frank.

"Of course," said Cheryl. "How else am I supposed to practice?"

"You see, Antoni. This Christmas tradition is not so much karaoke as it is the Cheryl Madison show. None of the songs will be in our key, I guarantee. So guess who ends up singing solo all evening?"

"We'll pass this year, thanks, Cher," said Johnny.

"Spoilsports," she said, screwing her face up and plonking herself down beside Trevor.

Instead of watching Cheryl sing, the crowd went back to their conversations. Sometime later, when Trevor looked over, Rudy seemed to be enjoying keeping Frank, Johnny, Mary and Karl entertained — something for which Trevor could hardly feel anything but gratitude. Out of loyalty and solidarity, Cheryl stayed beside Trevor, but when she yawned for the fourth time, he ordered her to bed. In two minds whether to do the same, he resolved to talk to Rudy once he could get him alone. He needed to know where they stood. All night he agonised over what to say and fretted about whether he should go to Rudy or whether he should let Rudy come to him. Eventually, just after midnight, with a backdrop of flurried snow, Trevor and Rudy ended up as the last two souls remaining, sat either end of the settee. They had not spoken since entering the living area.

"How did you get here tonight?" asked Trevor, throwing out an olive branch before taking a nervous swig from his beer bottle.

"In the Rover."

"Do you think you should drive back tonight? The snow looks really heavy and you've been drinking."

Trevor had been serious but turned to see Rudy grinning into the fire.

"Have you been keeping score?"

"No — I... Of course not. I — what I mean is," said Trevor, tripping over his words to explain himself, "you know this area better than anyone, but I'd imagine the roads can be treacherous in the dark, even without the snow. I'd never forgive myself if—"

"You may be right. I can always bed down here on the sofa."

"Oh," said Trevor and quickly turned away. "Of course. Or you could have your old room, if you want?"

"With you in it?" asked Rudy quickly.

At first Trevor wasn't sure how to respond, until the words slipped out.

"If—um—only if you want."

"Of course I want."

Trevor breathed a huge sigh of relief and smiled into the fire.

"In the bedroom with me, then," he said and turned to witness Rudy's smile become a full-blown grin. Of course, his smart mouth had to kick in before he could stop it. "But with you next to me, I'm not sure how much sleeping there'll be."

When Rudy's head swung Trevor's way, his smile dissolved and his expression morphed into a look of pure, wanton need. He stood abruptly, went over to Trevor, took the beer from him and placed the bottle on a surface before pulling him up from his seat.

"It was all for you tonight, Trev," said Rudy, brushing Trevor's cheek with his free hand. "Chatting with your friends and getting them to talk to each other. Something I've been told I'm pretty good at. But I need you to know that I did it for you."

Trevor's heartbeat sped up at the simple touch.

"Thank you."

He knew he ought to say more, but his brain couldn't find anything else to add.

"Come on. I can feel the bedroom calling," said Rudy. And this time, all the way to the bedroom, he never once let go of Trevor's hand.

But as soon as they reached the cool room, the atmosphere became less certain. After taking turns to use the bathroom, both stood fully clothed on either side of the bed, Rudy appearing as nervous as Trevor.

"Do you notice how the air in the room's cold, but the floor's still warm," said Trevor, in bare feet, scraping around for things to say.

"Underfloor heating," said Rudy, nodding nervously. "I told you. The water pipes run under the floor. Keeps the room warmer than most even after the cooker's no longer running."

Trevor began to remove his sweater but then stopped.

"Are you okay on that side of the bed? I mean, which side do you prefer?"

"I'm good. This is the side I'd normally sleep on."

"Fine, then."

"Or is this the side you prefer?"

"This side's fine for me."

Once again they both stood there, staring at the duvet cover.

"We don't need to do anything, if you'd rather not," said Trevor.

"You don't want to?" asked Rudy, his face falling.

"Well, no," said Trevor but then corrected himself. "I mean, of course I want to. I'm about to climb into bed with Rudy Mortimer, for heaven's sake. But I don't want to make you feel uncomfortable. And I get the impression you're a bit uncomfortable right now."

"It's not that," Rudy began. "It's just—I haven't done this in a while."

"How long's a while?"

"Six months, give or take."

"Well, I haven't had sex since January," said Trevor, grinning. "So I beat you on that score."

"But when you did, what did you prefer?" asked Rudy. Once again, he appeared unsure.

"Under the bedcovers was always a good start. Especially when the air's this cold."

"No, but sex-wise. In bed."

"The few men I've been with have always insisted on being in the driving seat, if you know what I mean?"

"And how did you feel about that?"

"Fine. In fact, I think I prefer things that way," said Trevor before looking nervously at Rudy. "Unless you—you know—prefer me to do the driving."

"No!" said Rudy urgently, before softening. "I mean, no, I'm very happy with that arrangement. I've had to be both in the past, but being the chauffeur is my preference, if you really want to know."

"So. Are we really going to do this?" asked Trevor.

"God, I bloody well hope so. Just looking at you, even with your clothes on, and I'm in danger of blowing my load. Do you have any—you know—thingies?"

Trevor stared, confused for a moment until he realised what Rudy meant. Condoms. And lubricant, hopefully.

"Box of twenty. Unopened. They come with me everywhere. And usually leave unopened. In the drawer your side of the bed. Although you might want to check the expiry date. And you'd better toss me the lube, so I can get myself ready."

"What? And spoil my fun?" said Rudy, opening the drawer. "No way. Are you ready to get naked, then?"

Trevor wasn't quite sure what Rudy meant about the lube. In the past, he had always prepared himself for Karl. But he decided to let Rudy take control.

"Fine. Quickly then. Ready, steady…go!"

Like a couple of school kids getting changed at breakneck speed after their swimming lesson in a cold changing room, they both shucked off their clothes and dove under the chill covers. As soon as they began to warm up, Rudy reached out and stroked Trevor's chin with his thumb and forefinger.

"Can I kiss you again?"

"Please."

Unlike the previous kiss, this one felt more tentative, more about asking permission. Trevor opened up then, pulling Rudy's muscular form over to him and deepening the embrace. And just like that, all of Trevor's doubts and insecurities melted away. Rudy's beer-flavoured tongue wrestled with Trevor's as their hands smoothed over each other's goosebumped flesh, their erections duelling beneath the covers. Rudy's body felt smooth and hairless but beautifully contoured with muscle, his large nipples standing erect from a combination of cold and arousal. When Trevor tweaked one of them, Rudy gasped, his eyes widening before he grinned and rolled purposefully on top of Trevor.

After firmly kissing Trevor then nipping his chin, Rudy disappeared under the sheets. Trevor wondered what was happening until he yelped with surprise at Rudy taking his shaft deep into his warm moist mouth.

Best fucking Christmas ever.

But Rudy had not even begun. After bringing Trevor close to orgasm — he seemed to know when to stop — he began to work his way down, across his balls, sucking on one then the other. Trevor barely took a breath the whole time, savouring the sensations.

"Fu—uuuck," cried Trevor, his eyes opening wide, his hands reaching for Rudy's head as Rudy's talented tongue ventured into his crack and started loosening him up, probing in and out, sucking and lapping hungrily around his entrance. Once again he brought Trevor close to orgasm but then stopped just before that happened. Trevor's heart hammered in the few seconds of respite before he felt cool gel being massaged into him, one finger exploring and caressing. Before long, one finger became two, and Trevor started to meet the thrusts into him until Rudy hit a particular spot.

"Mmm-ahh!" cried Trevor.

Beneath the sheets, without stopping, Rudy rumbled with laughter.

"Just saying hello to your prostate," came his muffled but humoured voice. And this time, Rudy took Trevor's shaft all the way down, while at the same time his two fingers smoothed confidently over the newly discovered sweet spot.

Arching his back and pushing onto the fingers, nerve-endings he didn't know he had sizzled with pleasure, giving him the most earth-shattering orgasm of his existence. As his body shook and spasmed in ecstasy, Rudy swallowed wave after wave of his load.

When Rudy surfaced from beneath the sheets, Trevor could neither move nor speak, feeling like his body had been filleted. Only after a deep, salty kiss did his conscious mind come back to him. But Rudy hadn't finished, and right then he was rolling a condom onto himself. Eager to reciprocate, Trevor began to turn onto his stomach, but Rudy stopped him with one hand on his shoulder.

"Where are you going, Trev?"

"You don't want me on all fours?"

Karl had always preferred sex from behind with Trevor's face buried in a pillow.

"God, no," said Rudy. "Not the first time, anyway. I want to be able to see your beautiful face. To kiss you, and lick you, and do all sorts of wicked things to you while I watch you."

"Oh," said Trevor, embarrassed, quickly flipping onto his back. "Okay, then."

Once they were both arranged comfortably in place, Rudy's grinning face appeared over Trevor's.

"Ready?"

Words had escaped Trevor and he could only nod. When Rudy dipped his head down and nipped at the side of Trevor's neck, Trevor almost missed the prod of the cock tip nudging his entrance. With what felt like practised ease, Rudy lifted Trevor's knees into the air before pushing slowly inside. Even as relaxed as he was from his orgasm, Trevor had to adjust to Rudy's size, but he had resolved to reward his new friend for the toe-curling early Christmas gift. When Rudy paused for breath with his whole length inside, Trevor pulled his head down for a kiss to let him know he trusted him. So began the slow push and pull, the rocking back and forth, bedspring squeaks gathering speed like the Flying Scotsman leaving its highland station. But once again Rudy surprised him, occasionally slowing, swapping long, unhurried strokes for shorter ones then ramming hard and fast. Before long, Trevor became hard again, and as Rudy began the erratic race for home, he grabbed Trevor's shaft and brought them both to a frenzied climax. A heavily panting Rudy fell on top of Trevor, who marvelled at the weight, the pounding heart and the musky smell of this new friend's torso. Rudy had brought his body to life in a way he had never before experienced.

If this is what great sex is like, he thought, *then let every day be Christmas Day.*

Chapter Nine

White Christmas

Trevor woke the following morning toasty warm with Rudy's body lined up against his spine. Voices sounded from somewhere outside the room. Others had already awoken, and there came distant barks of consternation and squeals of laughter—Jessica's and Antoni's voices. Were they opening their presents before everyone else? Cardinal sin, and something Mrs M would never allow to happen. Not that Trevor cared. He had the best gift of all lying in bed with him. As he listened, his senses waking to life, he realised the voices weren't coming from the kitchen at all, but from outside the lodge.

Trying not to wake Rudy, Trevor stretched out an arm for his phone and checked the time. Even that tiny action brought a tinge of pleasurable soreness from last night's exertions. Eight-ten already. After their second breath-taking lovemaking session, Trevor had finally begged for sleep. Next to him, Rudy stirred and turned onto his back, his messy, sleep-tussled burgundy hair nothing short of loveable and endearing. Trevor slowed his breathing and stared at Rudy, hoping there would be no awkwardness to spoil the awesomeness of the previous night.

"What time is it?" Rudy asked to the ceiling.

"Just after eight."

"What time did we sleep?"

"You eventually deigned to let us sleep at around two."

Rudy chuckled before rolling on top of Trevor and kissing him. Trevor's whole body relaxed at the embrace. He liked playful Rudy. Actually, Trevor liked Rudy. No adjective required.

"Do you mean I managed six hours of uninterrupted sleep? Unheard of. I have this odd but unshakable feeling that you're good for me, Mr McTavish. How are you feeling?"

"A bit sore."

"Bad sore?"

"Good sore."

"Any regrets?" he said, looking into Trevor's eyes.

"Nuh-uh. But I am waiting for you to say those two magic words."

Rudy looked quizzically into Trevor's eyes before a mischievous smile transformed his face.

"Cup of tea?"

"That's three."

"Any chance of a blow job?"

Trevor rolled his eyes. "That's five. Or is it six? And the answer is, yes, of course. Although we'll have to be restrained. If I can hear them playing outside, I'm sure they'll be able to hear us in here. But those aren't the words I'm thinking of. These two magical words go together and you only get to say them once – "

"Merry Christmas!" said Rudy, pinning both of Trevor's arms above his head and kissing him. "Merry Christmas, Trev."

"Merry Christmas, Rudy. And because you guessed correctly, and as requested, you get to receive your first present of the day," said Trevor, using his thighs to roll Rudy onto his back before heading south.

Rudy gasped and quietened in anticipation. On the way down Rudy's body, Trevor planted gentle nips and kisses, stopping to circle his tongue around each of Rudy's nipples, to follow his rippled stomach, then onto the money trail down towards his groin. Stopping before the bush of hair and the beautiful thick cock already straining at the leash, Trevor kissed both of Rudy's thighs and felt him shudder. Even though he had never once been sucked off by his ex-husband, he had perfected the technique on Karl. Without hesitation, he breathed hot breath along the length of the shaft, causing Rudy to groan. After allowing himself a second to smile, he drew his tongue slowly from base to tip a few tantalising times. Once he heard Rudy's breathing quicken, he pulled his mouth away, hearing a soft, frustrated groan. On that signal, he took him down to the root, opening his jaw to accommodate the entire length, and felt the bed shudder with Rudy's pleasure. Slow and long suction followed short and fast. Eventually, he used one hand to pull on Rudy's shaft while the other went to work his own until he felt the telltale vibration in Rudy. Trembling thrusts of the hips were followed by the stiffening of his body until Trevor's mouth filled with Rudy's salty cum, just as Trevor's orgasm joined in. Trevor took all of him, every drop, and only when Rudy stopped shaking did he remove his mouth with a pop.

When he finally joined him, Rudy's blissed-out expression was a picture of wonderment, which had Trevor grinning with pleasure.

"Where on earth did you learn to do that?"

"Boy Scouts."

"Seriously?"

"No," said Trevor, chuckling. "I had Karl to perfect my technique on. One thing in his favour. He never refused a blow job."

"Like the one you just gave me? Who in their right mind would?"

And with a simple gesture, Rudy surprised Trevor again. He snaked his forearm around the back of Trevor's neck, pulling his head down onto Rudy's shoulder. Submitting, Trevor nestled into Rudy's side, a gesture that felt so simple and yet so intimate. Breathing out a sigh, he wondered absently what he had been missing all this time.

"You can hear voices in the kitchen from this room. Did you know?" asked Trevor. "Is that why you always stay in here?"

"Actually, you can only hear the sound of voices. It's really difficult to make out exact words. Unless you're in the bathroom, which backs directly onto the kitchen. And even then, people have to be talking loudly for you to make anything out."

"Yes, I found that out already."

Trevor felt Rudy turn to look at him.

"When Mary and Karl arrived, I overheard Mrs M laying down the law. Let's just say voices were raised but she made sure to get her point across."

"I bet she did."

Trevor lay there, enjoying the warmth and listening to the steady beat of Rudy's heart.

"Can I ask you a personal question?" he asked.

"Uh-oh," rumbled Rudy's voice by his ear. "This sounds ominous."

"Not really," said Trevor. "It's just something you said. Yesterday. Wow, can you believe I've only known you for two days and here we are, snuggling like an old married couple?"

"I liked you from the moment I saw you. Waist-deep in bog water. But as soon as I lifted you out, your eyes had me snared."

"Really? You like my eyes?" said Trevor, genuinely surprised.

"Blue-grey? Trev, I could gaze into them all day."

"So you fell for my eyes?"

"To begin with. But when you made that quip about showering together, I was this close to—"

"No. Wait. I thought I'd disgusted you. When you backed out of the bedroom, I was crushed."

Rudy chortled then and turned his face away for a moment.

"You definitely didn't disgust me. When you took your shower, I came back to the bedroom to find you. You'd left the bathroom door open. You probably don't know this—how could you—but the mirror on the bedroom wall reflects the image from the mirror in the bathroom. And if you stand in a certain part of the room, you can see the reflection of whoever is in the shower. I stood there for a full five minutes watching you soaping up and washing, and I popped the biggest hard-on ever."

"In which case, you definitely should have joined me. I thought you'd gone to the kitchen."

"I had. But I came back. And later, when I was helping with your awesome decorating, I couldn't help noticing your amazing arse going up and down that ladder. One of the reasons I got you to go for a hike yesterday morning was so I could ogle your magnificent backside again."

By now, Trevor was laughing uncontrollably.

"Hang on. You insisted on me going up the hill first because you said it was safer."

"Aye, well, that's not strictly true," said Rudy, kissing Trevor on the side of his head. "I can be very single-minded and resourceful when I want something."

When Rudy went to do the same thing again, Trevor turned and met his kiss, which turned into a lingering one until Trevor gasped and pushed away.

"Hang on a minute," he said. "I wanted to ask you something."

"I'm not going anywhere," said Rudy, rubbing his nose into the side of Trevor's neck.

"You side-tracked me."

"I'm good at that—"

"No, I remember," said Trevor. "You mentioned you had an ex-girlfriend back in York."

"A what?" said Rudy, his chest rising and falling with laughter.

"No, seriously," said Trevor, even though Rudy was chuckling at the ceiling. "I'm pretty good with detail. You said you had an ex-girlfriend called Deb or Debbie back in York."

Suddenly Rudy quietened, the amusement draining from his face.

"Oh. I'd forgotten that slipped out. You remember?"

"Yup."

Somewhat sheepishly, Rudy shuffled onto his side to face Trevor and check his expression.

"So you're bi?" asked Trevor.

"Not even close. If you cut my leg off it would say 'gay' all the way down to the bone. That's one of the reasons I left the roost early and moved down to England."

"Parents didn't approve?"

"I didn't give them a chance either way. Went to study at York Uni. Guess I was too scared to tell them."

"Do they know now?"

"They do, and the funny thing is, they're fine. So is my brother."

"So who's this Deb?"

"Debbie. Oh God," said Rudy, rubbing his eyes with the palms of his hands. "I suppose you deserve to know. Debbie is code for my ex-boyfriend, a man buried so deep in the closet even his closest friends smelled of mothballs. Who, whenever he referred to me in company, even when I was in the room, used feminine pronouns — she, her, hers. To dupe people into believing he was dating a woman. And do you want to know the most fucked-up thing in all of this?"

"Go on?"

"I let him. I played along. But I could never do the same when I talked about him. It would have felt like lying."

"But you called him Debbie?"

"Everyone did. It was a nickname. Started by his mates long before I knew him."

"So what happened?"

"Trev," said Rudy, expelling the name through a breathy sigh, "do we have to spoil the moment? Walking away was really hard and put me in a dark place for a long time, something I never want to go through again. Just know that it's been over for more than six months."

Trevor thought over Rudy's words and needed to say something. Trying to help him understand, he placed the fingers of one hand against Rudy's cheek.

"I'm truly sorry, Rudy. Someone as amazing as you should never have to hide or settle."

"Fuck, Trev," cried Rudy, rolling onto his back, his hands covering his face.

"What?" said Trevor, trying to pull one of Rudy's hands away. "I'm sorry. What did I say?"

"Most people would call me all kinds of stupid. That I got whatever sick relationship I was prepared to put up with. But not you. Where were you six years ago when I needed you?"

Trevor didn't have an answer for that. Six years ago, he had met Karl. Six years ago, he had been about to embark on a relationship that was doomed to failure.

"And what are you looking for now?" asked Trevor.

"I'm not really sure. But definitely someone who doesn't hide who they are, and who doesn't need me to do the same. Someone who's fun to be around, if that's not too much to ask. Most of all I'm sick of feeling adrift. My days of one-night stands and casual encounters are well and truly over."

"This wasn't a one-off, then?"

Rudy smiled and landed back on top of Trevor. "I bloody well hope not. A whole headful of lustful ideas popped into my dreams during the night and I want to try them all out with you. Are you up for the challenge, Mr McTavish?"

A laughing Trevor lifted his groin to meet Rudy's.

"Permanently up around you."

"Trev," said Rudy softly, his smiling face hovering over Trevor's. "You are a truly beautiful man. And Karl's all kinds of an idiot for letting you go."

"Karl was being honest with himself. And me. I can't fault him for that."

Rudy moved back to lying next to Trevor but took his hand in his own and heaved out a huge sigh.

"You see, I don't get how someone could be in a gay relationship with another man one day, sharing the same bed and having sex — you did have sex with him, didn't you?"

"Of course we did. Not the best sex, but —"

"But then one day he just decides to switch lanes. Did you ever notice him eyeing up women?"

"Never. He may have his faults, Rudy — we all do — but he did not have a wandering eye. And I know what I'm talking about because I've watched a couple of our gay and straight male friends who are total players. Karl is not like that. He's inherently faithful." Trevor wondered how easily Karl had transferred that loyalty to Mary.

"Faithful but blind," said Rudy. "Because he clearly didn't realise what he had in you. Did he ever reciprocate with the blow jobs?"

"Not really his thing."

"But he must have got hard when he thought about having sex with you?"

"Of course. Look, the way I rationalise Karl is that if a tiny percentage of straight men have latent homosexual desires, then it only follows that some gay men have heterosexual ones. Maybe that makes them bisexual. I'm no expert. Of course, there are also those men whose only concern is getting off. The type who could just as easily get turned on fantasising about a piece of fruit or livestock. I like to think Karl was not the latter."

Rudy snorted, but wasn't letting up.

"And you never noticed anything strange when you were with him?"

"Like what? Chickens running scared in the backyard?"

This time, Rudy laughed aloud. "Come on, Trev. You know what I mean?"

"No, I didn't. Honestly. If it makes a difference, though, I was a late bloomer and Karl was my first crush."

Rudy stared at the ceiling, deep in thought, until Trevor disturbed him with another kiss.

"Come on," said Trevor. "We should get up and shower. It's Christmas morning. Look, Rudy — and I'm being serious now. What do you want to tell my friends? I'm happy to pretend you just crashed in here last night because you couldn't get home. That's not strictly a lie. If you'd rather people didn't know we slept together — "

"Trev," said Rudy, his beautiful green eyes staring earnestly at him. "Do you really think I'm going to be able to keep my hands off you today? As I said, I enjoyed what we did last night and hoped we might find time to be alone again today. I am into you and I'm sick of hiding how I feel. After your holiday, you'll all be heading back to England — we'll cross that bridge when we need to — so let's at least be together for Christmas and New Year. Are you okay with that?"

They had only just found each other. Trevor hadn't even considered the cold, finite dread of a deadline on their time together. At some point, he would also need to deal with that eventuality.

"Does it mean I can kiss you under the mistletoe?" he asked, smiling.

"As long as it's on the lips," said Rudy, playing along and, this time, causing Trevor to burst into laughter, quickly staunched by Rudy's kiss. "Come on, let's conserve water and shower together."

Twenty fun-filled minutes later, they stood on either side of the bed, getting dressed. Trevor grinned, watching an uninhibited Rudy pull on his jeans, remembering how nervous they had both been the night before. When Rudy reached to the floor for his top, Trevor stopped him.

"You can't wear the same shirt, Rudy. Apart from being creased to nothing, you'll so obviously be doing the walk of shame. Oh, hang on, I have the perfect solution. I know you're a few inches taller than me and broader around the chest, but try these on for size."

Trevor reached into his case and hurled across a plain white T-shirt and a thick knitted jumper. Intrigued, Rudy opened the jumper and instantly started laughing.

"Och, Trev! Are you kidding me? You really want me to wear this thing?"

"And I'll wear this one."

On one side of the bed, Trevor held up a black jumper with the cheerful, red-cheeked face of Santa Claus on the front, while on the other, Rudy's one in dark green had the smiling face of Rudolph, the Red-Nosed Reindeer.

"Monica used to knit me one every Christmas for my present. I've got three, but sadly the one of a Christmas pudding shrank in the wash. What do you think?"

"You're worried about me doing the walk of shame? If we're both wearing your clothes, your friends will know for sure we've slept together."

"Who cares? Let them," said Trevor, shrugging before pulling on his sweater. "I'm not ashamed. Quite the opposite, actually."

"Yeah?"

"Absolutely," said Trevor, smiling. "Come on, let's get some breakfast. I'm starved."

Luckily for them, everyone else had already awoken and sat either chatting or tucking into a light breakfast of scrambled eggs and smoked salmon on toast or crumpets. Conversations quietened around the table as Rudy and Trevor entered and took their seats, next to each other this time.

"Look what they're wearing. Santa and Rudy Rudolph jumpers," said Jessica, oblivious to the obvious and giggling into her coffee cup. Both hers and Antoni's cheeks were bright red, and Trevor guessed they had enjoyed playing in the snow that morning. "Totally lit. Love them."

At first Cheryl and Mrs M said nothing, but after a brief exchange of glances, both turned and grinned at Trevor. Cheryl got up and brought two champagne glasses of sparkling orange juice to them—at least, he assumed they contained juice—and nudged Trevor while placing one glass beside him. If others around the table suspected anything, they said nothing, either not noticing or deciding to be polite.

Until Irish Johnny piped up loudly. "Mary and Joseph! Did you two sleep together last night, Mac?"

"Sleep?" added Frank. "More like shag. Am I right or am I right, *Trev*?"

Trevor shuffled uncomfortably in his seat until Rudy took hold of his hand beneath the table.

"Yes," said Trevor, aiming for brevity. "Rudy stayed the night. In my room. With me."

Even though he had decided to leave out the part about shagging, he noticed Karl's unsmiling face. As though he had any right to a say in the matter.

"Good on you, mate," said Frank, beaming.

"Rudy," called Cheryl, slowly and meaningfully, from the end of the table. This time Trevor felt the blood drain from his face. "Can I ask you a question?"

"Cheryl, please—"

"It's okay, Trev. I've nothing to hide," said Rudy. "Cheryl, you can ask me anything you want. However, as you're in my home, and in my country right now, I reserve the right whether or not to answer."

"It's just, in the brochure, I saw this lovely table setting in the main room, overlooking the lake—"

"Loch," said Trevor, before turning to Rudy. "Actually, Cheryl's got a point."

"Except I notice the table's been taken away. Not that I'm complaining, but I thought we would be having Christmas lunch overlooking the loch instead of here in the kitchen."

"Well observed," said Rudy, his eyes flashing around the table. "As you know, I did forget to switch on the power when you arrived. But I kept the table a surprise, at the request of one of your guests."

Trevor peered to the end of the table.

"You knew, didn't you, Mrs M?" he asked.

"Of course she knew," said Cheryl, rolling her eyes. "They're as thick as thieves already, those two. I had a feeling something was afoot when I asked her this morning and she just shrugged."

"Even at my age, a woman's got to have her secrets."

"Quite right, Mrs M. So can I ask you all to top up your glasses with—" Rudy looked quizzically to Mrs M and tilted the glass.

"Mimosa—"

"Mimosa. Then wait for me by the Christmas tree in front of the raised floor section in the living room. I have a little surprise for you all."

Chairs scraped away from the table, and while everyone filtered out, excited and intrigued, Trevor grabbed Rudy's elbow.

"You planned this?" he asked.

"Not me. Mrs M asked me not to say anything to anyone, including you. I'm sorry, Trev. But the day I came and showed you where to find the fuse box and all the switches, she asked me to leave this as a surprise for everyone. In a moment you'll understand why."

Everyone had arranged themselves by the Christmas tree with its piles of brightly wrapped presents beneath. Wooden shutters covered the windows, blocking out any daylight, the only illuminations coming from the glowing white tree lights. Calling for quiet, Rudy instructed them to remain where they were while he walked to the other end of the raised floor.

"Why are the blinds still drawn?" asked Jessica.

"We'll open them as soon as lunch is served," said Mrs M.

"As you'll know," said Rudy, "nature laid on a surprise Christmas wonderland for you all—my family can't take credit for that—so Mrs M thought it might be nice to have Christmas lunch here, so we can we eat together and enjoy a view over the loch of the winter landscape."

"Before you say anything else, Rudy," said Johnny, "I am not carrying that bloody great kitchen table in here. Not risking getting a slipped disc on Christmas Day."

"You won't need to," said Rudy.

Holding a remote control in his hand, he aimed the small device at the ground and pressed a button.

At first nothing happened, and some of those gathered giggled. But then a mechanical buzzing kicked in, a vibration from beneath the smooth floorboards. Suddenly, to everyone's gasped surprise, a portion of the pine flooring began to ascend, a long oblong section rising slowly almost to waist height. Within minutes, a vast banqueting table clunked into place, with dining chairs stored artfully in the spaces beneath.

"Sick," said Jessica, mesmerised. "Just hides away when you don't need it anymore. That is well sick."

"The catch is you're all going to be tasked with helping get things ready," said Rudy. "And to begin with, the table will need to be cleaned and polished thoroughly—"

"Good enough that you could eat off the floor," said Frank, causing Johnny to laugh.

"Glad you think it's funny, Johnny," said Mrs M, "because you and Frank will be doing the cleaning."

"Not a problem, Mrs M. And I bet it'll look amazing once it's laid," said Johnny.

"Bit like Trevor?" said Frank to Johnny, clearly on a roll.

Even Trevor laughed, although his felt his cheeks burning. Rudy must have noticed because he strolled over, grinning, and put his arm around Trevor's shoulders.

"And while you're all busy in here," said Mrs M, taking over from Rudy, "I will be preparing everything in the kitchen. Lunch will be served at one. If you need drinks beforehand, use the bar in here once Frank and Johnny are done. Cheryl and I stocked the small fridge here this morning. Now let me read out the Christmas work rota."

Those who had been on the Christmas getaway before knew the drill and turned their attention to Mrs M. Only Jessica, Antoni and especially Mary looked on, intrigued.

"While everyone else clears out of the room, Johnny and Frank will vacuum everywhere, as well as cleaning and polishing the table and chairs. Once they've finished, Antoni and Jessica, you can lay the Christmas tablecloth and place table decorations, candles and Christmas crackers from the big cardboard box behind the bar. While they're doing that, Karl and Mary will collect everything we need — place settings, cutlery and wineglasses — from the kitchen and lay the table. You'll also get to choose the music for us all to listen to through lunch. Sorry, Cheryl, but we need someone else's selection today. Cheryl, Trevor and Rudy will be the only ones allowed to remain in the kitchen with me, because they'll be on washing up and vegetable-peeling duties — King Edwards, parsnips, sweet potatoes, Brussels sprouts, carrots and fresh peas. Any questions?"

Nobody spoke for a few moments and Mrs M took that as a sign of consent.

"In which case, Merry Christmas, everybody," called Mrs M, lifting her glass in the air, followed by a round of cheers from everyone.

"Now can we open our presents?" moaned Johnny. *"Please!"*

"Honestly," said Frank affectionately, putting his arm around Johnny. "You'd think I live with a child."

In their Secret Santa tradition, Cheryl had provided each guest with another person's name and a set spending budget. Presents often ended up being fun and more thoughtful than if there had been no limit. Mrs M always brought spares—thankfully, as this year's event turned out—in case anyone forgot or if there happened to be any unexpected guests. In a slight break from tradition and to make up for their surprise arrival, Frank and Johnny had brought something for them all, a present from their world travels.

Trevor ripped off the Christmas wrapping to find a cookbook entitled *Recipes for One* as his Secret Santa gift. He didn't even need to look up to rumble the person who had picked him because he knew Cheryl's humour all too well. Frank and Johnny had bought him a clay-modelled three-dimensional fridge magnet of Petra in Jordan, one to add to his already significant collection. Rudy was clearly delighted by their gift, a small bronze model of a Trojan horse, something they had bought from a gift shop in Turkey.

Once the gift opening had ended, Frank and Johnny shooed everyone out of the room and the work began. Giving holiday guests tasks to do on Christmas morning might have seemed unusual, but in the past nobody had ever complained, everyone happy to muck in before passing comment on what a good job each of them had done. The whole arrangement usually led to a far better appreciated and well-deserved Christmas lunch. As everyone headed off to start on their various duties, Trevor only heard Mary pass comment, grumbling to Karl about them being given the most arduous task and saying she would not be lifting anything heavy. She would opt instead to choose the music while he completed the rest. Karl, of course, agreed without objection.

Trevor shuddered to think what his ex's life was going to be like once their baby was born.

Chapter Ten

Baby, It's Cold Outside

Everyone went busily about their tasks while Trevor sat cocooned in the warmth of the kitchen next to Rudy, both happy to be together, their knees occasionally touching beneath the table. Time slipped by under Mrs M's watchful eye, and his hands ached from peeling and chopping vegetables—no frozen vegetables under Mrs M's watch. Only as they finished and received the seal of approval were they treated to a mug of hot tea. Frank appeared at the kitchen door as the hour nudged one and invited them all to witness the decorated table. With a nod from Mrs M, Rudy took Trevor's hand and led him away into the living area as everyone else gathered around.

Lit simply by lights from the Christmas tree together with clusters of candles down the centre, the Christmas table looked spectacular, like a scene from a Christmas lifestyle catalogue. Keeping the blinds closed had been a masterstroke because the softly illuminated decoration did not have to compete with harsh daylight. Someone—Jessica, he guessed—had continued Trevor's theme of nature. With the addition of gold and scarlet baubles set in clutches of wild green fir and arranged around the clump of blood-red candles, they had added glossy green and mauve tartan Christmas crackers, shiny stainless-steel cutlery and sparkling crystal glasses. They had even managed to add a garland of matching tartan around the rim of the tablecloth.

While he stood mesmerised, unable to speak, Rudy handed him a glass of champagne then used his phone to take a selfie of them both.

"Best Christmas ever," he whispered to Trevor, the warm breath and voice tickling Trevor's eardrum. Just having Rudy's body heat near sent shivered vibrations through Trevor's body.

"Okay, I know I'm a big softie, but I meant what I said, Rudy," said Trevor, turning to gaze into his eyes. "This whole trip had all the hallmarks of a train wreck. Until you showed up."

"When I said best Christmas ever, I was speaking for myself. And besides, I can't take credit for this," said Rudy, nodding at the table before clinking Trevor's glass with his own. After a brief, lingering stare, he leaned in and kissed Trevor full on the lips until he heard a soft gasp from someone.

"Is he gay now?" came a female voice.

Trevor felt Rudy's lips morph into a smile against his mouth. Moments later, he pulled away and turned to the voice. Mary. But Trevor answered her first.

"Of course I'm gay," said Trevor, grinning widely. "Ask your husband."

Everyone laughed good-naturedly except Mary who had not finished.

"Is it your mission in life to turn every straight man gay?" she asked. Trevor couldn't be sure, but he thought she might actually be joking. He was about to respond when he felt a warm arm wrap around his shoulders.

"He didn't turn me gay," said Rudy, grinning. "I came this way, and I plan on staying this way. Although, if you're referring to Trev making me gay as in happy, then the answer is yes, and I can't think of a better mission in life, can you? So how about we all help Mrs M bring food to the table and have a fun lunch together?"

"Well said, Rudy," shouted Antoni, clapping his hands loudly, much to everyone's surprise. Standing in front of him, Jessica pulled his head down and kissed him. Trevor and Rudy shared a knowing look. Perhaps their relationship had not been the only holiday romance.

One by one, they arranged dishes of food onto the table. Rudy came last, holding a large platter with the roast turkey surrounded by golden roasted potatoes and balls of chestnut stuffing. The whole arrangement looked like something found on a Christmas card. After they had all snapped photos, Mrs M joined them from the kitchen. Before they sat, Monica had always kicked off Christmas lunch with a short speech. Mary had already taken her seat at the table, her back to the window, complaining about aching feet. Hardly anyone noticed Rudy walk up to Mrs M and hand her the small remote control.

One by one, from left to right, the shutters on the windows began to slide open, revealing the incredible view of the outside world. Everyone still standing gasped in unison. Snow fell unending across the sweeping winter wonderland as bleached light flooded the room. Only Mary struggled to turn to witness the marvel. Eventually, she pushed back her chair, stood awkwardly and joined the rest of them.

"Come on," instructed Mrs M before long. "Let's eat before everything gets cold."

Turkey-carving duties performed, vegetables passed clockwise around the table, Christmas crackers pulled and generous glasses of wine poured, everyone got into the Christmas spirit, eating, chatting excitedly and laughing together. Mrs M had also created a leek, mushroom and goat's cheese roulade of filo pastry, which turned out to be one of Mary's favourites. By the time dessert came out—a homemade Christmas pudding the size of a bowling ball with a sprig of holly on top accompanied by a crystal bowl of pink and custard sherry trifle—everyone groaned aloud, some complaining about not being able to eat another morsel.

Jessica had assigned named place settings that put Trevor opposite Rudy rather than next to him. Now and again, they caught each other's eye and smiled. Despite having friends around the table who Trevor had known most of his life—and even an ex-husband—something about Rudy felt warmly familiar. At one point, as Trevor took a sip of wine while listening to Antoni gush about his new phone, he felt a socked foot beneath the table rub against the shin of his jeans before making its way up between his thighs. Spluttering his drink, he explained to a quizzical Antoni about his mild case of indigestion at having overeaten. Across the table, Rudy chuckled into his napkin until Trevor reached down and squeezed his big toe, making him yelp and yank his foot away. When, this time, Antoni looked puzzled across the table at him, Rudy said one word.

"Cramp."

After dessert, there came a selection of cheese, biscuits, dates and Turkish delight, courtesy of Johnny and Frank's Turkish adventure, accompanied by freshly brewed coffee, courtesy of Colombia. Mellowed by food and alcohol, everyone relaxed back in their seats, enjoying Mary's musical collection, which mainly consisted of modern pop songs. Maybe Frank noticed a nodding head or two because he decided to wake up proceedings.

"Truth or Dare!" he called. "Come on, it's a Christmas tradition."

"Truth or Dare is *not* a Christmas tradition," said Antoni.

"Actually, it is," said Jessica, turning to him, a hand on his arm. "At least, that's what my next-door neighbour told me. He said it's been played for centuries and dates back to the seventeen-hundreds. Used to be called Questions and Commands and was always played at Yuletide. But the rules are basically the same."

"Tradition or not, there is absolutely no way I'm playing," said Mary, her arms folded.

"Come on, Mare," said Frank, grinning wickedly at her—as her new best friend, he was the only one allowed to call her by the equine nickname. "You can start by challenging me. I'd be happy to go first."

After gentle goading from Frank, Mary finally grinned and caved in. Even Karl appeared surprised. As usual—not that the new crowd would have known—Frank went straight for a dare and ended up in his Calvin Klein underwear, outside in the snow beyond the living room windows. Given the freezing temperature, he provided a very passable *Gangnam Style* dance while snowflakes fell around him. Later on, Trevor went with a 'truth' choice when confronted by Frank, who asked about his night with Rudy, something he happily confirmed. Trevor dared Antoni to eat the remains of the trifle, which he did effortlessly, and Jessica chose to tell the truth about her virginity, something she had been saving until the right man came along.

"Mrs Madison," called Jessica, surprising everyone. "Truth or dare?"

"Am I playing?" asked Mrs M, woken from her daydream. Usually she would have been back in the kitchen with Monica, but she seemed to be enjoying the company this year.

"It's okay, Mum. You don't have to," said Cheryl, patting her mother's hand.

"Come on, Miss-Sem," called Frank, his words slurring slightly. "You remember Monica's rules. No spectators. If you're watching, you're playing."

"Frank," warned Cheryl.

"It's fine, Cheryl," said Mrs M. "Come on then, Jessica. I'll take truth."

"Okay," said Jessica, thinking long and hard. "What happened to Cheryl's dad, Mr Madison?"

Trevor sat up straight and drew in a breath. And he felt sure he wasn't the only one in the room to do so. None of their gay friends would have asked the question because they knew the answer. Although he wanted to intervene and roadblock the question, he had no idea what to say. Fortunately, Mrs M seemed unfazed.

"Actually," said Frank, apparently not too drunk to be remorseful, "I don't think that's appropriate —"

"No, it's fine, Frank," replied Mrs M matter-of-factly. "Truth is, Jessica, there never was a Mr Madison. Not in the picture, anyway. Madison is the surname I was born with. Cheryl was conceived out of wedlock."

"Oh," said Jessica, pulling a face, the reply carrying multiple insinuations. "I see."

"Well, no. I don't think you do see," said Mrs M, trying to close the conversation down. "But that's fine."

"And besides," intervened Johnny, speaking directly to Jessica, "Mrs M answered the question. The rest isn't anyone's business."

Trevor wanted to go up and hug him. But now Mary decided to join the interrogation.

"No, hang on, Mrs Madison. I'm intrigued. Tell us what —"

"Mary," said Trevor before glaring over at a stunned Karl. "Aren't you going to stop this?"

"It's okay, Trevor," said Mrs M gently, wiping her hands on her napkin before giving Mary her full attention. "We're all friends here. At least, I hope we are by now. I was thirty, Mary, a little older than Cheryl is now, and working as a nurse at a local psychiatric hospital. At the Christmas party, of all things, I had far too much to drink. And let's just say that Cheryl is a child conceived of non-consensual sex and leave things there. So, to answer your question, Mary. No, there is no Mr Madison. However, the true love of my life and Cheryl's other parent, Monica, who stood by me through the various stages of grief, the pregnancy, then motherhood, died in January of this year. Is there anything else you'd like to know, dear?"

Apart from the soulful song coming from the speakers, the room fell silent. Trevor noticed everyone looking anywhere but at Mrs M. Mary, whose face had drained of colour, suddenly shoved away from her end of the table and went over towards Cheryl.

"Cheryl, do you mind swapping seats?" she asked.

"Look, I don't think—" began Trevor.

"It's okay. Don't get up, Cher," said Mrs M, rising from her seat. "Mary. Why don't you and I go and chat in the kitchen?"

"No, Karl," said Mary, before Karl had even begun to rise from his seat. "Let me do this on my own."

As Mrs M led the way, the room fell quiet. Nobody spoke until they heard the door to the kitchen click shut.

"*Finally*," muttered Frank, breathing out a sigh.

"What do you mean?" asked Johnny, turning to him.

"We finally get this dickhead alone," he said, nodding at Karl. "Without him running off and hiding behind his girlfriend, or wife, or what-the-fuck-ever's apron strings. Time he answered a few questions."

"Frank—" warned Trevor.

"No, Mac. If he can sit there saying nothing while his wife fires off questions without caring who she hurts, then he can bloody well answer some, too. Besides, he owes us," said Frank before turning to Karl. "What the fuck, man. We go off on holiday for five minutes and suddenly you've transitioned from Mitch and Cameron in *Modern Family* to Gavin and Stacey. What the fuck happened?"

"And you don't get to answer for him, Mac," said Johnny. "*Capisce*?"

Trevor fell back in his seat and nodded. Right then, he felt the gentle weight of a foot on his own and looked up into Rudy's smiling eyes. Managing a smile, he nodded and relaxed. Maybe the time had come for Karl to answer for himself. When Trevor peered at him, Karl's face had gone pale, paler than he usually looked of late. Except that he slowly folded his arms and pushed his chin forward, a gesture of defiance Trevor had seen many times before.

"What do you want to know?"

"Did you cheat on Mac?"

"Never. I met Mary in April during a protest rally in London. We wanted to show our opposition to the police, crime, sentencing and courts bill. The passing of which would give the police powers to detain protesters at will if they consider gatherings are causing a public nuisance. Our freedoms are being flagrantly diminished in this country and neither of us are going to stand by and let that happen. This is not a police state, for fuck's sake."

"And you told her you were married? To a bloke?" asked Frank.

"Not at first, no. To begin with she was just a friend. But these things have a habit of overtaking you. When we met for the third time, I told her the truth about Trevor. But by then we both felt the same way about each other. I confessed to Trevor and moved out at the end of April."

"You made a commitment to him," said Johnny. "Did that mean nothing?"

"Of course that meant something. I still love Trevor. But I'm just not *in love* with him. I'm not actually sure we were ever *in love* with each other. Things just worked between us."

"Apart from the obvious," asked Frank, "what does Mary have that Trevor doesn't?"

"It's not like that. It's not about Mary having something that Trevor doesn't. I love her. She has a passion I've never known, and I love that she fights for what she believes in and for others, too. She's going to make a fearsome mother."

"She's a top, then?" asked Frank, and even Trevor rolled his eyes.

"You see? This is why I never said anything to any of you. Because I knew you would turn the whole thing into a joke. I fell in love with her, Frank. A woman. And, let's be honest, love is the most powerful force on the planet. We can't help who we fall in love with, can we?"

"Frank," said Trevor. "For Jessica's and Antoni's sakes, who have no idea what's going on here, can we please leave this be? Karl and I have both come to terms with what happened and moved on."

But Frank wasn't quite finished.

"Are you serious about her, about Mary?"

"We're *married*."

"Yeah, coming from you that argument doesn't hold much water—"

"She's having our baby. We're about to bring another life into the world together. And I am going to be a father who loves his wife and son, no matter what, with all my heart. Going to strive to give them both the best life imaginable."

Frank's eyes softened. "Good. Then I think we're done here."

Not long after, Mary and Mrs M returned to the table and appeared to have found their peace. Trevor had heard nothing of the conversation—nobody had—but he'd witnessed Mary giving Mrs M a heartfelt hug and returning teary-eyed to her seat. Christmastime could be such a mystery. Karl waited there for her, holding her cardigan, concern etched on his face.

After that, nobody felt like more games.

Later in the afternoon, once they had cleared everything and their Christmas table had once again become the floor, everyone except Trevor and Rudy retired to their separate bedrooms to relax or sleep off the big lunch. Trevor wanted to help Mrs M finish getting everything cleaned up in the kitchen before he dragged Rudy back to his bedroom. He joined him back in the main room at the large windows as the light began to drain from the sky, watching shimmer after shimmer of heavily falling snow.

"Are all your Christmas dinners as dramatic?" asked Rudy, slipping his arm around Trevor's waist.

"Sorry you had to hear that," said Trevor, squeezing his eyes closed.

"I'm not. Gives me a new understanding. And I see better what you mean, when you say that Karl was just being honest. Honest with you both."

Trevor opened his eyes and stared at Rudy, wondering how he could have been so lucky as to meet the man. He followed Rudy's gaze as he stared out at the scenery.

"Beautiful, isn't it?" said Trevor.

"Not if it keeps up like this," said Rudy, and Trevor noticed the concern in his voice. "Might look lovely now, Trev, but being snowbound up here in the highlands is no joke."

"You don't need to worry. Mrs M packed enough food to last until spring. And I'll happily keep you warm at night," said Trevor, weaving his arm around Rudy's waist, hugging their bodies close and making him smile.

"Thanks, Trev. I just don't want anything to spoil this break for you," said Rudy, nuzzling his neck. "What was that about Brenda, by the way? I didn't understand what was going on."

"Oh heck, Rudy," said Trevor, heaving out a sigh. "Our usual group knows the story. Mrs M took a group of orderlies back to her place from the Christmas party, to carry on the celebrations. She used to be pretty wild in her youth. But she passed out, and when she woke up in the morning to an empty room, she knew she'd been violated by one of the men. At the time, she felt so ashamed, she kept everything to herself."

"Bastard. And that's how Cheryl was conceived?"

"Twins, actually. But her brother, Connor, a beautiful but poorly child from birth, didn't survive the year."

"God, Trevor. Poor Brenda."

"That's why, you'll notice, she drinks very little. Everyone told her to abort them both. Except for Monica, who told her to follow her heart and not listen to others. Terrible ordeal at the time, she often says, but that's how she ended up with Cheryl and Monica in her life. And that's why she's *Mrs* Madison, because she and Monica got married as soon as they could."

"Thanks for telling me."

Once again, Rudy pulled his head around and kissed him, a more lingering kiss this time.

"Don't know about you, Mr Mortimer, but I think we should grab some us time in the bedroom before the evening celebrations—" said Trevor, before something in the sky caught his eye. "What was that?"

Rudy followed his gaze out of the window.

"What was what?"

"I thought I saw the shadow of a large bird in the sky."

"In this weather? Very doubtful—"

"There!" said Trevor, pointing. "No, not a bird, an airplane."

They watched in stunned silence as a light aeroplane—a seaplane—circled overhead through the snow before landing smoothly on the surface of the loch.

"Shit. In all my years coming back here, I've only witnessed that happen twice, and both times have been because of a medical emergency."

As they watched, the plane began to rotate ninety degrees and inch towards the mooring pier that belonged to Mortimer House.

"It's heading to the big house," said Rudy, the concern plain in his voice. "Why hasn't anyone called? Maybe they have no idea, either. Oh, God, what if it's my parents returned early? Or if something's happened to Millie or Tam? They're both in their late sixties. I'd better head back, Trev. I should really be there when they arrive."

An odd realisation came over Trevor then—that he had no idea about Rudy's real life. Everything between them had happened so fast.

"You want me to drive you?" he asked, turning and sharing the concern.

"No," said Rudy quickly, but he then turned and smiled before leaning in and kissing him. "Although I do appreciate the offer, I think you drank more than me. I only had two glasses. Besides, you should stay with your friends. Let me sort this out. It's probably nothing."

"Is your car going to be okay?"

"My car is going to be just fine," said Rudy, raising an eyebrow. "I have snow chains on the tyres. Remember who predicted the snow, Trev."

"Fair comment. Are you sure you don't want me to come?"

"No need, honestly. I'll call you once I've found out what's happening. And hopefully be back well before bedtime."

Finally, Trevor broke into a smile. "Promise?"

"Promise," said Rudy, adding a wink.

Chapter Eleven

Wintersong

After watching Rudy drive off, Trevor went to his room and tried to nap. Suddenly the bed felt too big for one. Time alone only made him stew about cold realities and how tenuous everything stood between him and Rudy. Trevor would be heading back to his tiny two-bedroom house in Kent in a week, to his uncomplicated job as a freelance accountant. Rudy would remain here. After which, was he ever likely to hear from him again? Probably not, even though the mere thought hurt his chest and made his stomach tighten. In all of his twenty-eight years, he'd never had such an instant and intense connection with somebody, had never known someone whose magnetic presence in a room set off currents beneath his skin and cast everybody else in shadow.

And in the bedroom? Right now, he didn't want to think about how wonderful last night had been. In a fair world, they should have been enjoying more of each other's bodies.

But the simple unromantic truth was they had different lives, different jobs, and lived at other ends of the British Isles. After tossing and turning for half an hour and hearing soft music from the kitchen, he decided to get up and seek out the company of whoever he found there.

Mrs M stood frozen at the kitchen sink, staring out of the window, the tap running and the dishwasher churning. She hadn't noticed him, and he observed her for a moment, then felt a wave of concern when she didn't move. Soundlessly, he went to stand some way off to her left before noticing a tear on her cheek.

"Mrs M?" he said softly.

She came to life with a flinch, then seemed almost embarrassed to have been caught, until she realised the person standing there was Trevor. Looking away from him, she turned the tap off before smearing the palm of one hand across her cheek, then down her apron.

"Are you okay, Mrs M? Is this about what you told Mary?"

She shook her head, chuckled, then let out a deep sigh before turning to him.

"Nothing like that. Don't mind me, silly old woman. Just having a moment. There I was, all alone a few minutes ago, washing cups and glasses, when Sarah McLachlan's beautiful voice came on the radio, singing something called *Wintersong*. Never heard the song before, and I don't usually listen to the words these days. Most of the time they're either vulgar or they make no sense. But hers hit me so hard. Could have been singing about Mon and me, especially something about lying awake at night or in the morning and trying to remember how her body felt lying next to me. I do that a lot, you know? Wake up and think she's still there. But when I reach out, she's not. Gets me every time. Incredible, isn't it, how a simple song can sum up what we're feeling in so few words?"

"Oh, Brenda," said Trevor, going over and pulling her around. "Give me a hug. I know you miss her. Believe me, we all do. But she was your Mon, first and foremost."

"She loved you to bits, Trevor," she murmured. Without making eye contact, she pulled away and wiping something from his shoulder. "I hope you know that. She'd want nothing more than to see you happy."

Selfless to a fault, Mrs M cared for everyone around her. In turn, Monica had been the one to care for her. Karl had cared for Trevor, but what Mrs M and Monica had was so much more. To break the awkward moment, he threw out an olive branch.

"I have to say, you outdid yourself this year. Lunch was outstanding. Do you need a hand cutting up bread or meats or things for tea?"

Traditionally, they had no sit-down dinner on Christmas night because everyone was usually still overfull from lunch. Mrs M still provided salad, French bread, filled vol-au-vents, plates of cold food including leftover turkey, cold-cut meats, cheeses, heated quiches and flans and pickles. And despite everyone's protests about having eaten too much and not being able to manage another morsel, most of the food disappeared.

"No need, Trevor. You've helped enough already," she said. "Anyway, Cheryl will be here in a moment. And Mary's also offered to lend a hand."

"How about you two?" said Trevor, smiling incredulously. "New best friends?"

"Let's not go that far, shall we?" said Mrs M, clucking her tongue. "Why don't you go and have a shower. When you come back, you can sit quietly at the table and enjoy the next episode."

Trevor laughed. That was more like the old Mrs M.

"Talking of new best friends, where's Rudy?"

Trevor's smile dissolved.

"He had to go back to his house. Somebody arrived."

"Is that his brother and the wife?"

"I don't know. Why? Did he say something?"

"He told me his brother and sister-in-law usually arrive a day or two early to help him with the arrangements for their New Year's Eve party."

Trevor looked away and huffed out a sigh. Why hadn't Rudy told him?

"He probably forgot to say anything because you've had better things to do together," said Mrs M with a smirk, once again reading his mind. "You really like him, don't you?"

Trevor nodded and grinned sheepishly.

"And he really likes you?"

"I don't know anything about him, Mrs M."

"That's the whole point, love. The fun is in getting to know someone."

"But we head back to England next week."

"Then make the most of your time together, because that's how you'll know whether there's a reason to stay in touch, or to want more. Trust an old woman when it comes to matters of the heart—"

"You're not old."

"Let me tell you something. I haven't seen you looking this happy in years. Yes, years. So go with your heart and tell that little man in your head to keep his big fat interfering mouth shut."

Trevor laughed. He had only ever told Cheryl about the critical little head voice who pitched in at the very worst of times.

"Okay, I'm going to shower," he said, heading to his room.

"Oh, and Trevor?"

He spun around in the doorway. "Yes, Mrs M?"

"You called me Brenda earlier? Do you remember?" she said, smiling and causing Trevor to laugh again. "I liked the sound of it. Is that something you're going to continue?"

"Sorry. You'll always be Mrs M to me."

* * * *

Served from seven-thirty, the cold Christmas buffet proved to be its usual resounding success. After napping or relaxing, everyone had worked up brand-new appetites, any tension from lunch forgotten. Mrs M, Cheryl and Mary moved around one another to serve the fare together with mugs of tea. Mary even rustled up a couple of hot vegetarian pasta dishes to share with everyone, which became an instant hit.

When the fourth person asked Trevor where Rudy had gone, and for the fourth time he had to explain, he checked his phone. Instead of checking in front of them all, he headed out into what could now officially be called a snow blizzard. One step across the doorstep the security light came on, and he scanned the display on his phone. No calls, no messages.

He thought about calling Rudy but decided not to pressure him, to let him deal with whatever had happened even though he longed to help out. Instead, he fired off a short message.

Trevor: Hope everything's okay. In case you're not back in time for supper, I'll put a plate of cold cuts in the fridge for you. Miss you.

On a second glance, he removed the last two words, even though he meant them. Standing there in the raw chilliness, he looked around himself and shivered. How could he have been gifted such a wonderful Christmas present only to have it taken away? Wrapping his arms around himself, he stared up into the night sky and did something he never did, something entirely out of character.

He asked for help.

"Monica? Tell me what to do?" he whispered, as flake after flake of snow landed on his face. "Because I really like him, and I don't know what to do."

He listened as the wind danced circles with spirals of snow, but no words came back to him.

Chapter Twelve

Fairytale of New York

Rudy didn't return that night.

Trevor woke alone, the way he had every night since Karl had left—every night but one. But today felt different. Something felt amiss. He thought back to Mrs M's words from the night before, about mourning the warmth of someone's body lying beside her, and wallowed in the dream of actually having Rudy permanently in his bed. Bleary with sleep, having stayed awake until after one, listening out for the sound of footsteps at his door, he had overslept. Now he rolled onto his back and stared at the ceiling. What had happened last night? Why had Rudy not returned when he'd promised he would? Or at least have gotten a message to him? Maybe they'd had a legitimate medical emergency, which was why Rudy couldn't return his text. Or had Rudy cooled off, realising their time together would soon come to an end and, rather than prolonging the ordeal, decided to stay away?

Wearing a tracksuit and dressing gown, Trevor dragged himself into the kitchen, where a drama appeared to be unfolding. Jessica and Antoni huddled together talking in urgent whispers. Mary and Mrs M worked with their backs to them at the kitchen counter, either oblivious to or, more likely, ignoring the situation.

"You're finally awake, Mac," said Antoni, looking up. "Big problem. We can't get out of the lodge."

"What do you mean?"

"The front and back doors are blocked with snow."

"Okay," said Trevor, shrugging. "Then dig the snow out."

"With what?" said Jessica. "If there are shovels, they must be kept outside."

"Oh, for goodness' sake," said Trevor, huffing and noticing Mrs M stifling her humour. "There are other ways of getting outside besides the doors, you know. Talk about a bunch of drama queens."

Without another word, he turned and headed back to his bedroom. He pulled open the short curtains to his window to inspect the scene. Even though the snow had stopped falling and the sun shone, overnight drifts had almost reached the windowsill. Almost. He pulled on the handle to the lead-framed panes and, despite letting a smattering of powdery snowfall onto the bedroom floor, managed to open the window. After throwing on a thick coat and boots and squeezing into warm gloves, he dragged a small chair beneath the window, clambered outside and ended up chest deep in snow.

Rudy had shown him the small lean-to container at the back of the house where they stored tools and gardening equipment, as well as shovels and salt grit in case of this very occurrence. He just hoped the structure had not been submerged too deeply in snow, which would be an inconvenience but not a showstopper. On his slow progress there – the back of the lodge had seen the worst of the blizzard, and walking was difficult, one deep footfall after another – he noted they would need muscle and hard work at some point to clear the cars of snow. However, the front of the building had escaped the worst of the drift, and someone had already cleared the container of snow. And, right then, he heard the sound of someone digging. Hurrying forward as best he could, his heart leapt at the anticipation of seeing Rudy again.

When he reached the lodge door, instead of Rudy, he found a red-faced Karl there, bent double and shovelling hard. In an unusual turnaround, his heart pinched with disappointment on finding his ex-husband there, something that had never happened. When he heard Karl mutter a curse, he laughed out loud, which instantly drew his ex-husband's attention.

"How did you get out here?" asked Trevor. "Did you clamber through a window like me?"

"Walked through the sliding porch door at the front. I overheard them fretting and thought I'd sort the problem out. Can't have Mary feeling trapped in the lodge, not in her condition. And if I'd been unable to get the porch door open, I'd have climbed onto the balcony of our bedroom and jumped off. Lots of soft snow to land in. Good to have you here, though, Mac. Another pair of hands never hurt."

Working alongside Karl felt familiar and awkward at the same time. Together they had decorated rooms in their old apartment, had laid a carpet in one of the bedrooms. Working side by side was nothing new.

But still.

"You like him, don't you?" said Karl out of the blue, pausing for a second to wipe his brow and puff out a steamy breath. "The Scotsman? I notice the way you look at him."

"I am allowed to look at other people, Karl. If you can—" Trevor realised how he sounded and stopped talking.

"I know, I know," said Karl, holding a palm up in defence. "I wasn't accusing you or anything. Believe it or not, I'm really pleased to see you looking happy."

"You are?"

"Of course I am," Karl said, leaning on his shovel and gently shaking his head. "Well, okay, at first I felt a little weirded out. Jealous, I suppose. Not sure I ever made you feel that way. Until Mary pointed out I was being a selfish prick and a hypocrite. As you can tell, she tends to say exactly what she thinks. And she asked me why I can't just let go and be happy for you. So that's what I'm trying to do."

Cheryl's recent words came back to him then, about how *we all need to grow up and move on at some point*. She had been talking about her and Hannah, but the same applied to him and Karl.

"Hope this doesn't sound shallow, Karl," began Trevor as they both continued to dig, "because I mean it as a compliment. But one thing I admired about being with you was that I could always rely on you for practical things. Mary's going to need that once the baby's born."

Next to him, Karl abruptly stopped digging.

"I'm terrified, Trevor. What the hell do I know about bringing up a child?"

"What does anyone? Talk to some people who already have kids. Mrs M, Mary's mum and dad. How about your brother and his wife? Don't they have two kids now?"

"Three."

"Three!" said Trevor. "When did that happen? Are they going for a football team?"

Karl chuckled and picked up his shovel again.

"We did a weekend with them and their newborn. And, of course, you know me — I did a heap of research with pamphlets and self-help books. The literature I could handle. Even the prenatal clinics with Mary and other mums-to-be were bearable with the toy baby doll. As for the practical experience? Scared me half to death. Seems to me that all babies do is eat, sleep, scream at the top of their lungs and shit on you."

"I hear that continues on into their teenage years. Metaphorically speaking, for the last one."

Once again, hearing Karl laugh lightened Trevor's mood.

"Don't forget I'm at the end of a phone if you need to vent, or talk — or whatever," said Trevor. "Not sure I'll be ready to babysit until he's at least on solids, using a proper toilet unaided and talking politics."

"Uncle Trevor," said Karl, testing the words. "Yeah, I like that. You know, Mary had been dead set on calling him Damian — you know, after Damian Ingram, the Bull's star player. But after Frank's comment about Rosemary's Baby she changed her mind."

"Yes, well, don't even think about calling him Trevor. Clever Trevor, when I got something wrong, Whatever Trevor when I tried to make a suggestion, or as the girls in high school used to called me, Never Trevor. Some girls can be so cruel."

"Point taken. But just so you know, I'd be honoured to have you babysit, whenever you're ready. Come on, let's get this finished."

Unblocking the pathway to the door proved a lot harder than expected, and half an hour later, they had both built up quite a sweat from the exertion. Just as Trevor scooped the last chunks away from the doorstep, his phone pinged in his pocket. While Karl stepped in front and took a couple of attempts to haul the door open, Trevor checked his phone.

RudyKing: Sorry. We're on our way over. I'll explain then.

"Rudy's on his way over with his brother," Trevor said after he had removed his boots and followed Karl into the kitchen. "Or his parents. Not sure which."

"Good," said Mrs M, looking up from the kitchen counter. "In which case, we may as well have an early lunch, as everyone seems to be up now. Rudy and his folks can join us, if they wish. Mary put together a spectacular curry sauce this morning, so apart from the leftovers and salad in the fridge, we're having turkey curry, aubergine masala and aloo gobi, with pilau rice, bubble and squeak and chunks of French bread. Hope you're all hungry. Frank and Johnny can set the kitchen table. Antoni and Jessica, put the kettle on and make pots of tea. Trevor and Karl are excused because they've been doing manual labour digging us out. Actually, Trevor, can you go and check on Cheryl?"

Trevor found Cheryl in her bedroom, sitting cross-legged on the single bed by the window, hugging a pillow. When he looked closer, he noticed her staring down at her phone.

"Everything okay?" he asked, waiting for her to acknowledge him before coming any farther into the room.

"Message from Hannah," she said simply, peering up.

"What's she done now?"

"She's miserable. Ever since they arrived, she's had nonstop disagreements with the new friend's family, especially the mother, who, apparently, hates her. She probably doesn't, but you know what Hannah's like. Now the new friend's not talking to her. They've all driven to the beach today, and left her alone in the villa. Didn't even ask her if she wanted to tag along. On Boxing Day. All she wants to do is get on a plane and come home. Says it's her worst Christmas ever."

"Uh-huh," said Trevor, coming over and perching on the side of the bed. "And how do you feel about that?"

"Oh God, Mac." She sighed and pushed a handful of hair across her ear. "I don't know what to think. I know I should be mad at her, should be feeling vindicated that she got what she deserved, but the truth is I feel sorry for her. Does that make me an idiot?"

"Of course not. They say Christmas is a time of forgiveness. Have you said anything to your mum?"

"No. Not yet. Because I know what she'll say. That I'd be a fool to even think about taking her back. But honestly, Mac, women aren't exactly falling over themselves to date me right now."

"You can't think like that, Cheryl. We have to be patient. Knights in shining armour and angels falling from the skies are the stuff of fairy tales. They don't happen in real life."

"Unless you count a certain lodge owner's son who appeared on horseback and seems to have rescued you."

Trevor couldn't help the smile that came so easily to his lips.

"Okay, sometimes they happen in real life."

"Seriously though, Mac. Do you think I'd be a fool to take her back?"

"I'm not sure you want to hear my opinion, Cheryl, because I might not tell you what you want to hear. It's a decision you need to make alone. But whatever you decide, I'll support you. I'll only say that if I was talking to Hannah right now, I'd be telling her exactly how much she hurt my best friend."

"I love you, Trevor McTavish," said Cheryl, after a moment of reflection, as a glimmer of a smile finally lifting her lips.

"We've always looked out for each other, Cheryl. That's something you can always rely on," said Trevor, just as Frank poked his head around the door.

"Sorry, Mac. Mrs M told me to come and fetch you. Rudy just pulled up in a bloody great Range Rover."

As soon as Rudy entered the kitchen and spied Trevor, his face lit up with a smile, his eyes softened and he mouthed the word 'sorry'. And just like that, Trevor's world fell back into place.

Behind him, two figures came in wearing winter coats, clearly too young to be his parents. His brother and sister-in-law, perhaps? Even though small in stature, the woman's comportment and appearance spoke of confidence and competence. With a tightly bound ponytail of blonde hair and natural classical beauty—not a trace of makeup—she could have seemed austere, but her expression held humour and composure. When the man behind her stepped forward and spoke, Mary dropped the cutlery she had been drying.

"Something smells friggin' amazing in here."

Instantly recognisable, even to Trevor, who was by no means a rugby fan, Damian Ingram smiled broadly at the group, his Northern accent catching everyone's attention and making them laugh. Ingram, with his mop of unruly brown hair, had a killer combination of incredible looks and muscular physique, as well as being a star on the field and a celebrity off. Lucrative modelling contracts for a famous national underwear chain and men's cologne brand kept his face on the pages of lifestyle magazines and posters nationwide. Not to mention being the primary reason for the phenomenal sales of the Bulls' semi-naked team calendar. Women and gay men — and, no doubt, a few straight ones — dreamed of getting into his designer underpants.

After the laughter died down and was replaced by a stunned silence, Rudy stepped forward to explain.

"Damian and Helen are here for my parents' Hogmanay ball. Some roads have been closed off, hence the somewhat dramatic seaplane entrance. We're putting them up at the house with other guests who manage to get through. Unfortunately, the house boiler took this moment to stop working — "

"Place is like a bloody morgue. Froze my ass off last night," added Ingram.

" —but the Fort William repair man's been called and he's coming tomorrow, if he can get through. So for tonight I'm going to put them up in one of the two-bedroom cottages we have down by the loch — "

"Why can't they stay here?" asked Frank, the diehard Bulls fan.

"That wouldn't be right. I mean, first of all, you don't have room — "

"Of course we do," said Mary, star-struck, a hand resting on her bump. "We can all shuffle around. Cheryl can bunk in with her mum. Jessica seems to be spending all her time in Antoni's room anyway. And, more importantly, as you can probably tell, the lodge's heating and boilers are working perfectly."

"Fine by me," said Jessica, unable to take her eyes off Damian.

Trevor watched Cheryl and her mum share a look before nodding. Rudy seemed to be more concerned about Trevor's reaction, his gaze and private shrug seeking an answer. Maybe he worried because Trevor had made all the arrangements and rented the lodge for their group's private holiday. Typical Rudy — he'd be more concerned about lumbering them with his parents' guests than the fact they'd be entertaining a celebrity. Trevor smiled and nodded his approval.

"At the very least," said Mrs M, breaking the collective trance by taking plates to the table, "your guests should stay for lunch while they think the plan over."

As expected, lunch turned out to be another huge success with the group and their guests. Also, as anticipated, Mary and Frank monopolised the conversation — interrogation, more like — firing question after question at Damian. Watching Damian holding court, Cheryl, who Trevor knew had no interest in rugby, chatted to Helen. After sampling her anxiousness about Hannah earlier, he was pleased to see her distracted and the two of them getting along.

During the meal, they learnt that Damian had cancelled a dream Christmas holiday at the Grand Hotel in New York because François 'Frankie' Debois, the member of the Bulls team invited to attend the

Mortimer family gathering, had pulled out last minute. That he and Helen were old high school buddies, and because he had finally got his pilot's licence, he could co-pilot the plane. That he knew Rudy from his time managing a gym in York when Rudy had offered the players a special Bulls team membership, and that he was not, in fact, dating the famous supermodel he had recently been photographed with at a charity event. All in all, he made light of the fandom and had everyone laughing by the end of the meal.

"Look, if you're all really sure," said Damian, after a whispered conference with Helen, "we would love to stay here and enjoy your company."

"Fucking awesome," said Frank, clapping his hands together with delight, followed by murmurs of approval from the rest of those gathered.

"But strictly no photo or videos posted on social media," said Mrs M. "I meant what I said the other day. And the rule still stands."

"Come on," said Cheryl to Helen, happily escorting her from the room. "I'll show you to your bedroom. Good job I made the bed and tidied this morning."

"Can I have a private chat with you?" whispered Rudy to Trevor. Throughout the meal he had sat apart from him, laughing along to Damian's stories and lighthearted banter, even though he had probably heard it before. Trevor cringed inside at hearing Rudy's polite, formal tone. "In your room, please?"

The minute they reached the bedroom, Trevor stood there and stared at the floor, sure the hammer was about to fall.

"Trev, look at me."

Eventually, Trevor managed to make eye contact, to find a gently smiling Rudy. Taking a step forward,

Rudy pulled Trevor into his arms and hugged him tightly.

"I'm truly sorry about last night, sorry about this mess," he whispered into Trevor's ear.

"Are you okay, Rudy?" Trevor stayed still, enjoying the contact. "You seem — I don't know — rattled? Did something happen?"

"No. Well, yes. Och, I'm just being selfish. I wasn't expecting anyone to arrive until later in the week, thought I would have you to myself before anyone arrived. Each year my folks invite celebrities to our annual Hogmanay celebrations. My mother's a bit of a collector like that, likes to show off people they've met during the year. Been trying to get some of the A-list royals, but as everyone knows they spend New Year at Sandringham. Damian's not supposed to be here until the thirtieth. Helen's his date to the party — even though they're not actually a couple — so because of the weather he got her to fly here a few days earlier than expected. At least they actually arrived. So I had to play host last night, trying to sort rooms out for them, running around, so busy I forgot to charge my phone. And then the heating packed up. But I wanted to come back, I really did. Please believe me."

"Of course I believe you. I just — I missed you."

"I missed you too. I'm so sorry."

"You're forgiven."

"Am I?" said Rudy, loosening his hug and facing Trevor. "So can I stay tonight? I brought a bag, if that's okay? Was going to show them to the cottage then come back to you."

"You'd bloody better stay. We've got serious some catching up to do," said Trevor, relieved, pecking Rudy on his smiling lips. "Go and fetch your bag, and I'll see what the others are up to."

As though Ben Nevis had been lifted from his shoulders, Trevor trailed behind Rudy into the kitchen, where Mrs M sat alone at the far end of the table, reading a magazine.

"Where is everyone?" asked Trevor.

"The woman pilot's taking a hot shower, poor thing. And Frank's showing the man to Jessica's room, while she packs her things. The rest of them are sitting in the lounge. I know he's a celebrity, Rudy, but I hope he's not expecting star treatment — room service and all that nonsense."

"Of course not, Brenda. If you like, I'll call our Millie and get her to fetch some food from the house."

"No, dear, that's not what I meant," said Mrs M. "I don't mind feeding them both — there's plenty of food to go round — but I'm not making any beds or doing laundry and ironing, no matter how important he is."

"That's not going to be an issue," said Rudy, laughing. "So, Trev, is it okay if I go and fetch my bag and take it to your bedroom?"

"Are you staying?" asked Mrs M, looking up, her eyes wide and hopeful.

Rudy appeared a little hesitant, and Trevor almost answered for him.

"If it's not too much bother?"

"Too much bother? Are you serious? One night you're not here, and I've never seen this one look so miserable. Of course you're welcome. But just so you know, you're both on vegetable-peeling duty again today."

"Anything you say, Mrs M," said Trevor.

Both Rudy and Trevor laughed, Rudy placing an arm around Trevor's shoulders. Everything felt right with the world again. Once everyone had settled, he and Rudy would carry on where they'd left off.

While Rudy went to the car to fetch his bag, Trevor strolled over to the door to the living area and, without anyone noticing him, propped his shoulder against the door jamb. Frank and Mary, the two he had been sure would end up hating each other, held court together, both clearly animated to have their hero staying with them. Karl sat smiling as he watched his happy wife, while Johnny, Antoni and Jessica appeared content simply to be a part of the fun. Breathing deep, he smiled at his friends gathered around the open fire, where Frank had them all laughing about a comment someone had made.

"Seriously, though, can you believe? That would be like me calling Johnny, Joanie or Sharon or Tracy!"

"You see?" said Mary smugly. "This is why I'm a better fan than you. If you really knew the Bulls as well as you say you do, you'd know his middle names are Edward Bruno. So his initials are D-E-B-I. Damian Edward Bruno Ingram. *That's* why Helen called him Debbie."

Despite the comfort and fierce warmth of the lodge heating, a sudden glacial coldness swept through Trevor.

Chapter Thirteen

Stay Another Day

Later in the afternoon, true to her word, Mrs M set Rudy and Trevor to work in the kitchen to ready food for their twelve guests. Twelve, Trevor mused. Finally, they had reached their traditional optimum number with this far from traditional crowd. Mrs M — usually flitting around the kitchen behind them — had been called to the shared bedroom by Cheryl for a private chat. A few minutes before he'd found out why when Cheryl had caught up with him in the hallway and whispered in his ear.

"Thanks for the chat earlier. I just had a stream of text messages from Hannah. She says she wants us to meet up when we're both home after New Year. To talk things through."

"Okay. That's progress, isn't it?"

"I don't know, Mac. Do I trust her? Not really sure. Does she deserve a second chance? After what she did, same answer. I'm going to have a word with Mum right now. If you hear raised voices or screaming, come and bail me out."

Trevor laughed and hugged her. "Helen's nice," he said.

"She is, isn't she," said Cheryl, brightening. "I'm so impressed that she's a fully licensed pilot. She says if and when the weather improves, she'd be happy to take me and a friend up in the plane, maybe get some scenic photos of the area. How nice is that?"

"Wow, I've never heard that line before."

"Trevor!" said Cheryl, shocked but laughing. "It's not like that!"

"Isn't it? How do you know?"

"Because she's not, you know, like us."

"Isn't she? Are you sure?"

"Stop sidetracking me. And while I have a talk with Mum, go and find lover boy. I think he missed you."

After she had gone, her words twisted in his gut when he thought of Damian and Rudy together. Now he and Rudy sat alone at the kitchen table, working quietly on the chores they'd been set.

"Are you sure you're okay?" Rudy asked for the second time, glancing sidelong at Trevor.

"I'm fine," said Trevor, continuing to concentrate on his task, letting peel fall into a pile on the table then dropping bald potatoes into a saucepan full of cold water. Seconds later, he flinched when Rudy placed a warm hand on his thigh.

"Okay, Trev," said Rudy, decisively putting down his peeler. "You're not okay. Tell me what the problem—"

"Your lordship," came a deep voice from behind them. Ingram stood there in tracksuit bottoms and a white T-shirt, his impressive pectorals and biceps on full display. Trevor could see the annoyance in the man's face—even the slight flinch as he noticed the hand resting on Trevor's thigh, something Rudy made no effort to remove.

"Yes, Damian," said Rudy calmly.

"I need your help. The shower in the room's not working."

"Really? It was working fine this morning."

"Yeah, well. It's not working now, is it? Can you give me a hand? You're supposed to be the maintenance boy around here, aren't you?"

Trevor frowned at the tone. But Rudy simply stood, removing his hand from Trevor's leg in the process. The coldness in its wake felt like an omen. When Rudy left with Ingram, Trevor put down the half-peeled potato he had been holding and let out a sigh.

Damian Ingram and Rudy? But then he thought back to his conversations with Rudy, about how his ex hadn't wanted commitment, how they never went out together in public. Moreover, he had insisted on being the active one in the relationship, forcing Rudy to adopt the passive role against his natural preference. And, most importantly, Rudy had said they had not been in contact for the past six months. So why in heaven's name would he come up to Scotland? Surely not really at the request of Rudy's folks. Had he come to win Rudy back? And if so, what hope in hell did Trevor have against a bronzed demigod?

Taking a deep breath, Trevor put his peeler down and stood. Without a second thought, he went out into the hall and stood by the open door to bedroom they had allocated to Damian.

" — not showering with you for old time's sake. I'm busy in the kitchen, as if you hadn't noticed."

"What about a blow job then? My balls are so blue, they're ready to burst."

"Damian! I'm warning you."

"Okay, but there are two beds in here," came Ingram's voice. "So you might as well spend the night—"

"I'm sleeping with Trevor tonight."

"Sleeping or *sleeping*?"

"None of your damned business anymore."

Silence fell, during which Trevor felt sure he could hear Ingram's pants of breath.

"You're an ungrateful little bitch, aren't you? I wasted money on two business-class tickets and a five-star hotel for Christmas in Manhattan. Why couldn't you at least have had the decency to honour that arrangement?"

"When are you going to get it into your thick skull? York didn't work for us, so why the hell did you think New York would? We're over, Damian, and have been for months. And I like Trevor. I really like him."

"That little runt? He's nothing like me."

"Exactly. He's sincere and honest. And happy to kiss me in front of people."

Ingram sorted loudly.

"Not that bullshit again? Can he give you what I gave you?"

"He gives me respect. That's worth more than anything I ever got from you. Now go and take your damned shower while I—"

Trevor heard a soft shuffle of feet.

"Get off—get off me," came Rudy's muffled cry.

"Rudy," called Trevor loudly before thumping on the door. "Rudy, are you there? Are you okay?"

Rudy staggered into the doorway, flushed and rattled. Without stopping, he stepped into the hallway and slammed the door closed behind him. Trevor headed back towards the kitchen, hearing Rudy following closely behind.

"Is this going to be awkward?" asked Trevor softly, turning to Rudy as they stopped at the kitchen entranceway.

"Is what going to be awkward?"

"The fact that Damian Ingram's your ex-boyfriend? He's the person you referred to as Debbie, isn't he?"

"Shit," said Rudy, pushing the palms of his hands into his eyes. After expelling a deep sigh, he turned to look at Trevor, his seriousness plain. "I'm sorry, Trev. I should have said something earlier."

"Ingram's gay? You were dating the Bulls' star international player and supermodel all that time? I'm just wondering how the hell am I supposed to compete with that?"

"You're not. You don't need to. And what me and him had was a far cry from dating, Trev. He used to treat me like dirt, ordered me around and – and sometimes try to force himself on me. Still thinks he can, if you heard any of that back there."

Rudy stood there looking pale and worried and, despite his own apprehension, Trevor's heart gave a tug.

"Look, if you want me to leave, I can go back to the big house –" began Rudy.

"You're not going anywhere," said Trevor adamantly, grabbing Rudy's hand and moving forward again. "First of all, you have no heating back there. Secondly, I'm going to keep you in my sights and if he so much as lays a finger on you again, he'll have to go through me. I know that doesn't sound like much of a threat but I have my resources. And last of all, you're not leaving me to peel the rest of the vegetables by myself —"

Trevor stopped when he saw Frank and Johnny standing frozen to the spot by the kitchen doorway.

"Ingram's gay?" asked Johnny, his eyes like golf balls.

"Shit," said Trevor, a hand briefly covering his mouth. "You heard that?"

"You can't breathe a word," said Rudy, fear shining from his eyes. "He's not out to anyone, and he believes his career would be over if people knew."

"You don't need to worry about us, Rudy. That's not our style. We're not in the habit of outing people. But did I hear that right, did he really push you around?" said Johnny, his eyes narrowing as Rudy nodded. "Jesus, Mary and Joseph, Rudy. Are you fecking serious?"

"Yes," said Trevor, before Rudy could answer. "You heard that part right."

"Water under the bridge," said Rudy. "Look, he's my problem to deal with and he'll be gone in a day or two. Back to the big house, and even then, only for a few days. After that, you'll never lay eyes on him again. Well, not in person."

"Rudy's right," said Frank, uncharacteristically calm, eyeing Rudy in a cold, measured way before turning to Johnny. "None of our business."

Trevor had often seen Frank become enraged when Johnny talked about the domestic abuse cases he dealt with at the shelter. Trevor put Frank's anger down to his personal experience growing up. Perhaps he had made an exception for one of his rugby heroes, or maybe he had learned to manage his temper better while travelling the world.

"But we're all here for you, Rudy," said Trevor, putting an arm around his shoulders, mimicking Rudy's gesture. "Aren't we, guys?"

"Dead right, we are," said Johnny, while Frank nodded.

"In which case," said Rudy, "can I ask you to continue being friendly and welcoming at dinner? As though you know nothing? You've had to put up with enough drama already, and I don't want to be the cause of more. As I said, they'll stay another day, then I'll drive them back to the big house. Can you do that for me?"

"Friendly and welcoming?" said Frank, holding his palms out to either side in a gesture of peace. "Rudy, they're our middle names, aren't they, Johnny?"

* * * *

After the heavy meals of the past few days, Mrs M had prepared a simple seafood pie and steamed vegetables for dinner that evening. When Helen admitted to being a vegetarian, Mary suggested they sit together and share her butternut squash and spinach filo pie. Although Helen accepted the food, she insisted on sitting with Cheryl. Trevor could not resist grinning smugly at Cheryl.

Unlike the night before, wine and beers made an appearance — perhaps in honour of their celebrity guests — and everyone loosened up considerably. Frank beat everyone to the spare seat next to Damian and enthusiastically engaged him in conversation. Perfect because between him and Mary, they knew pretty much everything there was to know about the Bulls' current season.

Next to Trevor, after a few furtive glances at the beginning of the meal, Rudy began to relax and appeared to stop fretting over Ingram's presence. But all the while, Trevor kept listening in on their conversation, even when Rudy placed his warm hand in Trevor's and squeezed.

At one point, at Frank's request, Johnny went to their bedroom to get the hoodie Rudy had given Frank because he wanted Damian to sign the front using a felt pen. At Mary's bidding, he also happily agreed to drop into her and Karl's room to bring back her Bulls team calendar. Trevor smiled at the interaction, wondered how Johnny might have responded on their first night together and marvelled at the difference a few days could make.

"Are you as good as this in the flesh?" asked Frank, opening to the semi-naked photograph of Ingram. Most others around the table held their own conversations, but Trevor kept an eye on them and noticed Frank flirting shamelessly. He cringed on hearing the suggestive remark, but the man in question grinned broadly, and leant back in his seat, appearing to enjoy the attention.

"Wouldn't you like to know?" murmured Ingram.

"Definitely," said Frank, the mischievous smile fixed in place. "So what do you think of the lodge?"

"Nice, very cosy. I'm downstairs—no view, but at least it's warm," said Ingram, looking around. "Felt a bit lost back in that old ruin. Bloody draughty, too."

"We got great views here. Our balcony overlooks the whole of the loch. Stunning panorama."

"Sounds great."

"Want to come up and have a look?"

Ingram faltered, looking awkwardly between Frank and Johnny.

"Uh, I'm not sure—"

"Johnny, is it okay if I show Damian the view from our balcony?"

"Of course," said Johnny, putting down his beer bottle. "Knock yourselves out."

Up to that point, Johnny had said nothing, nor did he appear to be concerned, chatting amiably with Mrs M and Cheryl. Every now and again he checked his phone beneath the table, something Antoni had been doing for the whole meal, probably playing another online game. Indeed, before long, as Frank and Damian left, Johnny turned his full attention to Helen, who had been sitting enjoying a glass of sparkling wine and savouring Cheryl's company.

"So, Helen," he said, "how long have you been flying?"

"Ten years," said Cheryl, answering first, her cheeks flushed with alcohol. She placed a hand over her mouth. "Sorry, Helen."

"That's fine," said Helen, grinning at Cheryl before straightening up at the question. "Cheryl's right. But I only obtained my commercial pilot's licence just over two years ago. Even so, I'm still mainly flying light aircraft in this neck of the woods. I was just telling Cheryl. That baby out there is an amphibious Cessna Caravan 208B. Has retractable landing gear for land or water landings. Flew her out of Glasgow with Daim, although she's normally stationed at Loch Lomond."

"How many people can she carry?" asked Karl.

"She's fitted to carry six, four passengers and two crew. But others are configured to carry up to nine."

"Do you fly for a living?" asked Antoni, finally putting his phone away.

"Heavens, no," she said, grimacing. "I'm a physiotherapist by trade. On the Bulls' payroll, thank you very much. Think if I flew for money, I wouldn't enjoy it so much. And at the moment, I absolutely adore flying in my spare time. I've flown light aircraft all over the world — Bermuda, Ottawa, Florida, Sydney and, my most favourite of all, Kenya. Flying at low altitude over the national parks and seeing the wildlife below."

"I bet that's amazing," said Cheryl. Trevor grinned. Damian Ingram was not the only new arrival being hero-worshipped. "What I wouldn't give to experience something like that."

"Maybe one day," said Helen, smiling at her.

Oh yes, thought Trevor, *definitely chemistry there*.

"Forgive me a moment, folks," said Johnny, standing up from the table and putting his phone in his pocket. "I'd better go and rescue Damian. Otherwise Frank's likely to bore the poor bastard to death."

"And if it's okay with everyone, I need to turn in. I'm feeling a little tired and out of sorts," said Mary, who did indeed appear pale.

"I'll take you up," said Karl, about to rise.

"No, you won't," said Mary, firmly, before kissing him on the cheek. "I'm only going to climb in bed and fall asleep. I'd rather you stayed and enjoyed the company."

Almost as soon as she had left, they continued the quick-fire questioning.

"Biggest plane you've ever flown?" asked Antoni.

"I co-piloted an ATR 72-210. Carrying around seventeen passengers."

"Scariest moment in the cockpit?" asked Jessica.

"Hot coffee spill in the co-pilot's lap," said Helen, causing everyone to laugh. "When he screamed, I nearly wet my pants."

When Helen started talking at length about some of the 'incidents' she had been involved in, everyone became so mesmerised they barely noticed the three men return. Johnny and Frank seemed fine, only Damian appeared a little flushed. For a fleeting moment, Trevor wondered what had happened, but then, after a few moments, he too started laughing along to Helen's aeronautical tales.

Later, when Mrs M herded everyone into the living area so she could clear the table, attention turned to Damian. Enthusing about his antics on and off the field, he had relaxed into his usual entertaining self. Rudy took the opportunity to pull Trevor away, to help Mrs M with the last of the dishes before leading him to the bedroom.

"Are you tired?" Trevor asked.

"Not in the slightest."

"You want to say goodnight to everyone?"

"Nuh-uh," said Rudy. "Let them chat. I've heard everything Damian's got to say a hundred times. And I want you all to myself. I've already missed one night— I'm not wasting any more."

"Just as well I'm not tired either."

"One thing, though," said Rudy.

"Yes?"

"Lock the door."

"Why? You don't think he'd try and come in here?"

"I don't know, and I don't care. I just know I'll feel safer if we're locked in here together. Tonight, I want to get in bed with you and wake up next to you. Totally undisturbed."

"Sounds perfect."

Chapter Fourteen

Santa Baby

A light sleeper, Trevor was awoken by a soft clunk just after midnight.

At first he dismissed the noise as imagination, or a creak in the bones of the lodge, or maybe snow falling from the roof. But then the same sound came again, this time from inside the room. Next to him, Rudy lay fast asleep, breathing evenly, a possessive arm draped across Trevor's waist. Without waking him, Trevor raised his head from the pillow and, using the soft glow of his phone display, illuminated the door. Very slowly, the handle moved downwards then back to its resting position. After that, soft footfalls padded away.

Trevor fell back into the pillow, awake now, and thought back to the previous evening. No matter how famous, rich and charismatic Ingram was, Trevor didn't give two hoots because Rudy had chosen him over the man. And yes, they had only spent two nights together, but already Rudy's body felt wonderfully familiar.

Trevor had never met anyone so considerate and selfless in bed. Not only had Rudy remembered all the things that had turned Trevor on the first time, but he had tested out new ways to give his body pleasures he could never have imagined. Last night they'd fucked long and slow, Rudy kissing and licking and nibbling, eventually sending them both over the edge by pulling Trevor's right foot from his shoulder and sucking on the toes. For someone so polite and formal by day, nothing in the bedroom appeared to be off-limits. After the second round, what was supposed to be a pre-slumber spooning session with Rudy's warm body aligned along Trevor's spine soon became something more. Trevor put everything down to making up for lost time. Gently fucking him from behind, Rudy had pulled Trevor's head around for a deep kiss, occasionally licking and nipping at his skin. Even as worn out as he was, Trevor's body had come alive again and hit boiling point as Rudy had thundered his own orgasm into him. After that, even though exhausted, neither could sleep for a while.

"Trev, can I ask you a huge favour?"

"Anything."

"Really?"

"Anything, Rudy. I owe you. You've made this Christmas special for me."

"Well, back at the house, with Millie's help, her husband Tam usually puts up our traditional decorations for the Hogmanay ball. They're fine, you know. Pretty tired now — the decorations, not Tam and Millie — because we've used them for the past fifteen years. But to be honest, they could do with a wee bit of freshening up, and I wondered if you might —"

"Of course I'll come and help. Can I add some new ones? I've got a ton left over that I didn't use. So long as I can watch your gorgeous bum going up and down the ladder."

Rudy had hummed with humour and rubbed his nose into the back of Trevor's neck.

"The other thing – and I need to get your opinion on this – is that I told my mother about you all, and she wants to invite everyone to the ball. It's just…they tend to be a tad formal, and I wasn't sure everyone would be up for that."

"If you're there, of course I'll come. And I think the best thing is to ask at breakfast tomorrow. Get their opinion. But I'm guessing that if Ingram's going to be there, Frank and Mary will come, which means Johnny and Karl will be there too."

"Hmm," Rudy had sounded doubtful.

"What?"

"To be honest, I hoped Damian would go home. Hoped he took the hint and has decided to head back to his friends in England. Even though my mother will be disappointed."

"Even if he does stay, we can manage him, Rudy. If they're going back to the house tomorrow, will you need to go and stay with them?"

"Not necessarily. Millie can feed them. And my brother and sister-in-law are supposed to arrive tomorrow. Mother and Father the day afterwards. As long as they can get through the snow."

"Let's sleep on it. And if the weather's good tomorrow, let's go for one of your early morning hikes before anyone wakes. Deal?"

"Trev, I can think of nothing nicer."

Minutes later, they had both fallen into a deep sleep.

Trevor sighed into the night as Rudy stirred next to him and murmured something inaudible. When Trevor leaned in close and asked him what he'd said, Rudy giggled in his sleep and pulled Trevor closer. Unable to resist, Trevor breathed out a sigh and snuggled in close, and within moments, slumber had taken him.

* * * *

How much later he had no idea, but he woke with a gasp and a jolt to someone hammering a fist loudly and repeatedly on their bedroom door. He shot up in bed, rubbing his eyes, about to shout expletives at Ingram.

"What the f—"

Rudy took a little longer to awaken but quickly jumped out of bed.

"Who the hell's there?" shouted Trevor.

"Trevor. Rudy," came Karl's muffled but terrified voice. "It's Mary. I think she's gone into labour. Can you open the door?"

"Shit, shit, shit," said Trevor, trying to hop into his jeans and falling back onto the bed. Rudy, who had already managed to dress, got to the door first, unlocked and hauled the portal open. Without stopping to talk to Karl, Rudy pushed past and headed straight for the kitchen. Karl stood open mouthed, watching Rudy go, probably wondering why he had said nothing.

"It's too early," said Karl, his attention swinging back to Trevor. "She's not due until March."

"We need Mrs M," said Trevor, doing up the top button of his jeans. "She used to be a nurse. If anyone's going to know what to do, it's her."

But they didn't need to wake her. They met Mrs M and a bleary-eyed Cheryl in the hallway as they were hurrying towards the stairs.

"Look, just so you know. I've had no specific training in midwifery, Karl," said Mrs M without stopping. "But I have had some experience dealing with childbirth — not just my own — during my days as a nurse. I'll do whatever I can. How far along is she?"

"Thirty weeks," murmured Karl. Trevor had never seen him look so pale and terrified. Until a blood-curdling cry of pain issued from the bedroom, and Trevor thought Karl might faint.

"Around ten weeks early?" Mrs M breathed out a sigh. "Then we really need to get her to a hospital with good maternity facilities. Let me check on her first of all, but if she is about to give birth to a preterm, then both she and the baby will need specialist help."

"Where is the nearest hospital?" asked Cheryl as they approached the room.

"I don't know. But I'm guessing Rudy will," said Trevor. "Did you see where he went?"

"He flew past me like a bat out of hell, heading towards the kitchen," said Mrs M, opening the door.

Without hesitation, she hurried over to Mary's side. Trevor faltered at the doorway, unsure how he could be of help, and noticed Karl had stopped there, too.

"Listen," said Mrs M, turning to address them both. "There's not much you two can do right now. And we're going to need a little privacy. So maybe Cheryl can stay and help while you go and make everyone some tea. Off you go."

Trevor thought Karl would object, but he nodded mechanically and quickly backed away from the room. After a quick shrug to Cheryl, Trevor followed suit.

"Well. That's told us," said Trevor, heading back down the stairs. "Are you okay, Karl?"

"I — I have no idea."

Trevor thought he might collapse, so he grabbed him beneath the arm and led him forward.

"I think maybe you need something stronger than tea."

"No," said Karl. "Need to keep a clear head. Tea's good, though. I'll make it. I need something to—"

"What the feck is going on?" came Johnny's voice, the man appearing out of nowhere with Frank trailing behind, taking them both by surprise. "All this crashing around in the middle of the night and people screaming like a banshee. S'like being back home in Finglas with me feckin' family."

"We think Mary's gone into labour," said Trevor. "Cheryl and Mrs M's at her bedside right now."

"Jesus, Mary. Has anyone summoned a priest?"

"Not funny right now, Johnny," said Trevor, who had also noticed Karl wince and turn away. "Sounds like she's in a bad way."

As they approached the kitchen door, Rudy came marching out.

"Where's Brenda?" he asked.

"In Mary's room," said Karl.

"Okay, good. Look, I've made a couple of calls. Doris Brennan in the village used to be our local midwife. Said she'll be here in around five minutes' time. She's retired now but helped deliver me and my brother. I also called the hospital in Fort William, in case we need an ambulance, but they said the roads in and out of Arkaig are still blocked. Nothing's getting through."

"Cheryl's mum says that if the baby's premature," said Karl, "they'll need a hospital that has the right facilities."

"There's a specialist maternity hospital in Glasgow," said Rudy, nodding to Karl. "My mother's on the board there. I could make a call?"

"What's the point?" said Karl, looking desolate. "If the roads are blocked, we can't drive her there anyway."

"No, maybe we can't drive," said Rudy, looking to Trevor, his eyes lighting up. "But we can fly. Let me go and wake Helen?"

By five-fifteen that morning, the lodge had become a hive of activity. Doris Brennan, a little woman with a heavy accent, arrived with her large medical bag. She had a short and—from Trevor's perspective—largely unintelligible exchange of words with Rudy before marching straight past the men up to the bedroom. Rudy came back with Helen, apparently having given her an update along the way, just as Trevor poured tea for everyone. Finally, Jessica, Antoni and Ingram—all woken by Mary's cries and other sounds of activity—sat at the kitchen table with Johnny and Frank. With mugs of tea in front of them, they looked so washed out and weary, an onlooker might think they had just given birth themselves.

Trevor didn't miss Ingram occasionally glancing at Rudy, but right at that moment, he didn't give a damn. More important things were happening. Almost an hour later, Cheryl—accompanied by Helen—came to the kitchen to provide an update. Between the two, she told them, Mrs M and Doris had managed to calm Mary and make her more comfortable. Even though her contractions had not been regular at first, they had increased slightly, and Doris agreed it would be safer for all concerned if Mary went to the hospital.

"We told her Rudy's plan," said Cheryl, grabbing two mugs of tea and giving one to Helen. As she continued talking, the kitchen phone rang, and Rudy got up from the table to take the call. "Mary wants Mum to go with her and Karl. Doris has asked to come too, to support Mum. She's such a love. I think Mum's really grateful to have her there. Even though we can barely understand a word she's saying."

Helen giggled and nearly spilled her tea.

"And this lovely lady has agreed to fly them," said Cheryl, looking fondly at Helen.

"Least I can do," said Helen.

"It's all arranged, Karl," said Rudy, coming back to the table. "There'll be an ambulance waiting at the seaplane jetty in Glasgow to whisk you and Mary to the maternity hospital. Can you ask Brenda to start getting Mary ready, and I'll bring the Rover around to the side of the lodge. I can get you pretty close to where the plane's moored. What do you need, Helen?"

"Just to warm up the engines. Should take about fifteen to twenty minutes. Then we can be off. I estimate around forty minutes' flight time. How many am I taking?"

"Karl and Mary," said Cheryl. "Mum and Doris, if you can fit them both."

"I'll stay," said Damian.

Trevor's heart sank at that remark, and if he'd got to know Rudy as well as he thought he had, his friend's face showed the same dismay.

"No, you won't, big boy," said Helen adamantly. "I need a co-pilot. You'll be flying next to me in case anything happens. That's one of the conditions of me bringing you here. So that's a full load of six. Rudy, can you drop us there now and come back for the others after?"

"Good idea," said Rudy, fishing in his pocket for his car keys. "Maybe I should go warm up the Rover engine now while you pack, so we don't have any delays."

"Cheryl," said Trevor, "can you take Karl and Jess with you to get Mary's bags packed and help her down when she's ready? Tell your mum not to worry about her luggage. If she hasn't returned by New Year, we can bring them back in the Volvo."

Cheryl, now accompanied by Karl and Jessica, headed back to the bedroom.

"Don't worry, Trev. We'll make sure Brenda gets back," said Rudy, patting a hand on Trevor's shoulder.

"Let's pack our bags, Damian," said Helen, turning at the kitchen door. "I'll see you back here in five."

"Rudy," said Ingram, standing. "A word outside?"

Trevor stood then, took his place next to Rudy.

"Anything you have to say to Rudy, you can say to me."

"It's okay, Trev," said Rudy, smiling gently before kissing him on the cheek. "I appreciate the gesture, but I've got this."

Rudy followed Ingram outside into the small antechamber and, once they had gone, Trevor moved to the doorway to listen. Even though they spoke in hushed tones, he could make out every word they were saying.

"We're not finished, you and me," said Ingram. "I didn't fly all this way here just to have you snub me. We've still got things to discuss."

"I've nothing to discuss with you, Damian."

"Yeah, we'll see."

"But you can make yourself useful and help me clear snow from the car."

Eventually, Trevor went back to the table. Only three others remained. Antoni had his head resting in his folded arms, his eyes closed. Frank and Johnny sat next to each other, each with their hands around a mug of tea, each gawping down at the table as though they wanted nothing more than to climb back in bed.

"I want to punch him," muttered Trevor, dragging out a chair noisily and sitting opposite Frank.

Frank lifted his head then and smiled. Swinging his gaze slowly around to take in Johnny, he nudged his partner's shoulder to get his attention.

"Hoi! That's the Bulls' star player he's talking about. Says he wants to punch him. Are we going to stand for that?"

"I don't care who he is," said Trevor, grimacing.

"Don't know what everyone sees in the prize fecking prick," said Johnny, pulling a face. "Body from *Baywatch*, face from *Crimewatch*, if you ask me."

"Do you want to show Mac, or shall I?" asked Frank with a smug grin.

"Show me what?" asked Trevor, his interest piqued.

"Not yet," said Johnny cryptically. "Wait until the bastard's airborne. But if it'll stop you being all uptight, Mac, just know that your Mr Fancy Pants back there will not be bothering you or your man ever again. Not if the shitehawk knows what's good for him. Nobody — and I mean *nobody* — fecks with our friends. End of story."

"Oh, my God," said Trevor, his jaw falling open. "What have you done?"

Chapter Fifteen

When a Child is Born

Half an hour later, after Rudy returned with the car, Karl carried a pallid and tired Mary in his arms down the line of sympathetic faces and out to the waiting Rover. Mrs M came back to say hurried goodbyes to everyone. Rudy also came in, mainly to hug Trevor and tell him he'd be straight back. Once the car pulled away, everyone left behind retreated to the heat of the lodge and headed to the living room windows, waiting to watch the spectacle of the plane taking off from the loch.

"And then there were six," murmured Frank to the darkness.

Someone other than Trevor chuckled.

"Seven when Rudy gets back," said Trevor. "What time is it?"

"Just after seven-thirty," said Cheryl.

"Is she okay to fly?" asked Jessica as they stood there listening to the distant thrum of the plane engines warming up.

"Bit late to be asking that now," said Frank.

"Mum spoke to the obstetrician in Glasgow, who said it's fine," said Cheryl. "On commercial jets, pregnant women can usually fly up to around thirty-two to thirty-six weeks into the pregnancy, as long as they're in good health. But this is a light plane, which flies at much lower altitudes. I just hope there's no turbulence, for Mary's sake. Helen says she'll be fine. It's a short enough hop."

"So now we've lost the evil twins, our celebrity and, most importantly, our master chef, what are we going to do for food? Me and Johnny existed on hotel food and take-out before we arrived. Don't suppose they have a pizza delivery service around here?"

"Fat chance," said Johnny.

"Mac and I can rustle up breakfast," said Cheryl. "As long as you don't expect anything fancy. And Mum said there are still cold cuts in the fridge, if we're okay with that. She'll be back as soon as she can. Problem is, Mum kept the Aga going and I haven't a clue how the thing works."

"Rudy will sort that out," said Trevor.

"Ant," said Jessica, nudging Antoni. "Tell them."

"Tell us what?" said Johnny.

"Go on," said Jessica, urging Antoni to speak, and when he wouldn't, she filled them in. "Antoni trained as a chef. Before he got into marketing. Didn't like the endless hours stuck inside the kitchen. But he can cook brilliantly. Tell them, Ant?"

"I'd be happy to cook for you. I never said anything because Mrs M's home cooking is the best. Simple and delicious. And, to be honest, sometimes it's nice not to have to cook. But, yes, I do enjoy being in the kitchen sometimes, and if you want, me and Jessica will take over food duties. Bit easier now that we don't have to worry about putting vegetarian meals on the table. Once we've seen the plane off—kind of looking forward to that—I'll get started on breakfast."

"Antoni," said Frank, putting his arm around him, "you have just become my new best friend. If it weren't for the fact that Jessica would punch me in the face, I'd give you a kiss right now."

"I'll pass, thanks," said Antoni, smiling, just as they heard engines revving from the loch.

Everyone fell silent, watching the silhouette created by the plane's lights against the dark surface of the loch. Over the edge of the mountain, like a prophecy of hope, a faint glow heralded the dawn of a new day. The engines throttling, the seaplane began to move across the water, all the time gathering speed. Even then, the vessel seemed to be travelling far too slowly, until the nose lifted and the plane glided up into the brightening sky. As they stood watching, the shape shrank to a speck on the horizon.

"Beautiful," came Rudy's warm whisper in Trevor's ear as his body squeezed in behind him, arms wrapping around Trevor's chest. Nobody had even heard him arrive. Trevor let out a sigh and rested his head back on Rudy's shoulder, their cheeks touching.

"You're not so bad yourself," said Trevor, breathing in Rudy's scent. Around them, everyone headed back to the kitchen, leaving the two of them alone.

"And he's finally gone. Ingram. Just you and me now. But he swears he's coming back for the party. I told him not to bother, that he was no longer welcome, but he insisted. Do you see now what a stubborn bastard he can be?"

Trevor said nothing, remembering what Frank and Johnny had told him. What the hell had they done to him?

"You okay, Trev?" whispered Rudy, kissing the side of his face. "I'm so sorry, I should have told you earlier. I think I was in shock. Or denial. Or both. And I thought he'd be on best behaviour, having Helen here with him. But leopards don't change their spots, it seems. Hope you'll forgive me?"

"There's nothing to forgive, Rudy. He put you in a difficult spot. Coming here wasn't particularly dignified. To be honest, I'm glad I was here for you. Hate to think what a living hell he'd have made of your life if we hadn't all been here."

"I know. And I need—" said Rudy, then stopped and leant back a little. "What's that smell?"

Trevor chuckled. If he wasn't mistaken, the smell of bacon or ham cooking had tickled Rudy's nose, that and something else, creamy and delicious.

"So in the few minutes you were gone, we found out that Antoni trained as a chef and is going to be wearing Mrs M's apron today. If I'm not mistaken, he's knocking up eggs Benedict right now."

"And coffee. I can smell fresh coffee brewing. Was going to suggest we go back to bed for an hour or two, but my stomach has just overruled my dick."

Back in the kitchen, Trevor had thought everyone would be sitting at the table, but Frank and Johnny stood at the cooker either side of Antoni, observing the master at work. Antoni was using a large pot of boiling water to poach eggs while reaching over from time to time to either stir the hollandaise sauce, check the asparagus or toss the mushroom and onion combination. Eventually, Jessica shooed them all away, back to the table, where she had placed doorstops of toast and a pot of freshly brewed coffee. After the seven had eaten their fill—and Antoni had been congratulated on his cooking—they all mucked in to clear the table while Rudy made his announcement.

"I mentioned to Trev last night that my mother has invited you all to attend our family gathering on New Year's Eve. Mainly family and friends, with locals and guests from out of town. The only thing is that it's usually a bit formal, and I thought you might find that a bit stuffy—"

"Will there be whisky?" asked Johnny.

"We have our own distillery," said Rudy, chuckling but rolling his eyes. "That's like asking me if there will be air to breathe."

"Then count us in. We've only got clean jeans, button-down shirts and jackets. Is that going to be dressy enough?"

"That will be just fine. How about you, Antoni?"

"I came here straight from work, so I've got my suit. Need to wash and iron my shirt and press the trousers, but I'm good to go."

"God, I finally get to wear a dress," said Cheryl, her eyes lighting up. "Did you bring anything, Jess?"

"I did, actually," she said, just as excited. "It's a not a ball gown, exactly—more of a cocktail dress—but I'm certain it'll be fine. Are we going the whole hog, Cheryl? Makeup and all? We can help each other. I've got some fab jewellery. Or is that too over the top?"

"Nowhere near the top," said Cheryl, pushing her chair back, clearly animated at the idea. "Come on, let's go and see what you've got."

"Antoni," said Jessica, "come and show me which shirt you want washed and ironed and I'll sort your clothes out for you. Least I can do to repay you for that amazing brekkie."

As they disappeared, Trevor kept quiet. At some point he would need to tell Rudy that he'd not brought anything even vaguely formal — unless you could count jeans with holes in them and a Father Christmas jumper.

"Look, guys, just so you know," said Rudy, checking over Johnny's shoulder to ensure the others were out of earshot, "Damian's probably going to be there too. Just treat him the way you did last night. Stroke his ego, Frank. He likes that."

"Not just his ego," said Frank, grinning.

"He'll not be coming back, Rudy," said Johnny firmly, folding his arms. "Not if he knows what's good for him."

Rudy stopped and looked to Trevor, who shrugged and shook his head.

"Is it showtime, Johnno?" asked Frank.

"You know what, Frank?" said Johnny, leaning back in his chair, "I think it might well be. Go get your laptop while I explain to Rudy why that fuckwit won't be messing with any of us ever again."

With Frank gone, Johnny explained how, last night, he had slipped away on the premise of getting Frank's hoodie, but mainly to set the stage — otherwise known as their nanny cam. Later, when Frank had fawned over Ingram — as rehearsed earlier that evening — he had offered to show him the view from their bedroom. Ingram, being the lecherous arsehole that he was, had finally agreed.

"But rather than explain what happened, probably easiest if we show you," said Johnny, as Frank came back into the room with his laptop.

Trevor watched the whole thing play out, incredulous, the camera placed in a clear vantage point to record everything in the room. Frank managed to manoeuvre Damian so that, after taking a cursory glance at the view, he sat on the edge of the bed facing the camera. Even though the lighting wasn't the best, there was no mistaking Damian Ingram's face and his field shirt with the very distinctive advertising logo. He sat asking highly inappropriate questions, such as how long had Frank and Johnny been sexually active, whether they fooled around outside of their relationship, whether Frank enjoyed certain sexual activities. Frank remained a tease throughout, saying Johnny loved him because he gave the best head out of all the gay boys he'd ever known. Of course, Ingram fell for that, stood, dropped his pants, and grabbed his already stiff dick.

"Show me."

"Is that it?" came Frank's disappointed voice. *"In all your underwear posters you have the hugest of baskets. And that's all you've got? You should be arrested for false advertising."*

Even Trevor spluttered when he heard Frank's remark.

Ingram literally snarled, lunged forward and pushed Frank by the shoulders down onto his knees in front of him.

"Shut up and suck my cock, you little faggot."

And right then, a loud pounding could be heard at the bedroom door, followed by Johnny's unmistakable voice. Ingram instantly began to hike up his trousers.

"Frank? Are you boring the tits off Damian Ingram? Come on down and stop sucking up to the poor guy."

"No chance of that. There's barely a mouthful," muttered Frank, for the benefit of the camera before going to the door.

Even though Trevor laughed along with Johnny and Frank, he noticed that Rudy had gone ghostly white.

"I placed the camera on the window ledge," said Johnny. "Beautifully captured, don't you agree?"

"The video?" asked Frank, laughing. "Or Ingram?"

Johnny must have noticed Rudy's face because he quickly explained.

"Don't worry, Rudy. This is just a little, um, insurance. Your man kindly gave Frank his personal email address before any of this happened. So we were simply planning to fire him a warning shot. Nothing's been sent yet, not without your consent. Here, have a read."

Johnny twisted the laptop so that he and Trevor could read. They both did so in stunned silence.

Dearest Damian,

Lovely to have met you at Stratham Lodge in Scotland. And such a shame that you had to leave so soon, just as we were really getting to know the real you.

Also, sorry we didn't get a chance to give you our little memento video we took of your time here, but happily, it's short enough for us to attach in this email message.

Best wishes for the New Year,

Johnny and Frank

PS: If you come anywhere near us again, or our friends, come to that – and I include Rudy Mortimer as one of our friends now – not only will this video go viral on all the gay porn sites that Frank and I frequent (and we frequent a lot), but I will also personally send it to my friends who work in the media, and who are always scavenging around for any salacious titbits.

PPS: Rest assured, as an out gay man myself, I am not in the habit of outing others, and would only do so if I thought the person dishonourable in any way. In other words, so long as you hold to your end of the bargain, this little clip will never see the light of day.

PPPS: Enjoy the closet.

Before Trevor had even finished the last line, Rudy reached a hand across the keyboard and hit the enter key, sending the email. Everyone else gasped in astonishment.

"Are you sure you won't regret this, Rudy?" asked Trevor.

"The only thing I'll ever regret," said Rudy, a wicked smile lighting his face, "is not being there to see the bastard's face when he clicks on the attachment."

Chapter Sixteen

Silent Night

Early the following day, Trevor woke to someone's mobile phone ringing faintly but persistently from the next room. Rudy stirred softly next to him. Trevor sat up and looked down at his beautiful holiday romance, and felt a moment of deep affection. For somebody who claimed he didn't sleep well, Rudy had unquestionably improved. Trevor smoothed a hand through Rudy's hair, causing him to emit a low purr before reclining back into his pillows.

Both had been exhausted from the previous day — and not from any excessive carnal activities, with only a comfortable session before both dropped off to sleep. Their dog-tiredness had come mainly from an afternoon of manual labour in Mortimer House. Everyone else had opted to catch up on lost sleep or await news of Mary and Karl and the possibility of a new arrival.

Rudy and Trevor had decided to get busy, working with old Tam and Millie to bring down decorations from the attic. After sifting through and cleaning them, or creating new ones, they had then spent three hours clambering up and down ladders. Trevor loved the old house, the musty smells and the sheer vastness of the place, full of oak panelling, faded tapestries and old family portraits—so different from the modernised lodge. Fortunately, they had no boars' heads or game trophies on the walls, something Trevor might have found distasteful. Chatting to Tam—whose accent he could just about understand—he had learnt little snippets about the Mortimer family, an old English gentry who had settled in Scotland in the early eighteenth century. Tam had also let slip that Rudy's father was the sixteenth Earl of Stratham. When Trevor had casually dropped this titbit into a conversation, Rudy had told him in no uncertain terms that if he even so much as bowed—or curtsied, come to that—to either of his parents, he would get the biggest wallop across his backside.

"Promises, promises," a grinning Trevor had replied.

Best of all, Rudy had taken Trevor to his old bedroom on the upper floor so that they could both clean up. Spacious and yet oddly austere, the room boasted two voluminous oak wardrobes along one wall, a free-standing mirror in between, floor-to-ceiling velvet curtains of deep scarlet outlining the French windows and a large double bed with a thick quilted bedspread to match the curtains. If a person viewed the room from the doorway, they would never have associated the space as a boy's bedroom. Rudy had admitted his family had decorated the room once he'd moved out but that things looked much the same. He'd had a strict upbringing, primarily where manners, tidiness and a lack of teenage paraphernalia were concerned. No posters had been allowed on walls, he'd had to hang his clothes up before bedtime, magazines and books had to be tidied away on shelves or — in the case of some of his more private collections — hidden away beneath his bed.

Together they had showered, smoothing and caressing the grime from the creases of each other's bodies — initially in innocence, until before long the ritual had turned sensual, both of them breathing hard with desire. Rudy must have known what would happen because he'd had the foresight to lock the bathroom door. After rolling a condom and plenty of lube onto himself, he'd turned Trevor's face to the glass cubicle wall and pushed slowly inside. Holding his hands above his head, he'd begun the slow back and forth until both of them achieved a mutual rhythm. Finally, they came together in shuddering spasms, Trevor's cock spurting abstract patterns onto the glass. For a long time, they clung to each other beneath the shower, letting the warm water wipe everything clean. While they'd both dressed in the bathroom, Rudy had confided in Trevor.

"I've dreamt about doing that with someone. But what we did was hotter than any fantasy I've ever imagined."

By seven o'clock that evening, Rudy had had to physically drag Trevor away from fussing over his decorative creations and order him back to the lodge. Antoni had prepared a mouth-watering salmon en croûte with a lemon parsley sauce, polished off by a dessert of Eton mess. Dinner had been a subdued affair, nobody having much to say after the craziness of the past few days, and they passed only a few comments across the kitchen table about Antoni's cooking skills. Eventually, Johnny had broken the virtual silence.

"Have you heard from your mother, Cheryl?"

"*Not yet. I tried calling earlier, but either her phone was switched off or she's forgotten to charge it again.*"

"*So we don't know what's happening?*"

"*No,*" Cheryl had said. "*I talked to her at midday, and they said Mary's contractions are coming more regularly now, so looks as though the baby may be early. They think Mary might have been further along than she thought. Mum said she's going to stay there with them until they know for sure.*"

"*Are they considering painkillers?*" Frank had asked.

"*I think she wants to avoid them as much as possible,*" Cheryl had replied, in all innocence.

"*I meant for Karl,*" Frank had answered, raising a collective chuckle around the table.

By ten o'clock that evening, everyone had decided to turn in, and for the first time that holiday, the lodge and its guests slept undisturbed, everyone enjoying a silent night.

* * * *

That morning, by the time the phone stopped ringing, Trevor and Rudy had thrown on dressing gowns and shuffled out to the kitchen. Cheryl was perched on a stool by the kitchen counter, talking animatedly into the phone — the call clearly from somebody she knew. While Trevor moved across to find out what was happening, Rudy flicked on the electric kettle. Seeing them both, Cheryl provided a smile and a simple wave of one hand before asking the person at the other end to hold on.

"Mum's on the line. Mary gave birth to a baby boy at four-thirty this morning. Premature and weighing in at three pounds, two ounces, so he's in an incubator for now, but all things considered, both mother and child are doing very well. Father passed out during the birth. Sorry, Mum, say that again."

As Mrs M spoke from the other end, Cheryl placed a hand across her mouth and tears sprang to her eyes.

"Oh, Mum. That's lovely," she said, clearly moved. Then, placing the phone against her shoulder, she told them, "Mary and Karl have insisted on naming him Connor. After the twin brother we lost."

Trevor reached in and gave her a warm hug. What an amazing Christmas. Behind them, Frank and Johnny entered the kitchen.

"Connor, eh? Now there's a good Irish name. So she's had the little devil, has she?" asked Johnny.

"His middle name's Karl," said Cheryl. "Plain and simple. And Mary's mum and dad are flying in at lunchtime. So Mum and Doris are about to make their way back by bus and should arrive at the Fort William station just after lunchtime."

"As long as the roads are clear, I'll come and pick them up," said Rudy, pouring boiling water into mugs.

"She says thanks, you're a godsend. Okay, Mum. Yes, I told him. See you later," said Cheryl, rolling her eyes, before putting down the phone. "She'll text me when they're half an hour away from Fort William. And Trev, she said to put some sparkling wine in the fridge, because we'll all need to have a wee tipple tonight, to wet the baby's head. *A wee tipple*? My mother's now officially Scottish."

After Rudy had made a couple of calls to confirm that the authorities had cleared the roads in and out of Arkaig and they'd finally received the text message from Mrs M, he asked Trevor to accompany him into town.

Sitting high up in the vehicle, warmth from the heater enveloping them, they listened to Rudy's choice of music. And Trevor found himself discovering a little more about his new friend, who was, apparently, a diehard country and western and country-rock fan, with song after song from old and modern artists — Blake Shelton, The Allman Brothers, Sam Hunt, Dolly Parton, Garth Brooks.

"You like country?" asked Rudy.

"I'm not too familiar. Except for the classics."

"Then maybe I'm going to have to educate you. What's your favourite music?"

"Rock and pop, mainly. I was a nineties child, so I was brought up on a diet of Radiohead, Nirvana—"

"Ah, the legendary Kurt Cobain. Dark and moody—"

"Keith Urban, Sheryl Crow—"

"Now we're talking—"

"Kylie, Cher and Mika."

"Huh? Are they like Crosby, Stills and Nash?"

Trevor pulled a face. "Looks like this musical education thing will need to work both ways."

When Rudy laughed, Trevor took the opportunity to turn and enjoy his profile. He navigated the small lanes well, entirely in control of the car, slowing at each turn and ever mindful of his speed. In Trevor's book, Rudy would be classed as a comfortable driver, aware of his skill and competence, completely at home behind the wheel. Cheryl, by contrast, was a nervous driver, something accentuated when anything unusual happened — a bump in the road, or a sudden downpour of rain.

"Rudy. Something I've been meaning to say. I don't have anything formal to wear for your parents' party. I didn't think to bring anything. But if we could stop at a men's clothing shop while we're in town, then maybe I could —"

"You'll do no such thing. Maybe I'm a little broader than you, but you can borrow something of mine. I've got suits I've barely worn back at the house."

"As long as you're sure?" said Trevor, relieved.

"Of course I'm sure. I'll even help dress you."

Trevor smiled at the thought. Another comfortable silence fell between them as Trevor hummed along to a vaguely familiar melody while watching out of the window as the highlands floated by.

"So are you inviting any of your friends along to the ball?" he asked.

"Apart from the Bulls team, you mean?" said Rudy without humour.

"Yes, well. Maybe not them. How about other friends?"

"I'd invite them if I had any."

"Come on, Rudy," said Trevor, shocked, turning to gape at him. "You expect me to believe you never made friends while you were at university? Or working at the gym? Even an idiot can see that you're friend magnet material."

"I did have friends," he said before looking away, his smile slipping. "But when you have to keep putting people off because your closeted other half won't be seen out with you, or won't allow you to invite friends home, then friendships become like autumn leaves in a storm, gradually dropping off and drifting away."

"Yeah, well," said Trevor, rubbing his nose. "We're going to need to fix that."

After around fifty minutes, more houses began to line the road as they hit the outskirts of Fort William. Trevor received a message on his phone from Cheryl to say Mrs M and Doris had arrived early and were waiting outside a supermarket along from the bus station. Rudy explained that the town centre had been pedestrianised, and how the bus station stood farther out, near the central train station. As they rounded the corner of a street lined with single and double-decker buses and coaches, Trevor spotted the two ladies chatting happily together, a clutter of full shopping bags arranged at their feet.

All the way back to the lodge, Mrs M kept them entertained with stories about the past twenty-four hours, about how the flight had been remarkably smooth and how Mary, for all her previous complaining, had been relatively calm throughout the whole ordeal. Trevor had to hold in a snort when he heard about Karl passing out cold when she finally gave birth. Fortunately, Doris had been there to catch him. Otherwise he might have given himself a nasty concussion. When asked about Damian, they found out he had been in an unusually foul mood, maybe because the incident had ruined his holiday plans. Out in the waiting area, 'he and the woman pilot' appeared to have 'harsh words', after which they'd both left. Mrs M had no idea what the argument had been about and didn't really care.

Neither did Trevor.

He just hoped Ingram had got the message that he wasn't welcome back.

Chapter Seventeen

Driving Home For Christmas

After the drama of the past days, a cosy lethargy descended on the lodge. Down to only eight, including Rudy, the remaining guests savoured the relative tranquillity of the slowly thawing highland countryside.

On New Year's Eve, the morning of the Mortimer Hogmanay Ball, Rudy drove Trevor, Cheryl, Frank and Johnny over to Mortimer House. Making up for lost holiday activities, he'd proposed they all go horse riding. Only Frank and Johnny had been keen to take him up on the offer, but Trevor and Cheryl had tagged along anyway. Rudy even approved of Trevor's decision not to ride because he wanted Trevor to give his final endorsement to the decorations viewed by daylight and make any finishing touches before guests started arriving at around six. Cheryl insisted on helping mainly because she wanted to have a nose around the 'big house'.

On the short car ride over, Trevor sat with Rudy upfront. Surface snow had cleared, and, with cloudless skies over the past few days, they hoped the threat of more snow had diminished. The night before, Rudy had likened snow to an occasional guest, someone who often brought pleasure with their arrival, but could soon become wearing when overstaying a welcome.

"It's quicker walking or riding to the house from the lodge," said Rudy, the car crawling and wobbling along the narrow lane. "With the Rover, I have to take the long way around. All of this land used to be a part of the Mortimer estate. But my father sold a lot off. The old house takes a lot of money to maintain."

"But he still owns the distillery?" asked Frank.

"Yes, Frank. Don't worry. He still owns that," said Rudy, chuckling. "You'll get to meet them tonight, my folks. They arrived back yesterday night to a house with fully functioning heating, thank heavens. But my brother, Ivan, and his wife were delayed because of a mix-up on flights times. They should be on their way now."

"I'm surprised they didn't insist you stay with them last night," said Trevor.

"I told a wee white lie. Said Millie needed time to prepare the bedrooms, including my own, for our other guests. And that you'd kindly allowed me to bunk in with you."

"And she believed you?" asked Trevor, grinning.

"Never know with my mother. Ah, here we are."

Down the short driveway, the impressive Mortimer House came into view. Trevor remembered the white building looking positively stately from the hillside, but up close the house looked more like an exclusive hotel. Three stone steps covered by an ornate portico supported by thick columns led to dark oak double doors. Above the top of the entrance sat the Scottish flag, the Union Jack and the flag of the European Union. Rudy noticed Trevor looking.

"Dad was proud to be a part of the European Union. He still can't fathom the fact that we're leaving. Says doing so won't do us any favours with our whisky export business. Whatever you do, avoid the subject tonight. You'll never get him to shut up."

Frank chuckled, which started Johnny laughing along.

"For future reference, Rudy," said Trevor smirking. "In case you haven't already got the message. Never, ever, tell those two not to do something."

Rudy pointed out Tam and Millie waiting at the front door to greet them. He steered the Rover to an empty parking area at the rear of the house then led everyone back to the front door. After exchanging greetings with them all, Millie explained that Rudy's parents had driven off early for the station to pick up his brother and sister-in-law. After a few private words with Millie, Rudy and Tam led the boys away towards the stables, while Millie accompanied Cheryl and Trevor into the house.

Cheryl gaped at the grand interior, exploring one room after another, and especially the main hall, which had been transformed into something befitting a Jane Austen novel—if she'd written one set in Scotland. Trevor had probably overdone the tartan theme, but Millie had advised him on the correct clan colours to use—scarlet and fir green—and he felt the old decorations had taken on a new lease of life with the makeover. Indeed the two massive Christmas trees at the far end of the main hall—previously adorned with simple white baubles and starry white lights— provided a focal point with their tartan bows of all shapes and sizes, as well as flashes of holly and purple thistle.

Beyond the main hall, Trevor noticed the dining room already being set up by catering staff, three huge tables each seating thirty guests. He realised the party planners had carried his tartan theme forward on the tables, probably at the advice of Millie. Rudy told him how his parents always employed specialist caterers to wait tables, to feed everyone and serve drinks. But ninety for Hogmanay dinner? Once again, Trevor felt a tremor of nervousness when he thought how different his world was from the one Rudy inhabited.

"What date did we arrive?" asked Cheryl.

"Evening of the twenty-second," answered Trevor.

"Can you believe this is our tenth day?" said Cheryl, bringing him out of his reverie. "Feels like months, doesn't it? I have to be honest, Mac, after that second night — after Mary and Karl arrived — Mum and I spoke about throwing in the towel, maybe driving home for Christmas. But I'm so pleased we decided to stay. I have a suspicion we're going to be dining out on this Christmas tale for years to come."

"I'm not sure anybody will believe you."

The four horsemen of the apocalypse — as Johnny had labelled him, Frank, Rudy and Tam — returned to the house just before midday. Millie arranged a light lunch of sandwiches and hot tea for them all, sat casually around the big oak table in the large kitchen. Rudy appeared to take pride in introducing his new friends, and both Millie and Tam listened patiently until he'd finished. Trevor could see how Millie doted on Rudy, the way she smiled at his enthusiasm and piled food onto his plate. Frank and Johnny — both red-cheeked from the chill air — stole the show, talking excitedly about their riding adventure, what they'd seen and where they'd been. Navigating the horse trails around rugged Loch Arkaig had provided a bracing contrast to their temperate middle eastern travels. When Cheryl offered to show the boys around the house, they jumped at the chance, leaving Rudy and Trevor together in the kitchen.

"Is yon bonny McTavish lad goin' tae the ball tonight?" Millie asked Rudy. Trevor had to listen carefully to her accent, much broader than her husband's or Rudy's.

"Yes, Millie. He's coming to the ball as my guest," said Rudy before turning to Trevor. "Millie's family name is also McTavish. Was, that is, until she married old Tam McDonald."

"Then he should be wearin' a Clan McTavish kilt," she said, folding her arms. "D'you no ken?"

"Aye, I suppose," said Rudy, with a smile and a shrug.

"Nae s'pose about it," said Millie, standing and grabbing Trevor by the elbow. "Come wi' me, young laddie. We'll make sure ye hae the right sett."

"What's happening, Rudy?" said Trevor in a panic as Millie led him away to one of the little rooms behind the kitchen.

"If I'm not mistaken, I think you're about to be fitted with a Clan McTavish kilt. Still, that sorts out your wardrobe for tonight. And I have all the right accessories to go with that particular outfit."

While Millie set about measuring Trevor and fishing out a large straw basket filled with cloth and accessories, she asked him questions. Rudy stood by to help out, leaning against the doorframe and grinning, his arms folded, enjoying watching her work.

Eventually, she found what she needed — a blue-and-red-checked material — and wrapped the cloth around Trevor's waist.

"You'll need tae drop yer troosers," said Millie, to which Trevor's eyes pleaded with Rudy for help.

"Do as she says, Trevor. Don't worry, she's seen worse before. Looking after me and my brother."

"Aye," said Millie, with a wheeze of a giggle. "That I have."

Oddly though, the more Trevor listened and tuned in to Millie's accent, the more he understood. She explained how the kilt typically fell to the centre of the knee, how the flat folds in the front were called aprons, while the sides and back were usually pleated. The one they'd found had belonged to Millie's late brother, who had stood shorter than Trevor and had been broader around the waist, but using the kilt pin fastened to the front apron, the result looked — and felt — both stylish and comfortable. She explained how he would need Rudy's thick belt to keep things in place, but both Millie and Rudy approved the result. When she inquired why he wasn't planning on bringing a Sassenach girlfriend or boyfriend to the ball, Trevor decided to tell her about getting divorced and having suffered a prolonged dry spell, which he thought might finally be looking up. From the doorway, Rudy snorted but Trevor ignored him.

"Aye, well," she said, unpinning the seam and taking the cloth over to the waiting ironing board, "it's a lang road that's no gote a'turnin."

Rudy nodded and hummed his approval.

"Too true, Millie. Too true."

When Millie left the kilt on the ironing board and disappeared into the utility room, Trevor turned to Rudy.

"Okay," he said, looking helpless. "I'm not sure I understood a word of what she just said. What was that about no goat or turnip?"

Rudy chuckled in his usual good-natured way.

"She said it's a long road that doesn't have a turn somewhere down the line. It's an old Scottish saying which means be patient even when things are going badly. Most roads have a turn in them eventually and things are bound to improve."

"Do you believe that?" asked Trevor, after thinking for a while.

As Rudy studied him thoughtfully for a moment, a smile like the sunrise blossomed on his face.

"I do," he said. "Aye, Trev, I think I do."

* * * *

When Trevor stood and stared at himself in the long mirror in Rudy's bedroom, he couldn't help his excited smile. Never in his wildest dreams had he imagined he'd be wearing a kilt. Well, maybe to a fancy dress party, but never formally. And the shade of blue—a dark cerulean—in the tartan of reds and blues matched the blue-grey of his eyes. Not only that, but his shock of unruly black hair complemented the white shirt, black waistcoat and matching jacket—all items borrowed from Rudy. Complete with silver buttons, the whole ensemble looked not only respectable but pretty darned sexy, even if the notion felt a little conceited. To complete the illusion, Rudy had helped him out with long black socks, garters, patent leather shoes and a sporran hanging over his family jewels. Yes, he rocked the part of the Scottish laird. Wait until Cheryl saw him.

"Look at you, Trev!" came Rudy's voice from across the room.

Trevor twisted around and hiked in a breath. If Trevor had thought he looked hot in a kilt, Rudy owned the image. In patterned scarlet and moss green wool check, Rudy looked entirely at home, moving naturally across the carpet. Although the kilt covered his thick thighs, his sexy muscular knees peeked from beneath above knee-length socks of thick oatmeal wool. Trevor felt his mouth go dry.

"You surely wear the style well, Trev. Remember, when you put on a kilt, don't be shy, wear the sett with pride. Own the outfit, and when people study you, they'll see a warrior or a nobleman, not a man in a skirt."

"Heavens, Rudy," said Trevor as Rudy came to a stop in front of him. "Forget about me. Look at you. Just looking at you is giving me a hard-on."

"Is it?" said Rudy, grinning. "Let me check."

Before Trevor realised what was happening, Rudy had reached a hand beneath Trevor's hem and was cradling his balls through his underwear. Trevor let out a soft yelp and grabbed Rudy's arm while emitting a chuckle.

"Och, not fair, Trev," said Rudy, smoothing a thumb over Trevor's semi-erection. "We agreed to go commando."

"In this draughty old place," said Trevor, pulling Rudy's hand away. "Not a chance in hell. Do you want me to catch pneumonia?"

"What was that about a commando?" came an unexpected voice from across the room. "You're not thinking about joining the army now, wee brother?"

Trevor turned to see a taller carbon copy of Rudy, same college boy-style haircut, same handsome grin, maybe a little leaner than Rudy. Dressed in an evening suit with a cummerbund in family tartan, rather than Rudy's traditional choice of a kilt, he would nevertheless turn heads.

"Ivan," said Rudy, going over and hugging his brother. "This is my, uh, friend Trevor. I was just explaining what a proper Scotsman wears beneath his kilt. He and his friends are staying at the lodge for Christmas and New Year. Mother invited them to dinner tonight."

"Did she now?" said Ivan, appearing genuinely surprised. "That's a first. You must have done something to impress her if she invited you for dinner."

Unlike Rudy, Ivan had no trace of an accent.

"Not sure about that," said Trevor, going over and shaking Ivan's hand. "I think maybe she took pity on us. Snowed in, and all that."

Ivan and Rudy shared a quick look before turning back to Trevor and saying, in unison, "No."

"Our mother doesn't work that way," said Ivan. "There'll be an alternative motive. It'll just have to remain a mystery until she lets on. Anyway, brother, I've been sent here to drag you down to face the masses. You know what Mother's like about having the whole family together for the meet-and-greets."

"Okay, I'll be down in a minute," said Rudy before placing an arm around Trevor's shoulders. "Let me have moment with Trev first."

Before Ivan left, he looked curiously at Trevor, then at their kilts, and finally at their faces, before producing a knowing smile.

"Okay. Maybe not so much of a mystery."

Trevor stared after the brother, wondering what he had meant.

"Just so you know." Rudy hooked both arms around Trevor's neck and drew him close. "Our family always stands at the living room doors and greets guests as they're seated for dinner. My mother likes to maintain certain formal rituals. We also usually sit together at one end of the table, as a family, but I've asked to be seated with you tonight. Mother's fine with that, because Ivan's here with his wife, Beth, so they'll sit with Mother and Father. As I said, it's all a little formal, but I promise it'll be a hoot."

"And what should I do in the meantime?"

"Are you kidding me? Go and join your friends. Have drinks and enjoy yourselves. I'm always going to come back to you."

Trevor warmed inside at those final words and almost said something mushy in response but changed his mind.

"I'm going to use the bathroom one more time," said Trevor, his nerves getting the better of him. "Go on down and do your duty, and I'll see you at the dinner table."

As the beautiful figure of Rudy strode confidently across the carpet, Trevor couldn't help watching him go.

"And, Rudy?"

Rudy stopped and turned back.

"Thank you. For everything. You've already made this Christmas the best ever. And now this. The absolute icing on the cake."

"Go on with you," said Rudy, smiling with pride at the compliment. "See you at dinner. Make sure you bring an appetite."

At six-thirty, on Trevor's way down the wide staircase that descended one side of the hall, he estimated around fifty people standing in small clusters, with serving staff dancing between and around them. Cheryl's loud laughter drew his gaze to where all of his friends stood, sipping champagne. Then, as he reached a point halfway down the stairs, Johnny turned and spotted him, producing a wolf whistle that had the others — and a few people he didn't know — turning to observe him. Self-consciousness didn't even begin to describe the hesitation that stalled him, but he decided to take Rudy's advice, hiked in a deep breath, held himself high and descended into the fray.

"Will you look at that," said Frank, the first to comment as Trevor approached. Frank wore black jeans, a white silk shirt and a navy corduroy jacket, looking smart-casual. "It's Robert the bleeding Bruce."

"I must say," said Jessica, wearing a pretty black spangled number, "you rock that look, Trevor. You're a true McTavish now."

"Actually," said Trevor, puffing out his chest with pride and grabbing a glass of sparkling wine from a passing waiter, "I am reliably informed that this is what is known as the McTavish sett — the correct tartan for the McTavish clan. But can I say, you are all looking amazing tonight. Let's have a toast to wonderful friends."

* * * *

After half an hour had gone by, as more guests arrived and the hall filled up, two men dressed in matching tartan kilts climbed to the landing on the stairs and began playing the bagpipes. One of the waiters stopped by and informed their group that the song was called *Flower of Scotland*, a popular tune for a not-so-popular instrument. Afterwards, and following a polite round of applause, the master of ceremonies summoned everyone to dinner, each person announced as they entered. The same waiter as before came over to their group and asked them to hold on until everyone else had been seated, which seemed odd, but nobody appeared to mind. Trevor looked over at Rudy's family, the father and sons dressed identically, his mother wearing an elegant, full-length evening dress in black velvet with a tartan sash matching her husband's worn diagonally from shoulder to waist.

At last, they approached. As Trevor went to shake her hand, she produced a gentle smile before taking his elbow and drawing him away from the line.

"So you're the young man my son keeps enthusing about who finally put a smile on his face," she said, her own smile so like her son's. When Trevor peered over her shoulder, he noticed Rudy shaking Antoni's hand but also turning to look nervously at them. "Honestly, when I saw him the other day, I barely recognised him. Since he came back last summer, he's been like a bear with a sore head. And Millie tells me I also have you to thank for decorating the hall. While you're supposed to be here on holiday enjoying yourself. Is that right?"

"Oh, no," said Trevor. "Well, yes, I did help Rudy spruce things up. But honestly, it was nothing. I really enjoyed myself and Rudy did most of the work."

"Well, it was certainly *not* nothing. I've had a stream of praise and questions from guests about our wonderful ornamenting this year, asking whether I did the decorating myself or used a company. And if so, which one? I feel like such a fraud. So when my husband does his usual Hogmanay speech — which will be traditionally long and boring — he has also been instructed to give you a special mention and a huge thank you."

"Really, you don't need to —" began Trevor.

"If I don't," she said, cutting him off, "my son will never talk to me again. And I've only just got him back. On another note, just a wee word of warning. I know you probably don't want to think about leaving yet, but as your time is drawing to a close here, Rudolph might start to get a wee bit sullen and moody when the reality hits home. If he does, don't take it to heart, it's just his way of coping. He refuses to think about things he considers negative until they're right upon him. Used to be like that when his father and I went off on business trips."

Trevor smiled at her and nodded his understanding. "Thank you for telling me. Sounds like we have more in common than I knew."

"Good," she said with a sigh before a smile lit up her face. "Now let's go eat, drink and be merry."

The rest of the evening turned out to be equally spectacular. As promised, Rudy came and sat next to Trevor, putting his hand on his bare thigh and squeezing. Trevor got his mention and a round of applause in Mr Mortimer's long but very entertaining speech and, according to Antoni, the food turned out to be good, if not great. When they finished the meal with a small plate of Scottish blue cheese, Dundee cake and a generous glass of Mortimer whisky, Frank looked as though he had died and gone to heaven.

After the meal, they retired to the main hall, allowing the doors to the dining room to be closed off, and a quartet on a small stage began playing. A selection of buffet finger food had been laid out on long tables and an amply stocked bar set up in a corner of the hall. Rudy explained about more guests arriving during the evening, having enjoyed Hogmanay dinner with their own families.

As the evening wore on, brave guests joined in with the Scottish country dances, where a couple of instructors demonstrated moves and called out directions to the group. Mrs M's friend Doris knew all the steps by heart and led Mrs M around with ease, giving only a few whispered instructions. Rudy did his best to direct Trevor — not the easiest of tasks — but then many of the dances seemed quite subtle, encouraging people to circulate and end up occasionally with a new partner. Nevertheless, each time Rudy would always end up facing Trevor again, his smile shining brightly, his eyes burning with affection. Eventually, Trevor stopped fretting about the steps and enjoyed the fun, knowing Rudy would always come back to him.

Rudy drew Trevor away into a small dark utility room at the back of the hall. Once inside, he hurriedly locked the door. Using his body, he squeezed Trevor up against the wall before clamping their mouths together.

"Mm-ouch," said Trevor through the kiss. Something sharp and hard was prodding him in the middle of his back.

"Sorry," said Rudy, nipping Trevor's bottom lip before pulling their mouths apart. "I've been wanting to do that all evening."

Out in the hall, the band had begun a new melody, a simple waltz.

"Something hard is digging into my back."

"Just your back?" said Rudy, rubbing his groin into Trevor's before bringing both hands beneath his kilt and cupping his backside.

"Ouch! Can we hold off for now?" asked Trevor, even though his body, despite the discomfort, began to respond willingly. "I'm in pain here. Can this wait until we're in bed together? I'll even wear the kilt, if you ask nicely."

"Och, I'm sorry, Trev," said Rudy, a warm hand retreating from his buttock before pulling him away from the wall. "I think you're leaning into a mop handle."

"Uh-huh. That would explain the agony," said Trevor, chuckling and pushing his face into Rudy's neck, his hand slipping under the hem of Rudy's kilt. "Best night ever, Rudy. I really like—hey!"

"What?"

"You're wearing underpants."

"Of course I am. It's too bloody cold to do otherwise. Now what was that you were about to say? Something you really like?"

"Cheater. I was going to say that I really like your family."

"They like you, too." Rudy reached down, took Trevor's hand and smoothed the palm over his erection. "My mother's a tough gig. Ask poor Beth. But she seems to have warmed to you."

"She's really nice. But come on, baby. Let's save this for later and go join the others. It's our last night here, and we should be seeing the New Year in soon with everyone else."

Rudy quietened a minute, and Trevor couldn't make out his expression in the darkness. After a moment, however, his body relaxed against Trevor's.

"Spoilsport."

"How about if I promise to make it up to you later? Somewhere warm and cosy that doesn't smell of bleach and mouse droppings."

Rudy chuckled into Trevor's shoulder.

"A deal. Come on, let's go."

Back in the main hall, only a scattering of guests remained, and Trevor wondered what had happened. He wondered if they had gone to watch the promised bonfire and fireworks display, or perhaps more highland dancing. Something significant had clearly taken them outside. None of his friends remained behind, and he was about to ask a waiter where everyone had gone when Rudy's brother headed towards them.

"Rudy, Trevor," said Ivan, his eyes wide. He moved slowly backward as he spoke not stopping on his way out of the door. "Everyone's on the front lawn. Someone's landed a seaplane on the loch. Mother thinks one of her special celebrity guests has arrived."

Trevor watched Ivan head out the door. He turned into the expression of an equally horrified Rudy.

"He wouldn't dare," said Trevor quietly. "Would he?"

Chapter Eighteen

Auld Lang's Syne

With their backs lit by the spotlights illuminating the old house, Trevor and Rudy stood together staring out across the loch, their shadows stretching towards the water. Then, like an accusation, lights glared brightly from the seaplane as the machine floated in the direction of the house. Trevor reached for Rudy's cold hand and squeezed. All around them, guests gathered in the chill air, immunised by alcohol, drinking still and chatting merrily, wondering with excitement who had arrived. Trevor heard somebody in the crowd voice the words 'famous rugby player'. He also recognised immediately the precise model of the plane and the unique number on the tail, something that sent a shiver through him.

Damian Ingram had arrived before in the same seaplane.

"Rudy," he said, turning, his heart giving a little tug to see Rudy's anxious profile and concerned eyes glaring at the loch.

When Rudy didn't answer, he pulled on the hand he held.

"Rudy," he said, a little louder, causing Rudy to turn his way. "No matter what happens, we'll get through this."

"I don't want anything to spoil tonight, Trev. That's all."

"Nothing will. I promise you."

"Why would he come back?"

"Because he's an insensitive prick. Because he's an asshole and an egotistical bastard who doesn't give a shit about anyone but himself. Pick any of the above."

Out on the jetty, a handful of people had gathered as the plane drew close. Fortunately, part of the pier's construction—inches above the surface of the loch—allowed for the aircraft to dock right alongside. Old Tam stood waiting to moor the craft, a rope in one hand, the other stopping his flat cap from blowing away. Others stood farther away—including Rudy's mother and father—waiting to greet the new arrivals. Lampposts along the pier illuminated the unfolding scene as the propellers slowed and stopped, as the doors opened and as, one by one, two bodies clambered out—a woman and a man. A tall and solid man. Mr Mortimer immediately moved forward to shake hands with the new arrivals before engaging the man in conversation.

"That's Helen, but I don't think it's him," said Rudy, breathing out a steamy sigh of relief. "I can't be sure, but I think that's François Debois. Come on, let's go and find out—"

But before they could move, a scream of joy pierced the air behind them. Cheryl had hiked up the hem of her red dress and was sprinting in high heels, unsteadily and unceremoniously—but without a care—towards the passengers on the pier. Many of those gathered giggled at the spectacle, but something had caught her attention, and Rudy and Trevor moved forward to find out. When Cheryl flew into Helen's arms, the penny finally dropped.

Cheryl's angel had descended from the sky.

"When did that happen?" asked Rudy as they strode towards the new arrivals, noticing his father and mother disengaging from them and heading back to the house.

"I'm not really sure. The two of them simply clicked, I suppose. At some point, I'm going to need to speak to Cheryl."

As they approached, he noticed Helen pulling bags from the plane and tossing them to the male passenger, as Cheryl stood by to help. After standing to one side for a moment, Rudy moved forward, and Trevor saw the smile of recognition light the man's face.

"Rudolph bloody Mortimer. How the devil are you?"

Trevor stood back as the man shook Rudy's hand forcefully then pulled him into a hug. Having finished, Helen grinned at the pair before closing the seaplane door and preparing to leap down onto the jetty next to Cheryl. After a couple of whispered words, a smiling Cheryl headed back to the house, with what Trevor guessed to be Helen's large red rucksack in her hand.

"Hey, François. I thought you'd cried off," said Rudy after releasing the fresh-faced rugby player. "That's what Damian told me. Said you pulled out at the last minute, which is why he felt obliged to come in your place."

"Pulled out? Damian told me I'd been officially dropped, that he was the one who'd been originally invited and was now free to come. Bloody annoying, actually. I'd cancelled other plans which were too late in the day to put back in place. But you know what Damian's like. Whatever he says goes."

"Damian is such a dick," said Helen, folding her arms. "On our way back to Glasgow, he was all for flying back for the party, but somewhere along the way he must have got a better offer. Flew off to New York two nights ago. I only phoned François on the off chance. I was really looking forward to coming back for the ball."

"Just the ball?" asked Trevor, which had Rudy chuckling. Helen grinned and her eye flicked up towards the house.

"And other things."

"Well, I'm really grateful to you both," said Rudy, standing between François and Helen and taking each of them by the arm while Helen took Trevor's arm. "I'm afraid we've already had dinner, but there's still plenty of buffet to be had. Come inside, into the warmth, and get something to eat and drink. I think we've got a bottle of our special twenty-year-old single malt you love so much."

"Now we're talking," said François.

At eleven-thirty, just as the earlier excitement had finally died away, Mr Mortimer announced the start of their traditional end-of-year firework display. Outside, in the middle of the lawn, Tam lit the carefully prepared bonfire contained within a brick housing, a knee-high fence marking out a perimeter to stop people venturing too close. Then, working with the entertainment specialists, Ivan and his father readied themselves to set off fireworks. Lights inside the house and spotlights around the grounds were extinguished one by one until the area lay in near-total darkness, with the only illumination coming from the brightly burning bonfire.

The moment everyone stilled and quietened, the spectacle began.

Pink, purple, red, blue, silver and gold — whizzing, fizzling fireworks raced for the sky before exploding into showers of glittery snowflakes reflected in the dark surface of the loch. *Oohs* and *aahs* and gasps of glee rose from the crowd. Mobile phones captured the moments, especially the second wave bursting into a kaleidoscope of colour above the house, illuminating the white walls and turrets in a panoply of hues, like something out of a highland fairy tale.

As the clock neared midnight, Tam commanded everyone back into the house, where Mr Mortimer provided the countdown to the New Year. Immediately afterwards, as everyone around the room cheered, the quartet began playing Auld Lang Syne, many of those gathered singing along. Trevor and Rudy wished a Happy New Year to all their friends — old and new — as well as the hosts and other guests before finding each other again. Back in Rudy's arms, Trevor felt at home, far happier than he had in years.

"You know, we sing this song every New Year, but I've never really understood the words," said Trevor, resting his chin on Rudy's shoulder as they slow-danced to the quartet's haunting version of Auld Lang Syne.

"Penned by our very own Rabbie Burns. It's a question, Trev. Should old acquaintances be forgotten, and never brought to mind? Then he repeats the phrase. Should old acquaintances be forgotten, as well as old times gone by? Obviously — for me, at least — the answer is no. We need to hang on to thoughts of friends and the times we had with them. If not, what else do we have when they're not here anymore?"

Something in Rudy's words filled Trevor with sadness. Would their time together be reduced to a memory next year? Of old times gone by? He peered out across the room and saw his friends dancing slowly together, with the addition of Helen and Cheryl. Then, softly, Rudy began to sing along to the music with such a beautiful baritone.

"For auld lang syne, my jo, for auld lang syne, we'll tak' a cup o' kindness yet, for auld lang syne."

"You're killing me."

"And surely ye'll be your pint-stoup!" Rudy smiled and brought their foreheads together. "And surely I'll be mine! And we'll tak' a cup o' kindness yet, for auld lang syne."

"I never knew," said Trevor, his eyes moist. "Such a beautiful song. We've sung the words countless times, and I never really knew what they meant."

"So what happens now?" said Rudy, his smile slipping.

"What happens now is that you take me back to the lodge and we continue this dance, but in bed beneath the covers and with no clothes. If you don't mind walking back."

"Of course not. But what I meant was, what happens to us? You all drive back to England tomorrow."

Trevor stopped dancing and faced Rudy. Lines of concern creased the skin between his brow, something Trevor wanted to smooth away. But, instead, he took both of Rudy's hands in his own and kissed him gently.

"I'm not going to lose you, Rudy. I promise." Trevor leant forward then and kissed Rudy between the eyebrows. When he pulled back, the crease had disappeared, and a small smile lit his face. "We've only just found each other. Let's agree to stay in touch at the very least. Until we can figure things out. Is that enough for now?"

"More than enough."

They carried on turning slowly until Cheryl and Helen came into view, standing before them. When Trevor looked over Cheryl's shoulder, he saw most of their other friends standing by the main entrance.

"We're going to stroll back to the lodge. Are you two staying here tonight?"

"No, we're coming too," said Rudy.

"Where are Frank and Johnny?" asked Trevor.

"They already headed back with Mum," said Cheryl. "Ivan dragged out a bottle of their premium thirty-year-old single malt, and between them, let's just say that Johnny got seriously over-refreshed, and his legs stopped working. So Frank loaded him into the back of Mum's car. She's dropping Doris off first then continuing on to the lodge. Said she'll put the kettle on and make tea for everyone."

"In which case," said Rudy, "we'll come, too. Just give us a moment to say goodbye."

After Trevor and Rudy said their thanks and bid farewell to the family, Rudy led the group down darkened lanes back to the lodge. Soft footfalls and murmured conversations and gentle laughter told them the others followed closely behind.

"So how come your name is hyphenated?" asked Trevor, their arms around each other's waists as they negotiated the lane.

"Mum's maiden name is King. Dad agreed to double-barrelling their family names when they got married, because Mum's family were all girls. They had nobody to carry on the family name. But you can tell they're down-to-earth people, Trev. You should see the piece-of-shit car he drives."

"I like your parents. They're good people. And I like your brother, too."

Just then, the moon poked out from behind a cloud, and pale light flooded the lane. Only for a moment, though, before the track fell back into the gloom.

"Does the darkness bother you?"

"No, not really," said Trevor before tightening his hold around Rudy's waist. "Not with you next to me, anyway. What was it Helen Keller wrote? Something about preferring to walk with a friend in the dark than alone in the light."

"Beautiful."

Before very long, they reached the crest of an incline in the lane and saw lights burning in the lodge below. Eager to get into the warmth of the kitchen, they hurried the last hundred yards and entered to find Mrs M pouring mugs of tea for everyone. Even though some complained of tiredness, they remained around the table, chatting and catching up on one another's stories. Then, just as Trevor had decided to drag Rudy away, they heard a clatter of feet from the hallway.

"Oh my God, you guys. You need to watch this," said Frank, rushing into the kitchen and spinning his laptop around on the table so that everyone could see the screen. One of the nation's leading news channels had a banner—Breaking News—across the top of the screen, and a female newscaster talked to the camera.

"News just in on the hour. A man charged with indecent behaviour in a New York public toilet is none other than the renowned Bulls forward Damian Ingram."

Right then, a headshot of Ingram faded into view.

"Ingram was caught during a police raid on the public restroom of a New York railway station. Sources say the area is a notorious meeting point for gay men. An undercover officer went into the restroom and witnessed Ingram publicly engaged in lewd behaviour with a younger man. The officer observed the act then arrested both men. Ingram posted bail and was released three hours after his arrest yesterday. The Bulls' press office has yet to release an official statement."

"He is so cancelled!" said Jessica.

Chapter Nineteen

Do You Hear What I Hear?

After a night of gentle lovemaking, Rudy finally dropped off at around two, wrapped in Trevor's arms. Trevor had lain awake for another half hour, not wanting to end the embrace or the day, knowing that when he slept, he would wake on their last day together. But, despite his efforts, he had finally given in to sleep.

"I don't want to move," said Trevor, lying next to Rudy the following morning, both of them staring up at the ceiling. "Not ever."

"Nor me," said Rudy. "This feels so—I don't know—natural."

"Doesn't it?" said Trevor, turning his head to Rudy and taking his hand.

"I heard my mother's voice."

"In your dreams?"

"No, in the kitchen," said Rudy, making Trevor chuckle then joining in. "She's probably here to say goodbye to you all before driving Helen and François back to the jetty."

"I suppose we'd better get up, then," said Trevor, with a sigh.

"I suppose."

While listening to the music of excited voices next door, they showered and dressed together. Rudy stood by solemnly watching Trevor pack his case, barely saying a word. After Trevor finished, he went around the bed and gave Rudy a reassuring hug and a kiss until he felt the tension in him dissolve.

"At least I don't have to repack this," said Trevor, handing the empty condom container to Rudy and raising an eyebrow. Happily, Rudy laughed at the gesture.

"I might keep this as a souvenir," said Rudy.

"Not sure about that. But I am donating my Christmas jumper to you."

Eventually, they moved out to the kitchen, where everyone had gathered, and where Rudy's mother sat drinking from a mug. On seeing them appear, she looked over and smiled affectionately before nodding a greeting. As they sought out seats around the table on that New Year's Day morning, Trevor smiled at seeing the happy faces — even Johnny, who appeared to find the daylight offensive — and realised they had worked their traditional Christmas magic. Okay, maybe not everyone seated was gay, but he could undeniably call them friends, or friends of friends.

Conversations buzzed with excitement, and Rudy and Trevor squeezed next to Helen, Cheryl and François. Mounds of buttered toast and pots of jam landed on the table, together with scrambled eggs, bowls of fruit, a variety of juices, yoghurts and heaps of fried food. Trevor guessed Mrs M wanted to use up as much of the remaining food as possible before the ride home. Nobody else appeared to notice, everyone content to tuck into the early morning feast.

"Do you hear what I hear, François?" said Frank, sat at one end of the table, turning up the volume on his laptop before twisting the screen around to face everyone. This morning, unsurprisingly, all Internet news stations ran the story about Damian. "The familiar name of that naughty teammate of yours. What New Year's resolutions do you think he might have chosen this year?"

François let out a heavy sigh, shook his head and put his mug down.

"He's such an idiot. Some of us knew his little secret, but you couldn't say anything to him. If you ask me, he should have come out years ago. Yeah, he'd probably have gotten stick from a few of the fans, but not the players. And now I doubt even the gay community will give him the time of day. Not after lying to them for so long, and after being caught in a public place. I bet money his sponsorships are drying up even as we speak."

"Couldn't have happened to a nicer bloke," said Johnny, then winked at Rudy. "What do you think, Rudy?"

Rudy merely shrugged, staring down at his mug of tea. Johnny threw a quizzical look at Trevor, who grimaced and shook his head before moving his eyes in the direction of Rudy's mother. She probably didn't know about Rudy and Ingram. Johnny understood instinctively, nodded quickly and didn't pursue the question. But Trevor realised there was more to Rudy's mood than Ingram's discretion.

As breakfast came to an end, Frank dialled up Karl, Mary and baby Connor on the video-conferencing app on his laptop. Still in the hospital, Mary appeared understandably tired. Karl turned the laptop camera to take in his newborn lying in a plastic-framed cot, the tiny body yellow-tinged. Karl, however, could not hold in his paternal pride. The girls all cooed in unison — causing Frank to choke on his tea.

"He's still in the incubator for now," said Karl, taking charge while a tired Mary sat nearby. "Classed as level-one neonatal because, as you can see, he has a slight case of jaundice. Other than that, he's doing remarkably well. His lungs are certainly strong enough. Hasn't stopped complaining since he arrived."

"Must take after his mother," muttered Johnny.

"Look," said Mary, leaning into view and eliciting a coughing fit from Johnny. "I wanted to thank you all for being so amazing. Hindsight is a wonderful thing, and if I'd realised the baby would be premature, I would never have considered coming in the first place. But as luck would have it, I couldn't have been in more capable hands. So thank you, Brenda and Doris, for taking care of me and the baby, and Helen for flying us to Glasgow. We will certainly have a story for Connor when he's old enough to understand. Thank you also, Rudy, who my husband tells me had the foresight and common sense to call Doris and the specialist maternity hospital, to figure out Helen could fly us to Glasgow when the roads were blocked, and arrange the ambulance at the airport."

"You did all that?" asked Rudy's mother, staring down the table at him, clearly impressed, once Mary and Karl had dropped the call.

"And so much more," said Trevor, turning to smile at Rudy, placing an arm around his shoulders. "He's gone out of his way to take care of everyone this holiday."

"I'll second that," said Mrs M, getting to her feet. "He's a credit to your family, Mrs Mortimer-King. And I'm sorry to have to do this, but I need you all to help me clean up the kitchen, so we can go and pack. I'm sure Rudy needs the place back."

With most of them familiar with the breakfast routine, they tidied up in no time. Having already packed, Trevor allowed Rudy to drag him away to the living area. Once again, he stood facing the large windows, his arm around Trevor's waist, studying the room.

"I thought I'd help get your decorations down," said Rudy. "So you can take them back with you."

"Don't you have more guests coming?" asked Trevor.

"Tomorrow."

"Then why not leave them up? Let someone else enjoy them?"

"Are you sure?"

"Of course. You and Tam can take them down on the twelfth night."

"A little reminder of you," said Rudy before pushing out a sigh. "This room is going to look sad and empty once they're down."

"Isn't that the beauty of traditions? They're short-lived and wonderful. And the space in between gives us something to look forward to. If you left the decorations up all year round, they would not only lose that element of surprise and delight, but they'd also lose their meaning."

"I suppose so. I'm terrified that when good things aren't there anymore, we might start to forget them."

Trevor understood Rudy's meaning and sought words to comfort him.

"Remember the night you showed me the snow falling?" asked Trevor.

Staring out to the scenery and without turning, Rudy nodded.

"The first time you kissed me?"

A small smile crept across his face. Trevor let out a soft sigh and followed Rudy's gaze. Out across the loch, two birds flew together—his osprey friend?—towards an overhanging tree, where they both settled.

"I want to do that with you every Christmas. Whether or not there's snow."

With that, he pulled Rudy around, wrapped him in his arms and kissed him. Rudy didn't fully return the embrace, letting Trevor hold his body but not hugging him back.

"Like I said already, I've found you now, Rudy, and I'm not letting you go."

"Come on," said Rudy, pulling away. "Let's go and say our goodbyes."

After the group brought their bags down and sat around the empty table, the last order of the day was to figure out how everyone would be getting home. Even though Cheryl talked about flying back to Glasgow with Helen and François—the latter also being a qualified pilot—she conceded that going with Trevor and her mum was the most sensible option, especially as she was a designated driver. Frank and Johnny had planned to drop off their hire car at the airport and catch a train back, but Antoni and Jessica offered to follow them to the airport then give them a lift back to London.

Once everyone had packed their respective cars, the farewells began. When Trevor went to shake the hand of Mrs Mortimer-King, she pulled him into a hug and whispered, "Come back and see us whenever you like. Rudy's been happier than I've seen him in forever."

"Not this morning."

"Oh, Trevor. I told you. He'll get past it, he always does. Poor boy takes things to heart. He's always felt things more deeply than Ivan. Just promise you'll keep in touch with him."

"I have. And of course I will," said Trevor. "But nothing I say seems to be helping right now."

Finally, everyone but Trevor's party had departed. After they'd packed everything into the back of the car, Trevor went over and gave Rudy a final hug. Once belted up in the back seat of the Volvo, he twisted his body around and watched through the rear window as the car hobbled slowly away from the solitary figure of Rudy in the driveway, framed by the beautiful wild scenery. Compared to the confident horseman he had met on that first day, the Rudy he stared at appeared defeated and broken.

Finally, Trevor's heart could stand no more.

"Stop the car!"

"What's the matter?" asked Cheryl, bringing the car to a halt. "Have you forgotten something?"

"Something like that," said Trevor, unclipping his belt and opening the door before poking his head back in. "Keep the engine running. I promise I won't be more than a moment."

When Trevor trotted back down the lane, Rudy's head came up, a look of quizzical surprise replacing the one of desolation. Trevor stopped in front of him and held out his hand.

"Give me your phone."

Baffled, Rudy did as asked. Trevor peered down at the screen.

"Can you unlock it for me?"

"Why? You have my mobile number. What are you going to do?"

"Do you trust me?"

"Of course I do."

"Then unlock your damn phone."

Rudy did as asked then handed the phone back.

Trevor found what he wanted, pushed his thumb on the app then raised the phone to his mouth, all the while smiling Rudy in the eyes.

"I love you, Rudy Mortimer. I love you more than life itself. If you're ever feeling down, listen to this and remember that I'm out there somewhere, thinking of you, thinking of your arm around me as we look out onto a snow-filled landscape. And somehow, I'm going to find my way back to you. That much I promise. Because I love you, Rudy, and I've never felt this way about anyone before."

With that, Trevor thumbed off the device and hit the play button.

"I love you, Rudy Mortimer…"

When he held out the phone and looked up into Rudy's eyes, a tear spilt down one of his new boyfriend's cheeks. The sight undid him, and he strode forward, folding Rudy into his arms.

"Rudy, I really mean those words," said Trevor, feeling the embrace returned. "We'll figure something out. But I need you to be strong. Can you do that?"

Instead of replying, Rudy nodded his damp face in Trevor's shoulder.

As Trevor went to move away, Rudy pulled him firmly back.

"I love you too, Trev. And I'm sorry I've been moody this morning, but I never appreciated how hard the reality of losing someone as special as you would hit me. But I also promise to work at us being together again."

Chapter Twenty

Close To You

Sunday in late January, Trevor sat in the booth of a closed restaurant on Edgware Road. On his day off, he had been doing the owner — his client — a favour, using his laptop and a portable scanner to finalise the restaurant chain accounts and getting everything ready to go off to the official accountant. But Trevor had an ulterior motive. During the week, he had received a message from Rudy to say he would be in Central London for the day — connecting from a business meeting in the south — and could they meet for a drink somewhere. Rudy had suggested a wine bar in Central London. What had gotten his attention was Rudy telling him the meeting was important. What did that mean?

Since the New Year, Rudy had been rushed off his feet, helping his father with the business while his brother and sister-in-law took a skiing holiday in Europe. Somewhat cryptically, Rudy had mentioned having something he needed to say, something that needed to be said in person.

After Trevor returned home, they had been texting and calling each other daily. Trevor warmed inside every time he saw Rudy's name pop up on his screen, the feeling intensifying whenever he heard Rudy's voice. Hesitant as always, Trevor wondered if, given time, Rudy would eventually cool off. But every communication since New Year had been upbeat and sincere.

Once again he read the text suggesting they meet in a wine bar not far from the restaurant. Trevor could hop on a bus and arrive well before one. A little after midday, and not only was his stomach churning but his heart felt just about ready to jump out of his chest.

A sound grabbed his attention, of someone unlocking the front door and stepping inside. To his surprise, the restaurant owner appeared. Marcus Vine and his chain of restaurants called Old Country had become a big name on the London restaurant scene, and despite his celebrity status, Marcus came across to everyone who met him as an everyman – genuine and down to earth. Trevor had even brought Frank and Johnny to the Shepherd's Bush chain once, where they had been treated like royalty.

After Marcus' hard work, the restaurant had finally won a Michelin Star award. The man knew how to put together incredible dishes. He also looked after his members of staff, and Trevor, as the man's bookkeeper-stroke-accountant – albeit a consultant – was treated as such.

"I thought you were supposed to be in Cairns," said Trevor, checking the date on his computer screen.

"Despite the wonderful weather – it's midsummer down under – plus the amazing seafood, wines and excellent diving, we flew back last week. On the eighteenth," said Marcus, parking himself in the other side of the booth Trevor had commandeered. "Tom missed the girls too much. So did I, if truth be told. Ah, here's the man himself."

Marcus' husband did not have Rudy's breeding, but there was something about his stature and his natural masculine attractiveness that turned people's heads. Togged out on this cold January lunchtime in simple jeans and a navy turtleneck sweater beneath a long grey trench coat, he moved with such ease and confidence. And Trevor couldn't help but notice the adoring looks from Marcus as Tom slid into the booth next to his husband and pecked him on the cheek.

"You've still managed to get great tans, both of you. I must look like a vampire by comparison. Now you're here, I might as well tell you what I told Michelle. Your books are updated for all four restaurants and in excellent shape. You've had record takings this holiday season, so well done. I've emailed everything to you in short form, and I've made a few recommendations of where you might want to offset some of your costs against tax when the time comes, but you'll have to let your official accountants decide whether that's feasible or not. Most important thing is that your accounts are up to date. Now it's just a case of keeping them that way until it's time to submit."

"See what I mean?" said Marcus, turning to Tom. "He's priceless. Do you want me to ask him, or will you?"

"Ask me what?"

"One of the reasons I'm here today, and not at home," said Tom, drawing Trevor's attention, "is because — and you can always say no — I need someone to look over my accounts. Marcus has been singing your praises about how much time and money you save him. At the moment, I've got a part-time bookkeeper, but I still spend almost a fortnight each year sorting through papers and invoices, and half the time I'm sure I'm missing things."

"You own a restaurant too?" asked Trevor.

Marcus laughed. "Try a building company."

"Oh," said Trevor, shrugging. Accounts were accounts at the end of the day, irrespective of business type. "No problem. What accounting system do you use?"

"Traditional. Pencil, book ledger, box files. And beginner's-level spreadsheets."

Somewhat dramatically, Marcus dropped his head into his hands. This time Trevor laughed.

"I know, Trevor," said Marcus, looking up through his fingers. "With the help of his daughters I've been trying to get him to embrace the twenty-first century, but it's been an uphill struggle."

"Is it that bad?" asked Tom.

"Not really," said Trevor. "Is your husband always this much of a drama queen?"

"What do you think?"

All three of them chuckled.

"But the truth is, Marcus is right. There are some great web-based systems out there that can save you a lot of time and effort. Depends on your business setup. Let's arrange for me to come and see you, check through your current system, work with you and your bookkeeper to assess where we are with your accounts right now, then I can make a recommendation and give you a quote."

Tom seemed genuinely relieved and grateful and sent a silent thank you to Marcus.

"Now that's settled," said Marcus, an unspoken message passing between the two men. "Are you going to tell us who this mystery man is that Michelle told me about? The one you're meeting today?"

"Oh, God, Marcus," said Trevor, raking his hands through his hair. "I am so nervous. We met at Christmas and had this intense connection. I know this sounds corny, but I just felt at home with him. I didn't have to be someone else, I could just be me. Everything felt so...so..."

"Natural?"

"Exactly. Do you know what I mean?"

"I think I get the gist," said Marcus, turning and smiling at Tom. "So you really like him?"

"Of course."

"Then I don't see the problem."

"He is so far out of my league."

"According to whom?"

"According to me! He's from Scotland, the son of the Earl of Stratham, for heaven's sake!"

Marcus turned to Tom, chuckling.

"Does he like you?" asked Tom.

"I think so. At least, that's what he told me."

"Where are you meeting him?" asked Marcus.

"In a wine bar. Off the Strand. In an hour."

"Cancel."

"What?" said Trevor, horrified.

"Tell him to come here instead. Not only can I feed and water you both, I can also give you my honest opinion. My gaydar relationship score out of ten."

"Marcus," said Tom, his eyebrows lowering.

"Okay, okay," said Marcus, holding his palms in the air. "No judgements. I'll just cook. You want to impress him, don't you?"

"I guess so."

"Then bring him here. Is he allergic to any foods?"

"No. At least, not that I know of. Oh heavens, I don't know. You see, that's the problem, isn't it? I barely know him."

"Trevor," said Tom, putting his arm around Marcus' shoulders and kissing his partner on the cheek. "Believe me when I say this. That's half the fun, really getting to know someone."

Mrs M had used almost the exact words to him over Christmas. Maybe he had been overthinking things— perhaps he should simply go with the flow.

"Right," said Marcus, pushing Tom out of the booth. "I have food to cook. And you, Trevor, have a text to send. Tom, come and help me in the kitchen."

Left alone at the table, he sent a text explaining him working in the closed restaurant and instructing Rudy to knock on the door. He received an instant 'okay' in response. Over the next half an hour, to keep himself busy, he finished off his work on the laptop and began process of closing up the scanner and putting paperwork into a file.

Maybe there had been a slight sound, a tiny rush of wind, or perhaps he had sensed someone else in the room, but Trevor looked up to find Rudy standing there, a small holdall hanging from his hand. Weather-proofed in a long overcoat of charcoal wool, smart jeans and an oatmeal crew-cut sweater, he wore a red-and-green tartan scarf loosely tied around his neck. Together with wind-rouged cheeks and slightly tousled hair, he looked adorable. Trevor stood instantly and smiled, even though a sudden burst of nervousness filled him. Rudy's grin grew wide, his eyes filled with happiness.

"You made it."

"I did. Front door was open. I've locked it behind me. Don't want any random customers walking in, do we?"

They smiled nervously at each other before Rudy's gaze dropped to the floor and the smile drained away.

"How's Cheryl?" he asked.

"Fine. She's already been up to see Helen. Talking about going up in a plane. But she says the distance thing is difficult. As we both know. Rudy."

"Yes," said Rudy, looking up hopefully.

"Any chance of a hug?"

Rudy dropped his holdall, strode forward, and took Trevor's face in his hands, kissing him firmly and passionately before pulling him into a hug. Then, standing with his arms squeezed around Trevor's torso, rocking him gently back and forth, Rudy let out a huge sigh.

"I can't do this anymore," he breathed in Trevor's ear.

"Yeah, I — I think I knew."

Trevor let out a sad sigh of his own and deflated, emptiness filling him. In his head, he had been half-expecting as much, but the sudden emotional wave that filled the empty void caught him unawares. Tears brimmed over while his body trembled uncontrollably.

"Trev? What's the matter?" said Rudy, his hands lifting Trevor's face and bringing their gaze level.

"I understand —" said Trevor, all he could manage, as tears ran down his cheeks.

"No, no," said Rudy, smiling and shaking his head, wiping away Trevor's tears with his thumbs. "I'm such an idiot. That's not what I meant. Look, I — I've just been for an interview with my old boss. That's why I've been down here. I didn't say anything because I didn't want to jinx things. But he's opening a new mega-gym in Shipworth—"

"In Kent?" said Trevor, his eyes widening. "That's the town next to mine."

"Yes, but let me finish," said Rudy, his hands draped around Trevor's neck. "He wants me to manage the whole thing—the fit-out, the operating systems, recruitment—then run the gym for at least a couple of years. It's similar to what I did in York, but on a bigger scale, so it's not going to be an issue. And I still get time off to help my dad when he needs me—although he's talking about selling up. But the only problem is, even though my old boss is not going to have the official opening until May, I need to come back next week to start things rolling. And at the moment, I don't have anywhere to stay—"

"With me," said Trevor quickly. "Stay with me."

A huge smile of relief blossomed across Rudy's face.

"I was hoping you might offer. He's giving me a decent housing allowance."

"Nuh-uh. There's only one thing I'll need from you. And lots of it."

Rudy pushed his nose into the side of Trevor's neck, his lips brushing beneath the ear.

"That's a given. But you need to let me take care of you, too, Trev. Deal?"

"Deal. And if you want," said Trevor, releasing Rudy, "I can come back with you and help you pack."

Rudy tilted his head in puzzlement before looking back at his holdall.

"I'm already packed."

"Back in Scotland. Help you pack for your new life down here."

"But I'm flying later this afternoon."

"I figured you were. And I'll need to buy a ticket at the airport if we're flying together. Or don't you want me to come back with you?"

"Of course I do," said Rudy, aghast now. "Mother would be over the moon to see you. But don't you have other things to do?"

"Not really. Yes, the house will be empty, but Cheryl can go and feed the goldfish if I ask. I've got all my work here on the computer. And next week I don't have to physically visit any clients, so the least I can do is come help my new partner—wow, I really like the sound of that—pack for his future life with me."

While Trevor had been talking, a broadly grinning Rudy had been checking something on his phone.

"How about a compromise?"

"Go on."

"If I stay one more night—at your place, perhaps—to give you time to pack and me a chance to check out the bed in my new digs—"

"Our bed."

"*Our* bed. Then we can both take the six-thirty train up from Euston tomorrow."

"What about your plane ticket?"

"Not booked yet. I was going to get a standby at the airport."

Trevor laughed happily. "Then it's a deal."

Across the restaurant, he barely heard the two men framed in the open kitchen doorway, standing shoulder to shoulder, laughing too and clapping their hands.

"Are you done yet? Can we bring the drinks and appetisers?" asked Tom.

After pleasantly surprising Trevor with a very drinkable sparkling wine produced by a vineyard in

Sussex, Marcus impressed Rudy with a traditional Scottish soup of seafood with crab and rice, one he introduced as partan bree. Trevor thought the name sounded like cheese, but Rudy knew better, though he had only ever tasted the one made by their housekeeper, Millie. When the main course came along — Marcus serving his delicious spin on the Scottish classic of haggis, neeps and tatties — Rudy insisted Tom and Marcus join them. Trevor sat back at one point, listening to the easy conversation between the three men, with Rudy promising to bring them to Scotland one day. He would introduce Marcus to Millie so he could grill her about recipes while Tom went fishing on the loch. While Marcus and Tom cleared plates and prepared dessert in the kitchen, Trevor and Rudy found themselves alone again. A very happy Rudy reached across the table and grasped Trevor's hands in his own.

"I love your friends. They're such easy company."

"Technically, Marcus is my client. But I know what you mean. Isn't it great to have clients you can categorise as friends?"

"Sure is. And what I meant to say earlier — and messed up monumentally — is that I couldn't stand this geographical distance between us. I need to be close to you. I'm not sure I really believe in fate, but somehow everything feels right when I'm with you, when we're together, Trev. And I want to see where this goes."

"So do I." A warm feeling of optimism filled Trevor, and he lifted his wineglass in the air. "Let's do this, Rudy. Together. For the sake of old times gone by."

Rudy raised his glass and clinked it with Trevor's.

"To old times gone by. And new ones to come."

Chapter Song List

Season's greetings to one and all. Brian Lancaster here. In case you wanted to enjoy this story over Christmas accompanied by the music title I selected for each chapter, here's the song list (mostly Christmas songs) by the artists I had in mind:

Last Christmas – Wham!
2000 Miles – The Pretenders
Deck The Hall – New Philharmonic Orchestra
Mary's Boy Child – Boney M
Winter Wonderland – Tony Bennett
Imagine – John Lennon
Let It Snow – Joe Williams
Dear Santa (Bring Me A Man This Christmas) – The Weather Girls
White Christmas – Bing Crosby
Baby, It's Cold Outside – Chris Colfer & Darren Criss
Wintersong – Sarah McLachlan
Fairytale of New York – The Pogues featuring Kirsty MacColl
Stay Another Day – East 17
Santa Baby – Eartha Kitt
When A Child Is Born – Johnny Mathis
Silent Night – G4
Driving Home For Christmas – Chris Rea
Auld Lang Syne – Mairi Campbell
Do You Hear What I Hear? – Carrie Underwood
Close To You – Carpenters

Want to see more from this author? Here's a taster for you to enjoy!

Any Day
Brian Lancaster

Excerpt

Sunday morning, Leonard Day lowered himself into the plush black leather chair at his sixteenth-floor office desk. Still wearing his warm grey tracksuit and saffron Bluetooth headphones, he sank back into the soft padding, pressed a button to boot up his laptop, then placed his phone and car keys alongside the mouse mat designed to resemble a Persian rug.

Issuing a bark of laughter only he could hear, he ripped off the two fluorescent-pink Post-it notes, one stuck in the middle of each of his monitors. Both carried warnings in vivid purple felt-penmanship—one to 'Go Home!' and the other to 'Get @ Life!' Shaking his head but still grinning at being caught out again, he dropped the notes into his wire wastebasket as his gaze trailed to the day outside the room.

Framed by the tinted office windows, a beautiful spring morning had woken to life. Sunlight glistened off the rain-slick roofs of regimented rows of South London terraced houses. From a music app playlist on his smartphone, the opening strains of Vaughan Williams' *Symphony No. 5 in D major* provided the perfect soundtrack to the tranquil morn.

Naive perhaps, but he used to think none of his staff knew about his habit of slipping into the office on Sunday mornings. He went there not so much to check figures and plan the week, but to avoid being at home on what had once been his favourite day of the week. The easiest way to change a habit is to create a new and better one, his late Qigong teacher had once advised. So after performing a regular morning routine of gentle moves and stretching exercises in the back garden and after locking up the house, Leonard escaped to his office, the perfect distraction and a familiar sanctuary in his otherwise solitary world. And his team were none the wiser.

Until the day Kieran had rumbled him.

His young, energetic marketing manager, who had impeccable attention to detail, had caught Leonard out a few months ago. Kieran—dropped off at the office each weekday morning before anyone else arrived—had noticed reports on Leonard's desk on Monday morning, ones that hadn't been there the previous Friday because Leonard had been travelling. Confronted, Leonard had confessed but had tried to fob off the action as a one-off urgent business need. Kieran hadn't bought the excuse, and, like the Post-it warnings this morning, he often booby-trapped Leonard's desk. *'If you insist on everyone having a work–life balance,'* Kieran had stated aloud at a staff meeting, *'then you should set an example and live by your words.'*

Had Leonard listened to the office designer's recommendations, he would now have a lockable corner office. But ever since taking the floor space, Leonard had insisted on open-plan for everyone, the only enclosed spaces being a fish tank—glass conference room—at either end of the office. Leonard's desk sat in the middle of the open space, the same size as everyone else's, surrounded by a team he considered his surrogate family. And he loved being in the thick of things. None of his team just *worked* for him. They contributed, not one of them complaining about extra effort when business ramped up, not one having anything but positive things to say about their working environment. Leonard preached work–life balance — even if he didn't exactly live by his own ethos — and made sure nobody stayed beyond five-thirty every day unless absolutely necessary. And every Friday, to show his gratitude, he either prearranged snacks and drinks in the office from four-thirty if he happened to be away or took them to a local wine bar. In the office, at least, Leonard found smiling effortless.

But Kieran didn't miss a trick. On his day off, he'd brought his Cockapoo canine rescue called Ed into the office — a fiery red bundle of havoc — and had tried to persuade an amused Leonard to get a pet dog himself. Leonard blamed his schedule, which meant him being regularly away from home, travelling to various parts of the country for a week or more, assessing listed buildings or attending antique shows or car auctions. Kieran hadn't bought the excuse.

'*Sorry, Len,*' he'd said one Friday evening as the whole team had gathered around a wine bar table for drinks. '*But I'm calling bullshit for three very distinct reasons. First off, you can employ a dog sitter for when you're travelling. I can even provide names. Second, did you or did you not employ Izzy here as your assistant director for the sole purpose of reducing your workload?*'

Only Kieran dared challenge him publicly this way, always in a light-hearted, tongue-in-cheek manner. He'd wanted intelligent, creative, personable Kieran as his number two. But when Kieran and his husband

Kennedy had added twin boys to their family unit, many of their priorities had changed.

'*You already know the answer to that.*'

'*Then let her. She's more than capable of hunting out grubby antiques around the country, or looking over run-down, borderline derelict properties.*'

Isabelle had sat smiling down at her glass of Merlot and said nothing.

'*Remind Kieran again what they're called, will you please, Isabelle?*'

'*Listed buildings,*' Isabelle had said, laughing along with the rest of the team.

'*We call them listed buildings, Kieran. But thank you for your advice. Your point has been made and will be taken into consideration.*'

'*Then I rest my case,*' said Kieran, folding his arms and sitting back.

'*Hang on, you said three reasons.*'

'*Ah, yes. Thirdly – and most importantly – Ed needs a playmate.*'

'*Of course he does. Let me think about it.*'

Leonard raised his gaze to Kieran's haphazard workspace and smirked. The monitor had been plastered randomly with an assortment of colourful Post-it reminders in his distinctive handwriting while trade magazines lay open across the keyboard. Pride of place on his desk sat a large, framed photo of him, his husband and their kids. Another showed their cheeky-faced mutt with what looked like a television remote control in his mouth. Thirty-two years old and Kieran had surrounded himself with so much love. The quiet young man Leonard had first encountered on a cruise ship had blossomed into a doting husband and father. Leonard turned forty-seven in May, and what did he have? A handful of successful businesses, but there it ended. At home? Not even a goldfish. Then again, perhaps he'd already had his time in the light.

The real reason Leonard had not followed through on the dog plan was because he didn't share Kieran's affinity for pets. During his childhood he'd broached the subject once only — he must have been seven or eight at the time — and both parents had stated their disgust at domestic animals, dismissing them as unruly and unhygienic. There the conversation had ended. Both accomplished scientists — microbiologists — they'd lived in a simple semi-detached a few miles away from the university campus. Work had been their lives. His father specialised in mycology, the study of mushrooms, toadstools and other fungi, and particularly how various species can kill or cure. At the same time, his mother, more interested in classification, had concentrated her efforts on microbial taxonomy — the naming and classification of micro-organisms. As couples went, they could not have been a more perfect match.

For a few seconds, he stared at his Cisco desk phone, toying with the idea of ringing them. Usually the call entailed dull generalities and awkward silences, neither party having much of any interest to share. Both parents had retired from university life. Heaven only knew what they talked about at home.

Being an only child, Leonard wondered if he had been an experiment rather than a child born of intimacy. Neither parent had demonstrated the kind of tactile warmth or fondness he had witnessed in other families. Not that his were uncaring or cruel in any way. Nutrition and learning had been equally valued in their house. As academics, they had encouraged his studies, praising him for good grades while trying hard to mask their disappointment when he failed at any subject related to the pure sciences. Their frustration had been mitigated when he'd excelled at mathematics, social sciences and, in particular, business studies.

After a quick check of message headings in his inbox, most of which he had already opened and drafted replies to—he never sent his team emails over the weekend—he returned to the one containing attachments sent by his finance officer. Spreadsheets often proved too long and detailed to open on his home laptop but displayed adequately on his two monitors. End-of-month figures popped up on his screens, much as Leonard had expected except for the incredible numbers on their latest venture, the online auction. Between the two of them, Isabelle and Kieran had come up with the idea as an extension of their antiques and artisans site. Traffic had increased tenfold, but more importantly, sales in both had skyrocketed. He folded his arms, sat back in his chair and allowed himself a private moment to gloat.

Fortunately for him, a single-minded determination to focus in the field of business management had allowed him to study for his undergraduate degree in Bournemouth, far enough away that his parents only deemed the occasional visit home necessary. When the time had come to leave at the age of nineteen, he had been able to fend for himself, had learnt to appreciate his own company. A more challenging lesson had been in realising he had developed a singular attractiveness in his late teens. One female college student had referred to him as the sexy lone wolf, but despite getting plenty of offers from girls, his heart hungered only for other boys.

After scanning other columns of figures, and satisfied all of them headed in the right direction, he checked the time on his phone—ten o'clock. An hour before he needed to set off for the hotel in York to spend two days in business meetings and viewing potential properties around the area. Far enough from home he might even try for a random hook-up using the app he had recently discovered and downloaded. Kieran had been right about one thing. At some point, he needed to get himself a life.

Although made in jest, a quip about him by a male friend on a cruise holiday still stung. Thinking Leonard to be out of earshot, someone had asked this friend why he'd nicknamed Leonard 'Any Day'. He had replied, *'Because any day is better than Lenny Day. The man is a walking misery.'* Overhearing this, he had been shocked to the core. When had he changed from being a sexy lone wolf to a *'walking misery'*? Naturally Kennedy had stepped in to defend him even though, in fairness, the friend had less-than-respectful names for all of their acquaintances. The main problem? Leonard had sensed the truth behind the quip. Maybe he needed to make more of an effort to be cheerful outside of his day-to-day.

As he closed down programs on his laptop and pulled off his earphones, he raised his head and froze, his attention drawn to a distant sound.

Barely audible beyond the building's thick glazing, somewhere out there in the suburbs, cutting through the constant hum of traffic, came the peal of church bells. For as long as comfortably possible, he held his breath, squeezing his eyes shut and absorbing the simple melody.

Church bells, like Sunday mornings at home, reminded him of Kris. And without warning or witness, he was overcome by the kind of immobilising grief that he had hoped would have receded after the death of his lover ten years ago. He rarely allowed himself to wallow in thoughts of their time together, but the memory blindsided him and filled him with such warmth and love and togetherness. And when those tender recollections inevitably melted away they would leave him emotionally desolate, standing alone in the stark coldness of reality. But for now he would allow himself to listen to the bells, and wallow and remember…

Until the shrill ring of his desk phone drowned out everything.

For a moment, he sat there, appalled at the intrusion, glaring at the device, deciding whether or not to answer. Eventually, after several rings, he relented.

"Days-Gone-By Enterprises," he answered gruffly, ripping a tissue from a box on his desk and dabbing at his eyes.

"Leonard," came his mother's stern voice. Although no explanation had been forthcoming, she no longer called his mobile phone. "I tried you at your house but you weren't answering. You need to come home. Your father passed this morning, and I need your help arranging things. When can you be here?"

"What?" said Leonard, caught off guard. "Oh, God, Mum. Dad died? I'm so sorry. What happened?"

"Not now. When can you be home?"

"I—I can come now." He had a case in his car for the business trip. By some stroke of fate he had even packed his black Hugo Boss suit for meetings. With a few clicks of his phone he could cancel the York trip. "I suppose I could be there around three or four. Traffic willing."

"I'll get your room ready."

"Mum, what—?"

Before he had a chance to probe any further, she ended the call.

Annoyance bubbled in him. Most of the time he accepted his mother's natural candour, and admired her ability to view and deal with the world dispassionately. Right now, he wished he had a parent who could be sensitive to the emotions a son might be feeling at the passing of the only father he would ever have. Perhaps she knew without asking that he considered grief an old friend.

As he left the office, he did something he hated and called Isabelle on her day off to hand over the reins for the week ahead. At home, his own house, everything would be fine.

Striding across the empty car park, Kieran's words came back to him and cemented inside. He needed to find a life. At the moment, he seemed to be surrounded by too much death.

About the Author

Brian Lancaster is an author of gay romantic fiction in multiple genres, including contemporary romance, paranormal, fantasy, crime, mystery, and anything else that tickles his muse's fancy. Born in the sleepy South of England where most of his stories are set, he moved to Southeast Asia in 1998, where he now shares a home with his husband and two of the laziest cats on the planet.

Brian loves to hear from readers. You can find his contact information, website details and author profile page at https://www.pride-publishing.com

PUBLISHING

Sign up for our newsletter and find out about all our
romance book releases, eBook sales and promotions,
sneak peeks and FREE romance books!